HER EVERY DESIRE

Miriame did not protest when his hands moved to touch her breasts under the linen of her shirt. She arched her back, thrusting them into his hands. She would die if he did not touch her, if he did not take her breasts into his hands, and smooth his callused palms over her sensitive nipples.

It was as if he could read her mind and knew every desire that she felt but could not put into words. His hands moved exactly where she wanted them to go. They touched her just where she ached to be touched.

Jean-Paul's fingers moved down to the waistband of her breeches, and paused. For one heartbreaking moment, she thought he would stop there, but he did not. "I cannnot think of you as a wench when you are garbed as a man," he growled into her ear. "You will have to take those breeches off, or I shall do it for you."

BOOK YOUR PLACE ON OUR WEBSITE AND MAKE THE READING CONNECTION!

We've created a customized website just for our very special readers, where you can get the inside scoop on everything that's going on with Zebra, Pinnacle and Kensington books.

When you come online, you'll have the exciting opportunity to:

- View covers of upcoming books
- Read sample chapters
- Learn about our future publishing schedule (listed by publication month *and author*)
- Find out when your favorite authors will be visiting a city near you
- Search for and order backlist books from our online catalog
- Check out author bios and background information
- Send e-mail to your favorite authors
- Meet the Kensington staff online
- Join us in weekly chats with authors, readers and other guests
- Get writing guidelines
- AND MUCH MORE!

Visit our website at
http://www.kensingtonbooks.com

THIEF OF HEARTS

Kate Silver

ZEBRA BOOKS
KENSINGTON PUBLISHING CORP.
http://www.kensingtonbooks.com

ZEBRA BOOKS are published by

Kensington Publishing Corp.
850 Third Avenue
New York, NY 10022

All Kensington titles, imprints and distributed lines are available at special quantity discounts for bulk purchases for sales promotion, premiums, fund-raising, educational or institutional use.

Special book excerpts or customized printings can also be created to fit specific needs. For details, write or phone the office of the Kensington Special Sales Manager: Kensington Publishing Corp., 850 Third Avenue, New York, NY 10022. Attn. Special Sales Department. Phone: 1-800-221-2647.

Zebra and the Z logo Reg. U.S. Pat. & TM Off.

First Printing: March 2004
10 9 8 7 6 5 4 3 2 1

Printed in the United States of America

Chapter 1

The air was fetid with the stench of the open sewers that ran through the narrow streets. Only the barest hint of moonlight glimmered through the thick clouds that lay heavily over the sky, reaching down with foggy tendrils to drift over the very rooftops of the houses that lined the way on each side of the roughly cobbled road.

Miriame stepped carefully on the raised middle of the road, avoiding the edges where the muck thrown from the overhanging second and third stories of the houses pooled into a reeking mass of filthy mud. It had rained early that evening, washing down the raised cobbles, but making them slippery and treacherous. Just one false step and she would find herself up to her ankles in slime and mud. She had no boots—they had finally fallen apart the week before so that no mending was possible—and her feet were wrapped only in rags.

That was, indeed, the reason for her mission tonight. She needed boots for the coming winter or her heels would crack until they festered, and her cracked, red chilblains would return with a vengeance at the first hint of snow on the streets, itching to the point of madness.

She had seen it happen time and time again to those poor souls who lived on the street and were too clumsy or too foolish to steal themselves a pair of boots. Their toes festered in the cold, turning black and ill smelling, until the poison from the evil humors in their feet made them sick and they died.

She was not going to let that happen to her. If she didn't have boots, she would be stuck inside all winter long. If she didn't have boots, she would have no way to make a living during the dark days of winter. Then she would die anyway. Starvation would kill her just as swiftly and surely as blackened, rotted feet would.

By whatever means possible, she had to have those boots and she wanted them tonight. Judging by the chill in the air, winter was well on its way. She did not want to be caught unprepared by an early snow.

She trudged on through the night. The streets were starting to get wider now and the cobbling less rough, though the cobblestones were not noticeably cleaner. She was invading the part of town where wealthy merchants and the gentry lived.

The pickings were richer here, though the danger was greater as well. Wealthy folk didn't like to share what they had with those who needed it. Even less did they like to have a tiny portion of their wealth stolen from them, though what was a mite of luxury to them might well mean the difference between life and death to her.

As far as she was concerned, wealthy folk could spare her a little out of their excess. If they would not give it to her, she would steal it without compunction. She would rather steal bread from those who could well afford it than take bread from the mouths of those who were just as poor and hungry as she was. She would not steal from beggars. That was as much morality as she could afford.

She drew her cloak around her with a bravado she did not feel. She stuck out in this part of town as she never did in her own shabby quarter. Here, people didn't wrap their feet in rags for the want of a pair of boots, or wear filthy breeches and coarse woolen shirts that would fall to pieces if they were ever washed.

No, the men dressed in fine buckskin breeches and fine white linen shirts and wore powdered, curled wigs on their heads. Their fingers were loaded down with glittering jewels, and, best of all, no doubt their boots had been made specially for their feet. The jewels she would rather have than not, but it was their boots she lusted after with all her heart and soul. Their soft, leather boots—how she envied them their boots . . .

If the men were finely dressed, the women were dressed even finer, she thought, as a couple of ladies minced past her on their way to their coach. The jewels that just one of them was wearing round her neck would have bought her a dozen pairs of boots with enough left over for a hearty feed at the alehouse, even after Conard the fence had taken his cut, grasping old rascal that he was.

There was no point hankering after those particular jewels though. The ladies were well-guarded by a couple of stout footmen with cudgels. She gave them a careful look. They looked more liked hired bullies than footmen, with their small heads set on huge necks, their thick shoulders, and their beefy hands. She knew their type—faster than they looked and merciless as the Devil himself if they ever laid hands on you. Little hope there of doing a quick snatch and an even quicker scarper down the road and into a dark alley where they wouldn't find her.

Still, the jewels looked like they would fetch a fair price. She hadn't seen anything as fine for a long while. Conard would pay her well for such quality. Perhaps if she distracted the attention of the footmen somehow, she might stand a chance . . .

A cuff about the ears brought her to her senses again.

A third footman had come up behind her and caught her eyeing the jewels with obvious desire. "Get out of here, you nasty little rat," he growled at her, swinging the cudgel at her again. "Don't try it on, or you'll be swinging from the end of a rope faster than you can blink."

Her head still ringing from the first blow, she made sure to duck fast so his cudgel hit only empty air this time around. The footman swore at her as she scampered off down the street.

She tossed a few choice epithets back at him as she rounded the corner and slowed down to a walk again. The night was still young, and well-dressed women were not that uncommon. She would find her boots sooner or later. No bastard son of a stinking two-sou whore would stop her from getting her feet done up warm and watertight for the winter.

She wandered around for a while, meeting with nothing promising. A fine young gentleman with a lace cravat and well-polished boots stumbled by her, his breath stinking of ale. "Fine night, ain't it. Jes' fine," he slurred at her, waving his hand in her direction. She picked his pocket with a practiced hand as he passed, but his wallet was suspiciously light and gave out nary a jingle, even when she gave it a circumspect shake.

She scuttled round the corner to inspect her booty, and muttered under her breath in disgust. He must have drunk or gambled away all his money already. His wallet held nothing but a couple of pewter buttons. Damn, how she hated to risk her neck for so little.

She didn't mind risking her neck for a decent reward. She was not overly afraid of ending up on the gallows tree—death came to all. Do what she will, she would meet the grim reaper sooner or later. She would gladly risk her life for a handful of gold coins, or a pair of stout boots, or even for a hot meal that would fill up her hollow insides with a warm, full feeling for a few delicious hours. She risked her life every day, just so that she could survive.

She put her whole hand inside the empty purse just to make sure she hadn't missed anything the first time she had looked in it, but no matter how hard she looked, it was still empty. She gave a disappointed sigh and let her shoulders slump in defeat for the barest moment.

Just surviving seemed to get harder and harder each day. She would risk her life a thousand times over for the chance to get out of the stews of Paris—to have her own room in a house that didn't leak, sharing it with people who didn't stink of despair and cheap wine, and to have a decent meal once a day without having to steal it. But to risk her life for a pair of tarnished pewter buttons not even worth the price of a mouthful of bread? That was truly absurd.

However absurd it was, she still had to get her boots. She would not let a little piece of bad luck upset her. She threw the purse to the ground in disgust and spat on it for good measure. She hoped the young fool she had stolen it from died of the pox. To have such wealth and to let it fall from his fingers so easily? He didn't deserve any better fate.

The theaters were emptying now and the streets were busy for a time. Trade was poor when the streets were busy. Too many eyes were around to catch her. The chance of getting noticed in her thefts was greater, and getting away again could be a problem when there were too many people around. In her rags, she couldn't blend in with the crowds here—she would have to rely on her speed to escape.

She didn't know this part of Paris as well as she should if she was going to make it her more permanent hunting ground. She would have to come here in the daytime and scout it out better—find out which alleys were blind and which walls she could scale to get away from pursuers, which roofs were easy to climb and which would lead her into a sudden precipitous drop just at the wrong moment.

Even better, if she could once make a lucky hit, she would invest in a properly made suit of clothes so, guilty or not, she didn't have to run for it every time someone missed his wallet.

She wandered around for some time, looking over the terrain, until the streets started to empty out. A good time to be making her hit.

She took up her position in a niche in a stone wall that kept her sheltered from the bitter night breezes and waited for suitable prey to wander by. No one would notice her there, or give her any trouble. If she stayed there long enough, like a patient spider, some fat fly would blunder into her web sooner or later.

Her muscles were starting to grow stiff from the cold when she heard the hoofbeats of a lone rider coming through the street, the horse's iron shoes clattering on the cobblestones. Damn it all. She could hardly rob a man on horseback.

Then her ears pricked up. The rider was being followed, she was sure of it, though she doubted that he could hear over the noise he was making. Five or six men, she would say at a guess, with soft shoes on, so they could follow after him without being noticed.

The rider went past her, and sure enough, close by after him came a group of six men, slithering by in the shadows, their breath misting the chill night air. She shrank back into her niche in the stone wall as they went by. They didn't see her.

On quiet feet she followed after them, thankful for the rags that made no sound as she walked. The man on horseback must be carrying great wealth if he was worth six stout ruffians to take him down. With any luck, there would be a few crumbs left over for her to pick up when they were through with him.

She crept along behind them through the dark streets. The man they were following stopped a couple of times at crossroads, turning his horse's head first one way and then the other before deciding on a direction to take. He evidently didn't know exactly where to go.

Miriame smiled to herself in the darkness as the man on horseback passed through the wealthy streets of the town and began to skirt the edges of the slum that she called her home. She couldn't imagine his business there, alone and in the dead of night. He must be lost.

More fool he not to stop at a respectable inn and wait for day to break before he carried on his way. Strangers to Paris were the easiest game of all.

She hoped the ruffians would take him down soon before he attracted the attention of more thieves. She would rather take her pickings quickly and leave again—though she would fight for them if she must.

Just as she was starting to think that the ruffians would never make their move, they pounced.

The man on horseback had stopped one more time, looking around him as if he knew he had lost his way, and wheeled his horse around to retrace his steps. In that moment, the six men set upon him with a ferocity all the more fearful because of its silence.

The man drew his sword and tried to beat them back again. "Help, murder, thieves!" he yelled at the top of his voice, but there was no one to hear him. No one but Miriame, and she could not help him even if she would.

He was no match for his six burly attackers. One of them hung on his sword arm so he could not raise it, another held his horse by the bridle so he could not spur away, and the other four dragged him off his horse.

He landed on the cobbles with a nasty crunch and lay limp, his furious cries of protest suddenly stilled.

Miriame crept forward, her senses in high alert, watching for the gold or silver gleam of any stray coins that might roll her way, or for the opportunity to grab some loot while their attention was distracted. Her fingers itched to snatch whatever she could, and her legs trembled with their readiness to sprint off into the darkness to get away.

"Is he dead already?" one of them asked in a hoarse whisper. He sounded eerily disappointed, as if half the fun of the robbery was in killing the victim.

Mere robbery, however, was not on the minds of the ruffians. As Miriame watched every move they made, in a fever of impatience to steal enough to get the boots she craved, one of the six drew a knife. The blade gleamed wickedly in the moonlight as it plunged into the chest of the stranger lying still on the cobbles.

The man with the knife spat on his blade and wiped it clean on his jerkin before sliding it back into the sheath at his belt. "He will be now."

She stifled a gasp and crept back into the shadows. Murder was a far greater crime than robbery was. You would hang for simple robbery, sure enough, but for murder? By the time the torturers had finished with you down in the dungeons, you would be begging for death—if you even had a tongue left with which to beg.

She shuddered, hoping that the six would not find out they had a witness to their crime. If they found her now, she wouldn't wager a single sou for her chance of living till the dawn.

"Are you sure he is dead?" she heard one of them ask in a whisper. The accent was cultured and pure, as if he came from the court of the King rather than from the slums where hired murderers were more often to be found.

Miriame gave a start, her blood freezing in her heart. She knew that voice, she was sure of it. She had last heard it on the day that Rebecca had died, laughing over her poor dead sister's body. She made herself as small as a mouse, hoping none of them would think of checking the shadows that surrounded them. If they found her, she would soon be as dead as the man they had just knifed. Heaven help her if they discovered she was a woman before they killed her. She would rather kill herself now—a nice, clean, quick death—and be done with it.

The man with the knife nodded. "As near as makes no difference. He'll be dead before dawn."

One of the others reached toward the rings on the man's hands. Even from this distance, Miriame could see the gleam of avarice on his face.

The man with the cultured voice cuffed him viciously around the head. "Leave them be." His voice, even in a whisper, had the ring of authority—the tone of a man who expected instant obedience.

If Miriame had had a knife in her pocket, he would be wearing it in his chest at that instant. She hated him with a deep, abiding hatred that went deeper than her instinct to save her own life, deeper than her very soul. One day, she promised herself, keeping her fear in check with her fantasies, one day he would find death at her hands. She owed Rebecca his life.

"But the rings alone must be worth—"

He didn't finish his sentence. The leader drew his knife and pressed it to the man's side. "Are you arguing with me?"

The man shook his head sullenly and sidled away from the knife. "No."

"Good. Because if you are I shall slit your throat as easily as your comrade knifed that fellow on the ground." He gave the body a contemptuous kick. Miri-ame shut her eyes for a moment, willing herself not to see the body of her sister in the man's place. "Our or-ders were clear. Nothing was to be taken from him but his papers."

He reached into the man's jacket pocket and with-drew a packet of papers. Blood dripped down from them onto the cobbles. He gave a grunt of satisfaction. "That's what we came for, lads. Now let's get the hell out of here."

He turned to face the man who had tried to steal the stranger's rings. "I would counsel you not to return to rob the body. It will be death for anyone caught with his possessions, and you will be tortured first to tell all you know of his death. I am not willing to risk my life on your silence in the hands of the torturers. If I so much as sus-pect you of robbing him of even a single sou, I will kill you myself. Do you understand?"

They shuffled their feet uncomfortably, and the man who had tried to steal the rings backed away into the darkness toward where Miriame crouched in her hiding place. She shut her eyes and willed him not to come any closer or to turn around and see her hiding there.

"Let some other poor bastard come along and rob him. Someone else can hang for his death, not you or me."

All five of them nodded, and without another word being spoken, they melted away into the dark again, leav-ing the street bare and empty.

Miriame breathed a sigh of relief. By a miracle, she had escaped with her life. She waited in her hole in the shadows for some minutes, but nothing stirred. Her fear and hatred for the man she had just seen warred with her desire for a pair of boots, and eventually the boots won.

As silent as a ghost she crept out again, carefully balancing her weight on the balls of her feet so she could take off running if the leader was still lurking around, waiting to make sure that his instructions were followed.

Not a sound reached her ears but the rustling of the wind and the bark of a lone fox in the distance.

She reached open ground and knelt carefully beside the body. His rings were indeed very fine. She did not wonder at the killer risking a knife blade in his side to get his hands on them. She herself would risk death for them twice over. She pulled them off his fingers and stowed them away in her rags. She'd have a pair of stout new boots before the week was out.

Carefully she felt in his pockets in his greatcoat, dragging out his wallet. It was heavy with gold pieces. She looked inside, and her eyes opened wide. Never in her life had she seen so much wealth. How foolish they had been to leave the money here. One man's gold piece looked the same as any other. They could never pin aught on a man just for a purse full of gold. Her heart hammering, she tucked the wallet away next to her skin.

A rustle of papers caught her ear. She patted his greatcoat and his jacket, finding no pocket.

They must be sewn inside his lining. She felt around on the ground around her until her fingers found a sharp stone. With the tip of the stone she ripped the lining of his jacket, put her hands inside, and drew out a packet of papers tied with ribbon and a couple of loose sheets.

He had been murdered for his papers. They must be even more valuable than the gold she had tucked away. She pulled out all the papers she could find and transferred them from his coat to her own.

Just then, the body gave a feeble groan and stirred slightly. Miriame gave a start. She had thought he was dead and gone already.

She bent her head towards his chest and felt a faint stirring of his chest as he labored to draw his last breaths. He was still alive. Not very alive, and not likely to live for long, but still alive for now.

"Can you hear me?" she said into his ear. "Can you understand what I am saying?"

He gave the tiniest nod, so small she didn't know whether or not she was imagining it. His eyes flickered open for a brief moment, and then shut again, and he groaned again. He was definitely alive.

She sat back on her heels wondering what to do. She had no qualms about robbing a corpse—she was just taking things that were of no use to their owner any more. But to rob a dying man and leave him to breathe his last in the mud of the roadway? Living on the streets as she did, she could not afford many morals, but somehow that didn't sit quite right with her.

Besides, the man she hated from the very depths of her soul wanted the man dead. That was reason enough for her to want to save his life.

She touched her hand lightly to the wound on his chest and drew it away again, sticky with blood. With a grunt she tore a strip of wool from one of the shirts she wore and bound it tightly around his chest to stop the bleeding. She had taken enough wealth from him to replace her garments with better ones twenty times over, but even so she sacrificed it with some unwillingness. She hadn't survived on the street for this long by giving her clothes to strangers.

"What the hell," she muttered to herself, as she heaved him to his feet with all the muscles in her strong, wiry body. "You've done me a good turn by giving me your wallet. The least I can do is help you to die in your bed, not die like a dog in the gutter."

His brief moment of lucidity had not lasted for long.

He was quite insensible now, flopping against her shoulder as weak and spineless as the rag doll her mother had once made for her, long, long ago when times had not been so bad. He did not even groan when she accidentally knocked against the wound in his chest, making it bleed anew.

The stranger's horse was still standing nearby, nosing around the cobblestones in the vain hope of a blade of grass. Miriame called softly to it. "Come on, my pretty girl, come over here a moment," she called, and it ambled over in her direction.

Somehow she managed to wrestle the stranger onto his horse's back, until he was lying face down over the saddle. His face bumped against the horse's flanks on one side, while his knees bumped against the other side. He could hardly be very comfortable, but they only had a short way to go. She knew of an inn not far away where he would be well looked after. The landlady there was kind enough and more honest than most. She would take good enough care of him if she were paid well to do so. She would not take his money and throw him out on the streets again to die, as would some others Miriame knew.

More worrying, the wound in his chest had begun to seep blood again. The horse flared its nostrils and sidestepped uncomfortably down the street with its strange burden, but Miriame held tight to its reins and forced it to follow along behind her. "Come," she murmured to the horse, "go softly." The horse snorted uneasily, but did not panic or throw off its burden.

The dark of the night was starting to lighten slowly into the gray of a new day when the lights of the inn flickered in front of her. Miriame banged on the door and a sleepy-eyed scullery maid opened it a crack. Her eyes went wide when she saw the horse with its burden, and she opened her mouth to scream.

Miriame had no patience for her hysterics. "He's alive, you fool," she said shortly, "but he won't be for much longer if you don't get a move on. Fetch your mistress, and right smartly too, or it'll be the worse for you."

The girl stuffed her apron in her mouth to stifle her sobs and scurried away as if the devil was after her.

The landlady came down the stairs shortly afterwards, a clean apron stretched over her ample hips and her mouth stretched in a yawn. She cursed loudly when she saw Miriame in her ragged clothes, but there was no malice in her words. "What do you think you're about, waking me out of my bed at this ungodly hour, you young scamp," she grumbled. "Go on, be off or I'll give you a smack to learn you better manners."

Miriame hushed her and gestured to the horse and its grisly burden. "We need a room."

The landlady waddled over the threshold of the inn and looked more closely at the stranger. "He's dressed fine enough. What's the matter with him? Drunk or sick?"

"Not drunk, anyway. Someone tried to murder him in the street. He needs nursing."

The landlady's eyes narrowed. "And who'll pay for that? I'm no charity, to be paying for the nursing of half-dead strangers who pass by my door in the middle of the night."

Miriame sighed at the thought of parting with any of her newfound wealth. "We can pay you well enough."

The woman still looked suspicious. "So you say. Until you've eaten my food and slept in my bed and used up the best linen and hot water until your master there breathes his last, and then you claim you've been robbed and don't have a sou to pay your debts. Aye, I know all your tricks."

Miriame drew a small coin from the bag hidden in her shirt and handed it over. "Does this look like a trick to you?"

The landlady grabbed it eagerly, sniffed at it, and gave it a bite with the few teeth she had left. Satisfied that it was genuine enough, she tucked it into her large bosom. "Well, mebbe you're one of the honest ones," she admitted grudgingly. "But you can't blame a poor woman for looking after her own interests." She turned back towards the inn and raised her voice into a bellow. "Luc, Mathieu, drag your lazy carcasses out here and give me a hand to get this young gentleman up to bed."

The two men who appeared at her call lifted the stranger as if he were a featherweight. Miriame took the saddlebags off the horse, gave it into the care of a stableboy to be fed and brushed, and then followed the men up the stairs and into a chamber with a large bed in it.

The landlady drew back the counterpane and spread out some old rags on top of the sheet. The men deposited their burden roughly on top of the rags and shouldered their way out of the room again.

"No sense in getting the sheets all bloody," the landlady remarked to no one in particular, as she lighted a tallow candle and bent to her work, stripping off the stranger's boots and breeches, and baring the wound in his chest. She poured a bowl of water from the pitcher on the washstand and began to sponge off the blood around the edges of the cut.

For the first time that night Miriame got a good look at the man she had rescued from the streets. He was young enough by his looks—barely three-and-twenty, she would guess. His cheeks were pale from loss of blood and his face was drawn with pain, but even this could not hide the beauty of his features. His eyes were framed with long eyelashes, dark brown to the very tips. His mouth was full and red, despite the paleness of his face, and his teeth, when he grimaced slightly in pain, were white and straight. His hair, once they had got his hat off, fell across the bolster in brown-blond ringlets, streaked golden with the sun.

The landlady seemed equally struck by his handsome features. "He's a right looker, ain't he?" she said, as she wiped a lock of hair off his face with a clean corner of her washcloth.

"Indeed," Miriame agreed. It wasn't just his face, either, that held her attention. His legs in his silk stockings were long and straight and his thighs and calves firm with muscle.

Slowly she raised her eyes from his legs again. His belly was flat and his chest as broad as any woman could want, but his chest was disfigured with the nasty wound. A pity. She doubted that he would live until the morrow.

Even half-dead as he was, she couldn't help but stare at him. No wonder a gang of thugs had set on him in the street—no doubt some slighted lover had ordered them to get rid of his rival. He was as beautiful as an angel in Heaven—enough to inspire desire in any woman—or murderous jealousy in any man.

The landlady was looking curiously at her, and she snapped her mouth shut again. She had been caught gawping at him like any girl. The woman would be suspecting her disguise, or suspecting her of worse than that, if she were not more careful about where her eyes wandered.

"Shall I make a pallet up on the floor for you?" the landlady asked, satisfied that she had done what she could for now. "You can watch over your master until the doctor comes. I'll send a boy for him as soon as it gets light."

Miriame shook her head vehemently. She would never stay around a man with a death warrant marked on his very face. She was only too used to being blamed for anything that went wrong, whether it was her fault or no. Still, if the landlady thought she was the stranger's servant, her robbery would be all the easier. "I must get away," she muttered hastily. "He give me a job to do afore the thugs got him. Says I must do it for him or he'll feed me liver to his pet stoat, so he will."

"I can't stay with him till the doctor gets here," the landlady grumbled. "It's not yet dawn and I've got other guests besides him to look after."

"I'll stay with him till then," Miriame offered with some reluctance. She was itching to get clean away with her loot. Besides, she had little intention of staying long. Let her just make sure that she had taken everything she could, and she would be off. The unlucky stranger was going to die whether she waited and wept over his soul or not.

"I'll leave you with him then," the landlady said as she backed out of the door before Miriame could change her mind, the basin of bloody water in her hands. "I'll send the doctor up when he comes." She nudged the door shut with the back of her shoulder and Miriame could hear her plodding down the stairs to the kitchen once again.

Saddlebags first, Miriame thought as soon as she was alone with the stranger again. If the stuff in it was worth stealing, she would take it gladly. If not, the heavy bags would only slow her down and she would leave them behind.

She thrust her hand in the first one and drew out a large packet of food wrapped in a coarse cloth. She wouldn't bother to take that with her—she'd eat it there and then. The bread was white and sweet and still soft, the cheese was ripe and moist, and the meat was thickly sliced. She wolfed it all down in less than a minute and finished it off with a sweet, wizened apple. She sat back and patted her stomach with satisfaction. She hadn't fed so well in a long time. Her robbery was going well so far.

Apart from the food, that saddlebag was empty. She thrust her hand around in it to make sure that she wasn't missing anything, but there was nothing else there.

She thrust her hand into the second saddlebag, smacking her lips in anticipation. She wouldn't say no to more food like that she had just devoured. If she could eat like that every day, she would soon be even fatter than the landlady.

No food in this saddlebag, but there were clothes. She drew them out eagerly. Half a dozen shirts of lace-trimmed white linen, softer than silk. A pair of brocade waistcoats. More silk stockings than she could count. A pair of breeches identical to the ones the stranger wore. Even a tortoiseshell comb and brush, and a pretty jeweled knife, more like an ornament than a weapon despite the sharpness of the blade. She sighed in wonderment over such riches, wishing she could wear them instead of taking them off to Conard to be sold.

She shook her head at her foolishness. In the slums, people would knife her in the back for the lace on just one of the sleeves. She could never wear them, but she'd get a good price for them, and buy herself a coat to keep the winter cold from her bones instead.

Her curiosity about the saddlebags satisfied, she drew out the papers she had taken from the stranger earlier. She pulled the ribbon from the packet of papers and a bundle of letters spilled out on to her lap.

A noise outside in the corridor startled her and she leaped up in a sudden fright to bolt the door, cursing her own greedy impatience. The stranger had been knifed for his papers. Those who had done the deed might have found out by now that they hadn't got all of what they came for and be on the hunt for him again. At any rate, she ought not to take any chances.

The door once safely bolted, she sat down cross-legged on the floor to puzzle over the letters. Her mother had taught both her and her sister Rebecca to read a little when they were small, but since their mother had died, she had had precious little chance of reading anything. What use was it to her when all she had wanted to do was protect her sister and feed them both? Her life had been one long struggle to survive.

She puzzled over the fine handwriting, making it out with some difficulty. Obviously the letters were from some woman to the handsome stranger lying on the bed, judging by all the "darlings" and "sweethearts" that lay sprinkled over the pages. They were signed "Francine," every one of them, with an ornately curved F at the beginning. She riffled through them, and then tossed them aside with a snort of disgust. What a sentimental young fool the stranger was, carrying them in the lining of his cloak, as if they were more precious than the jewels he wore in plain sight on his fingers.

Only the two single pages were left. She picked them up, hoping they were worth rather more than the love letters she had tossed aside. No one would kill a stranger for a passel of old *billet-doux,* to be sure. The thugs in the street must have stolen the right papers after all.

The two loose sheets seemed to be written in the same hand, but they were rather more difficult to make out. The words were writ smaller, and they were much longer and more complicated. At least, Miriame noted with a shrug of satisfaction, there were no "darlings" or "sweethearts" on these pages. They were filled with serious words—words, she hoped, that might mean money.

With a sigh, she settled down to painstakingly read

through the pages, her finger pointing to each word in turn as she spelled them out one by one.

The dawn was beginning to break in earnest by the time she had finished. They had given her an idea—a wild idea, an unthinkable idea, an impossible idea—but an idea nonetheless.

She stood up and stretched, her legs stiff from sitting cross-legged on the floor for so long. The man on the bed was still lying there with his eyes closed. His chest labored up and down with each faint breath he took. He was still hanging on to life, but only by a thread.

Young and strong though he was, he could not expect to live. His Maker was even now preparing him a bed in heaven, where he would be the most beautiful of all the angels, she had no doubt. Except for Rebecca—she would always be the most beautiful angel of all with her dark eyes, her long curling hair the color of a raven's wing, and her sweet, sweet smile. A pity that death would take him so soon, in the first bloom of his youth, just as it had taken Rebecca . . .

She shook her head. She had no time to think about Rebecca now. Her sister would have cautioned her to keep her mind on the task in front of her and not to let herself be distracted. She would do so still, for the memory of Rebecca, if nothing else.

The man on the bed, Jean-Paul Metin, from the South of France, according to the letters he carried, was likely to die. His letters could not serve him now. He was a stranger to Paris, from the provinces. He knew no one and no one knew him, save for the mysterious Francine of the letters. There was no one but Francine to know if she, Miriame, were to take his place. No one but Francine to suspect that Jean-Paul Metin was not the person he claimed to be.

If she were like other women, this Francine would be sure to lose interest in poor, murdered Metin if he never replied to her letters. Indeed, Miriame could not answer them in his name even if she would. They were not furnished with an address. Poor Francine would have to live disconsolate without her "sweet cherub" beside her.

Shaking with wonder that she would dare to attempt the trick she was contemplating, she ran down to the kitchen. "Have the maid bring me a tub of water, as warm as you can make it," she instructed the landlady, who was standing at the bench, her arms covered to the elbow in flour. "I need a bath."

The landlady snorted at her impudence, but Miriame pressed another small coin into her hand. The landlady took it with her grimy paw, dropped it in her bosom and went back to kneading the dough. "One tub of water, will be brought right up."

The water arrived quickly, but not quickly enough for Miriame. She had been pacing up and down in the chamber, one eye on the door and the other on the wounded stranger. Jean-Paul Metin. The name had a nice ring to it. She wouldn't mind being known by such a name.

His brow was white and covered in sweat. He looked to be in terrible pain. She hoped for his sake that he died quickly—she didn't think a man should suffer when his time had come. It crossed her mind to give him a quick tap on the head to ease him gently into the afterlife, but something stayed her hand. He had done her no wrong. She would not be his murderer.

At last came a knock on the door. The maid wrestled in a small hip bath, following it with jugs of steaming water. "Shall I stay and help you wash?" she asked in a bored voice, as she tipped the last of the water into the tub and began to roll up her sleeves in expectation of an invitation.

Miriame waved her away. "No, thank you all the same." She had a character to preserve now—one that she would easily lose again were someone to see her naked.

When the maidservant had left, she bolted the door once more. Just for good measure she drew the coverlet off the bed and hung it over the door to make sure that every little peephole was safely covered. Only then did she begin to undress.

One by one she shed her ragged clothes and put the tip of her toe into the water. She had never had a whole bath before. Even when her mama had been alive, the most she had done was sponge herself all over with a washcloth.

She looked down at her feet. They were gray with grime, their nails black with accumulated dirt. She would not be so disrespectful of the stranger's soft leather boots as to put her unwashed feet into them. Besides, no one would ever take her for a member of the gentry with a dirty face and her hair matted and tangled with the filth of the streets. "Like it or not," she told herself firmly, "you have to wash."

Gingerly she sat down in the bath and rubbed herself all over with the sweet-smelling soap the maid had given her. The water was warm. She found to her surprise that washing wasn't as bad as she had expected. Lying back in the warm water, her legs bent right up under her chin and her head resting on the edge of the tub, it was almost pleasant.

Or it was until she got soap in her eyes. She screwed up her face and bit back a wail as the harsh soap burned her. She splashed water on her face and blinked furiously until she could see again. Men did not cry because they got soap in their eyes in their bath. She scrubbed her face furiously, roughening the tender skin under her nose and around her chin, to make it look as though she had shaved herself closely.

Once her hair was washed, too, she got out of the tub and rubbed herself dry. Wrapping herself in the towel, she took the wide-toothed comb from the saddlebag and began the long, laborious task of combing through her hair. She had kept it short for years, hacking it off above the shoulders so no one would ever suspect she was a woman. She didn't like what happened to women on the streets—no more than she liked what happened to pretty boys—and was determined that no one would ever so much as suspect her disguise. Even despite the ragged haircut, though, it took her some time before the comb would go through it without getting snagged on a nasty snarl.

She drew out some fresh linen from the saddlebag and put it on, feeling more like a thief than she ever had before. Taking a man's money was nothing, but taking this man's linen as he lay back on the bed, dying by inches, gave her an uncomfortable feeling. She shook it off as well as she could. She had done him no harm, but tried her best to save him. His murderers should be the ones to harbor a guilty conscience, not she, who merely had the good fortune to profit from their crime.

The jacket fitted her well enough, buttoning across her front to hide the fact that she was a woman, but the breeches were far too big, bagging around her waist and bottom like a saggy skin. She knotted a leather tie around her waist to keep them up, and as an after-thought, pinned a pair of rolled-up stockings in the front to give a realistic bulge. She would defy anyone to catch her out now.

Boots now. With a reverent sigh she took the stranger's boots and drew them on over her calves. They were slightly too long in the foot for her, but she hardly noticed. They were boots. Real leather boots, rich and brown, and as soft as her new-washed hair.

Her disguise was nearly complete. A scrap of leather to tie her hair at the nape of her neck, the stranger's feathered hat to clap on her head, his greatcoat to throw around her shoulders, his rings to go on her fingers, his letters to be tucked inside her jacket, and his well-stocked wallet to be worn inside her shirt next to her skin.

She made an awkward bow to the wall, wishing she had a looking-glass to see her disguise in. No matter, she had passed as a lad in rags for years—why would anyone suspect her now she was dressed as a gentleman?

The landlady was cutting up vegetables and tossing them into a stewpot when Miriame went into the kitchen. Her eyes widened when she saw Miriame in the doorway. "You do clean up nice," she said, as she went back to her chopping.

Quick as a wink, Miriame snaffled a couple of carrots and a turnip and stuffed them into one of the pockets of her greatcoat. They would do very well for her to munch on for her supper that night. "Thank you," she said gravely.

"What can I do for you, Monsieur?" the landlady asked, putting down her vegetables and wiping her hands on her apron, when Miriame made no move to leave.

"My master upstairs is gravely ill and likely to die."

"Aye, that he is," the landlady agreed, absentmindedly sharpening her vegetable knife on a long steel that hung in a corner of the kitchen. "Them as murdered the poor lad did their evil work well. He'll be lucky to last until tomorrow morn."

"I must leave him now to carry out a commission that he entrusted to me, but I would have him well looked after in my absence." She held out the smallest of the stranger's rings—a circle of gold with a dark blue stone embedded in it. "Care for him well. Cure him if you can. This should more than recompense you for your trouble."

The landlady put aside her knife and took the ring with a glint in her eye. Any protest that she might have made was instantly stifled at the sight of the jewel. "I shall."

"And if you cannot cure him, then see he is decently buried."

The landlady looked up sharply. "You will not be coming back, then?"

Miriame smiled to herself. Not if she could help it. She knew that the landlady suspected her theft, though she had bought the woman's silence for the present time. "My journey must needs take me to the farthest corner of France, but I will return when I can for news of him," she lied.

The landlady nodded, seemingly satisfied. "God speed you on your journey, then, Monsieur," she said, chopping her vegetables with her newly sharpened knife with renewed vigor.

Miriame tipped her hat as she left, the purloined carrots giving her pocket a comforting weight. She would not starve tonight.

The horse was well rested and well fed when she made her way to the stables. She tipped the stableboy a few sous for looking after it so well, and he saluted her with a tip of his dirty cap.

He looked after her with admiration as she clambered awkwardly onto her horse. "Where be you off to then, Monsieur?" the lad asked, as she tightened her knuckles around the reins and urged the horse out of the yard.

She gave a big belly laugh as she rode off, clinging to the horse's back like a beggar to a rich man's leg. She could hardly believe it herself. "Me? I'm off to join the King's Musketeers."

Chapter 2

The cardinal's lips curled up into a sneer and he tossed the packet of letters onto the table in front of him. "What is this rubbish you have brought to me?" He swept his long robes around himself with a mutter of disgust and went to stand in the window, the harsh midday glare lighting up his malformed body and shrunken features with all nature's indifference and lack of mercy.

The messenger in front of him turned his hat over and over in his hands as beads of sweat started to appear on his forehead. "The letters you asked for, your Excellency, the ones we were to take from the young man."

The cardinal whirled around and fixed the unhappy man with a baleful glare. "The letters I asked for? Pah! What nonsense! Why would I want such drivel?"

"They were from the right man, I would swear to it," the man protested. "We never lost sight of him for an instant. Besides, I would know his pretty face anywhere." His voice was rough with disgust. "Dress him in a gown and you'd mistake him for a girl."

"They may be from the right young man, but they are not the right letters." His voice held all the ice of a pond in midwinter, a coldness that no winter sun could melt. "Did you bother to look at them?"

The messenger shrugged uneasily. "Wouldn't do me any good if I did."

The cardinal stalked back to the table and slammed his fist down on the top. "Why must I be served by idiots and fools? Is there not a single literate thief or cutthroat in the whole of Paris?"

The messenger wisely held his tongue.

The cardinal picked up one of the letters, shook it open, and began to read. "'My dear son'," he began.

I hope this missive finds you well and in good health. God has seen fit to bless me with a fit of the rheumaticks this season, but other than that I am as hale and hearty as ever an old man can expect to be. By the grace of God your mother has been cured of her cough. The brindled cow had a calf last night. With God's grace it will grow up to be a fine young bull.

Your loving father,
Henri.

He shook the letter at the thief. "What good is this to me? How can I use the ramblings of a doddering old fool to discredit the King's mistress? You have failed in your task. Failed. You do not deserve a single sou."

"We did not fail altogether," the messenger complained, his face dark at the prospect of missing out entirely on the promised reward. "You asked us to do away with him, and we did that right enough."

The cardinal's face was suffused with anger. "You murdered him before the letters were in your possession?"

The messenger misread the signs of anger on the cardinal's face. "He won't be bothering you now, for sure," he said, his voice thick with satisfaction. "We left him a-lying on the streets, dead as a doornail."

The cardinal clenched and unclenched his fists as if he would love to strike the other man dead on the spot himself. "You are a fool. A triple fool. Where are the papers now?"

Comprehension flooded the messenger's face. He went red and stood as if rooted to the spot. "I . . . I . . ."

"You don't know." It was a statement, not a question.

The man was silent, not able to deny it, but fearing to assent.

"Out of all the people in Paris who may have come across the body of the young fool, you have no idea which one found him first. You have no idea who may have stolen the horse or searched the body, and found the very papers we seek? You do not know if they are in the hands of our enemies even as we speak? You do not even know if they have already been destroyed?"

The messenger shook his head and drops of sweat started to run down his forehead. He wiped them away with the back of his sleeve. The stench of fear hung in the air. "I do not know, your Excellency." His voice was the merest thread of a whisper.

"It seems to me that you have just made your task a good deal harder than it was before." The cardinal's voice was smooth as silk and as menacing as the hiss of a viper. "I want those papers. Do you understand me?"

"But how can I possibly . . ." The man's planned protest trailed away into silence at the look on the cardinal's face.

"How you find them is your own affair. You lost them once through your stupid carelessness. Do not lose them again. And remember," the cardinal said, fixing him with a cruel stare, "I will not be a happy man if you have wasted my chance to ruin the King's harlot through your stupidity. I do not tolerate failure in my servants. Not a second time."

* * *

Miriame cocked her hat at a jaunty angle and whistled a little ditty as she rode into the barracks, though inside she was shaking like a leaf in a storm. A couple of soldiers were lounging around in the yard when she dismounted and stretched ostentatiously, as if she had been riding all day. Her backside was damn near numb anyway. She had never been on the back of a horse before and right glad she was to get off it again. She wasn't sure she liked sitting all the way up there close to the sky. The ground was such a long way down.

She glanced sideways at the uniforms as she stretched. Very soon now, if she played well the hand that Fate had dealt her, she would be one of them.

Never again would she go to bed hungry at night for want of a bite to eat for supper. Never again would she shiver in her thin blanket as the hail and sleet battered through the thin roof of the room she lay in, huddling against the filthy lice-ridden bodies of her fellow beggars to keep from freezing to death. She was going to be a soldier. Not just any old soldier, either. She was going to join the elite of the elite—the King's Musketeers.

She was crazy to think that she, a beggar from the streets and a woman to boot, could get away with such a crazy plan. She wiped her sweaty palms on her breeches, hoping they wouldn't leave a mark. She couldn't go back now.

The other soldiers were watching her with absent-minded curiosity. She gave them a lazy salute, hiding her fear as best she could. "Hey, where's the captain?"

"You joining up?" one of them asked her. He was a short, squat, muscular looking fellow, almost as wide as he was tall.

"If the captain'll have me."

The other one, a brute of a man with powerful-looking legs and hands the size of bear paws, looked mildly interested. "Can you fight?"

She thought about that for a moment. She'd learned early on in life that it was usually smarter to run away if she could. "When I have to."

The smaller soldier looked at the bigger one, and the bigger one gave a brief nod, as if giving his permission. The smaller one drew his sword out of its scabbard, tossed it lightly from one hand to the other and grinned at Miriame. "So draw your sword and show me."

She was startled out of her rather fragile composure. "Now?"

"You're not scared, are you?" the squat man taunted.

Scared? Of him? She laughed out loud. She was scared of hunger and of cold, of the man with the cold voice who had raped and knifed her younger sister, and of the King's executioner in his black hood with holes cut out for him to see his victims, but she wasn't scared of anything else. She simply didn't see the point of wasting her energy fighting when she didn't have to.

Now, it seems, was one of those times when she had to fight rather than run. How hard could it be? All she had to do was to look reasonably convincing . . .

She looped her horse's reins over a post by the water trough, took off her greatcoat, slung it over the horse's back and whirled to face her opponent.

He was waiting for her in the center of the yard, his legs apart and his sword in his hand. Miriame hefted her blade in her fist, feeling its weight. She'd not used a sword before, having only had a little knife she carried with her, sharpened to a wicked point on a flint she'd stolen. She waved it a few times in the air, testing its weight. She found it rather awkward.

The squat man laughed at her and flicked his sword expertly in the air.

To Miriame's surprise, the sword in her hand was suddenly on the ground and her opponent's sword was at her neck. She blinked. She hadn't even seen it coming.

The squat man laughed again and turned towards the bearlike soldier. "What do you say, Captain? Are you desperate enough to take on an untried youth who can't even hold a sword? Or shall I send him back again to where he came from with a flea in his ear for wasting your time?"

He should not have turned his back on Miriame. Once the sword was out of her hand, she could fight the way she was used to. Without making a sound to warn him, she kicked out viciously at him, catching him on the back of the knee and making his legs buckle. He fell to one knee and turned his head in astonishment, sword still in his hand. "What the . . . ?" he started to say.

Miriame avoided his sword deftly and chopped his wrist hard with the edge of her hand. He gave a yelp of pain and his sword fell to the ground into the dirt of the yard. "What do you think you're doing?" he spluttered.

With a quick movement she drew the knife out of her boot, crouched on her heels by his side, and pressed the tip of the blade into his neck, just below his ear, hard enough to nick the skin. "This is the way I fight," she hissed into his ear, as his face turned slightly pale. "I give no quarter and expect none in return. When I fight, I fight to kill."

"Enough, enough," the bearlike man called. "Put your weapon away."

Miriame dug the point of her knife in just a little harder, to teach her opponent a lesson he would not forget in a hurry, and leaped to her feet, her knife disappearing into her boot again in a flash.

"You fight like a savage, not like a gentleman," the squat man complained as he got to his feet again, but there was a measure of respect for Miriame in his eyes that had not been there before.

"True enough," Miriame agreed equably. "But I had you for all that."

He shrugged. "Only because I let you go and turned my back on you for a moment."

"Idiot."

"Any gentleman would have confessed himself beaten already and honorably surrendered his sword."

Miriame snorted. "Then 'any gentleman' would be a fool. And so are you, for trusting me to behave like one. Your trust could have gotten you killed just now."

He opened his mouth to argue, then shut it again. "I won't make that mistake a second time, Monsieur Savage."

She smiled with all her teeth bared. "Few people do."

His comrade in arms interrupted their argument. "So, Renouf," he said, "are you still of a mind to send the boy home again with a flea in his ear?"

"No, Captain," the squat man answered. "Let him stay so that I may have the pleasure of teaching him better manners. He fights like a rabid dog."

The other soldier grinned as he ambled over to Miriame. "Captain D'Artagnan at your service, Monsieur Savage," he said, as he held out his hand. "Welcome to the King's Musketeers."

Miriame suppressed her grin of exultation and fumbled in her pocket for the letters she had stolen. She held them out to the soldier. "Thank you, Captain. Do you need these to vouch for me?" She could hardly believe how easy it had been to fool them both—surely he would want to at least read her precious letters before he accepted her into his company.

He waved them away with his huge paw. "All the flowery phrases in the world can't tell me whether you can fight like a man or not," he growled. "Put 'em away again. I don't care a toss for them, be they from the King himself."

She tucked them carefully back into her pocket again. Mayhap she could get the name changed on them by a forger of her acquaintance, and sell them for a good profit in case of hard times ahead. No one else was to know they were worthless. She made a note to see to it in the coming days. Though better than begging or thievery, soldiering was a chancy occupation at best. She wouldn't starve, but she would have to use her wits to make her fortune still.

"Monsieur Savage is a fitting enough name for you, but hardly suitable for the barracks," the squat man said. "I am Saphon Renouf, lieutenant of the company. What name are you called by?"

Miriame doffed her hat. "Jean-Paul Metin at your service."

Renouf took her arm in his and marched off with her across the yard. "Welcome to the barracks, Metin, my friend. Come, let me show you around."

Jean-Paul Metin blinked his eyes slowly, feeling as though he had just waked from a long and troubled dream. Phantoms had been dancing around him just out of sight, evil phantoms that had brought nothing with them but pain so great it made him, a grown man, want to weep.

Thank the Lord he was awake now. That was the last time he would eat toasted cheese before going to bed. The bad dreams it gave him weren't worth it. Besides, cheese was reputed to make a man melancholic and give him worms.

He reached out with one arm, feeling blindly for the sensual goddess who had shared his bed for the past month. He had never known such pleasure could exist as she had shown him. The touch of her soft, red mouth on his body would more than make up for all his bad dreams. He could not feel her beside him. "Francine?" he asked, puzzled. She was as indolent as a pampered cat and never ever got out of bed before he did in the morning.

The phantoms returned when he moved, sending flashes of fiery pain through his entire body. He squeezed his eyes tightly shut, willing the tears of anguish not to fall. He would not want her to see him weep like a babe.

"There ain't no Francine here," a rough voice came from somewhere to the side. "Just me."

Her voice was coarse and uncultured, not like the cultured softness of his Francine's sweet speech. From somewhere deep inside him, away from the pain, he found the strength to ask. "Who are you?"

"Louise, if it please you, Monsieur."

"Where's Francine? What have you done with Francine?"

"I don't know no Francine, Monsieur."

He heard a rustle of her skirts as she moved away. He was suddenly filled with an unreasoning panic that she would leave and he would be left alone with his phantoms again. "Where are you going? Don't leave me."

"I'm just going to fetch the doctor, Monsieur. Your lad told me as I had to fetch the doctor if ever you woke up again, though he didn't think it likely."

"The doctor? Have I been sick?" That would explain the pain he still felt, even though he was awake now. "Have I been poisoned? Where is Francine?"

"Not sick, hurt bad. We all thought you was a-going to die. We already had the sexton bespoke to bury you in the churchyard and all."

His mind was struggling through the fog, but he could make no sense either of her words or of his jumbled memories. "What happened to me?"

"Don't rightly know, Monsieur. Mebbe the doctor can tell you. He'll be here in a trice." With a final rustle of her skirts she was gone.

Metin lay awake for a bit after she had gone. He tried to move again, to sit up and look around him at least for his Francine, but the phantoms were still too watchful. They circled around him warily, ready to deliver a jolt of pain to his body when he moved so much as a single muscle. He lay as still as he could in the hopes they would weary of their game and leave him be.

By the time the doctor had climbed up the stairs, wheezing heavily in his tight waistcoat, Metin had fallen asleep once more.

When he woke again it was daylight. The sun streamed in the open window, taking the chill off the autumn day. The brightness made his eyes water and he blinked several times and turned his head away from the light.

"Ah, you're awake, I see," a gruff voice came from the other side of the room. "I was beginning to wonder if the maid had been telling stories."

It was not Francine's voice this time either, but the voice of a man. "Where's Francine?"

"Francine?" The gruff voice sounded puzzled. "Who is this Francine you speak of?"

He opened his eyes just a crack and peered around with growing puzzlement. None of his surroundings were in the least bit familiar. The chamber he was lying in even smelled strange—like heavy stone and damp wood and rat droppings. He missed the scent of fresh tilled earth and green fields that he was used to. "Where am I?"

"You're at the Bull and Goose in Fauborg Lane."

"Fauborg Lane?" He had never heard of such a place.
"In Paris."

He shook his head, wincing at the pain that the slightest movement gave him. The last thing he could remember was drifting off to sleep, with the delectable Francine clasped in his arms, back in her chateau in the south of France, where she had been in exile from the court for displeasing the King. How could he suddenly have been transported half the breadth of the country? "What am I doing in Paris?"

"I was rather hoping you could tell me that."

He went to sit up, but the pain in his chest made him gasp, and he lay back down on his pillows once more. "What happened to me?" he said, when he could finally control his voice for long enough to speak. "Why does my head hurt so much? And my chest?"

"You are lucky to be alive at all. You have a nasty wound just by your heart that would have made an end of most other men. An inch further to the side, and no one could have saved you."

He touched his hand to his chest, encountering thick layers of wrappings instead of the skin he expected to find. "Wounded," he said in wonderment. How and when had this happened? He could remember nothing of it.

"Indeed you were," broke in a female voice.

He turned his head a little to see a buxom woman in a voluminous apron bring a tray in through the door. He sniffed at the savory, meaty aromas wafting through his chamber and his stomach rumbled. His belly was growling as if he hadn't eaten for a week.

She set the tray down on the bed with a thump, seated herself next to it, and held a spoonful of beef broth to his lips. "We all thought you was on your way to heaven," she said, as she slipped the spoon into his mouth. "I'd never seen a man wounded as bad as you were that lived to tell the tale. For all that, I couldn't leave you a-lying in the street waiting to die, so I hoisted you up and brought you here, put you in this here chamber and looked after you as if you were my own son, and all the while thinking you were a-going to die and none but God in Heaven to recompense me for the trouble I've taken over you and the expense I've been to to see you right.

"I've had the doctor around every day, so that I have, and a maid to sit with you to see you didn't do a mischief to yourself, and here you are better again." She crossed herself piously with the spoon still in her hand. "I'm right glad to see you on the mend again, Monsieur. Sure as there are angels in heaven, you won't forget a poor woman who's gone without herself in order to bring you back to health again."

He swallowed down the three or four mouthfuls she fed him as she talked, before turning his head away. Hungry as he was, his stomach felt too delicate for even such light fare as weak broth. "How long have I been here?"

"Five days ago you was brought in, looking like you needed an undertaker more than a doctor. Still, as I thought to myself, where there's breath, there's hope, and I sent for the doctor anyways, and lucky for you, Monsieur, that I did."

Evidently he had been lying insensible for five days in a ramshackle Paris inn after someone had tried to murder him. He lay back on the lumpy bolster. It was all too much for him to comprehend while he was still so weak. "I thank you for your care of me," he said as he shut his eyes and let his mind fade into blessed darkness. "I will make sure you are fairly recompensed for the trouble you have been to."

He would attend to the mystery of his wounding and his whereabouts some other time. He hurt all over, so badly that he could not turn his mind to aught. He had not even the strength to ask after Francine again. He needed sleep now, more than anything.

Miriame liked her new life in the barracks. What, after all, was there *not* to like about it? She was being paid a small fortune to fight for the King, so fight for him she would, with all her heart, and trust in him to help her make her fortune.

With the ready money in her pocket she had taken from the dying man, she got herself a tiny attic room close to the barracks and as far away from her old haunts as she could get. She doubted that her old acquaintances would recognize her now, dressed in the uniform of the King's Musketeers, but she wouldn't take the chance. Her old life was gone—she wanted nothing and nobody to remind her of it ever again.

Her new comrades had sniffed at the poverty of her room, but she had dismissed them with a rude gesture. To her, her little attic room was a palace. It kept her warm and dry all winter long—and it was hers and hers alone. No one else could set foot in it without her permission. How she treasured the privacy her tiny chamber gave her.

Renouf, true to his word, had taught her how to fight like a gentleman. She didn't think much of a gentleman's way of fighting—it was more like dancing than the rough and tumble brutality she was used to—but she learned it quickly all the same. Soon she could handle the long sword with passable proficiency. She had to learn quickly—Renouf never again turned his back on her until they had put down their weapons and called a truce.

As far as hand-to-hand combat, she could teach Renouf

a thing or two. She had not grown up on the streets for nothing. Her proficiency with a knife had saved her neck more than once before. She knew every dirty trick there was to get the better of an opponent, and she practiced them on Renouf until they were an equal match—his squat strength matched against her agility and speed.

Best of all, she drew regular pay for her efforts. With satisfaction she watched the pile of gold and silver coins that she hid behind a loose brick in the wall of her attic room mount up. She took out her pile most every evening and counted it over and over again.

The pile was growing, to be sure, but too slowly still for her liking. Who knows how long she would be able to remain a musketeer? She might fall ill, or worse, get hurt. Doctors cost plenty, and what if she had to spend all of her hoarded savings on a doubtful cure, and then starved to death on the streets afterwards?

At the thought of going back to living on the streets again, perpetually cold and hungry, she redoubled her efforts to save her money, volunteering for every unpleasant or dangerous duty that would earn her a few extra sous.

To keep her hoard growing, Miriame pilfered food when she could, unwilling to pay for it while she had two good hands and a quick eye. The time would come only too soon when she could no longer steal what she needed. Then and only then would she break into her ever-growing store of coins and buy what she must.

Even so, for the sake of comradeship she could not always save her money. Once in a while, Renouf dragged her off to the local tavern and they sat together drinking ale until the early hours. Miriame always tried to pay for these excursions by picking the pocket of some of the other patrons there. The cardinal's guards were her favorite targets. There was no love lost between the King's guards and the cardinal's. She felt an almost righteous pleasure in robbing them of their pay and spending it for them on good ale for her and her comrades.

Neither did the innkeepers always get off free. She was honest enough in those taverns that treated her right, didn't water the beer or serve her dry, week-old rabbit and swear blind that it was fresh-killed beef. But inns that shortchanged her would find their cellars a bottle or two of good wine short, or find their storerooms not quite so full of onions and hams as they had thought.

One night, in her least-favored tavern, she excused herself from the table where she had been drinking with a group of her fellows on the pretense of needing to relieve herself, and took advantage of a sudden uproar in the tavern to sneak unnoticed into the storeroom.

She hated this innkeeper and positively enjoyed stealing from him. Not only did he water his beer, he also treated his maidservant like a slave and she was sure that he beat his little daughter, a pretty wee thing of six or seven years. Miriame had more than once caught sight of her tear-stained face peeking round a corner, but whenever she had beckoned her to come closer, the little mite had disappeared again.

She was thinking about stuffing a couple of good Spanish onions into her jacket pockets and wondering whether the innkeeper's daughter would like to live with her instead, when the door suddenly sprang open and two musketeers almost fell over themselves in their haste to get inside the storeroom and bar the door again.

Miriame straightened up with a start. There was something definitely odd about these musketeers. She blinked, shook her head, and blinked again, hardly able to believe her eyes. It wasn't just the slight roundness of their hips, their lean shoulders or their smooth cheeks. Such a combination was possible in a man, though hardly usual. It was their eyes, the watchful, wary look in their eyes, that gave their secret away. She knew that look only too well. There had been a few other women who lived on the street as she had—she had always been able to pick them out from the crowd. Besides, she saw that look each time she caught a glimpse of her own face.

The onions she had picked up dropped from her hand, unnoticed. She was so stunned and surprised that either of them could have knocked her over with a feather and she could not have so much as stretched out a hand to save herself.

She swallowed the words that were about to burst from her throat, turning them instead into a strangled gulp.

By God, she thought she was the only woman with enough daring to join up as a soldier. It seems she was mistaken. There were at least two others with as much courage as ever she had.

She stared at them from the corner of her eye, taking in their appearance without seeming to look at them. They were done up like men, right enough. The tall, blond one even had a moustache glued somewhat crookedly on her upper lip. Musketeers though they were, they were women, and, once she had recovered from her surprise, she realized that they were evidently in trouble.

With a sigh of annoyance she picked up the onions again and stuffed them into her jacket pocket, tucked a bottle of wine into her shirt, grabbed her sword and started to get to her feet. Had they been men, she would have left them to their own devices with perfect indifference, but once she had realized they were women, she could not stand back and let them fight through their troubles alone. If women did not protect each other, men would not do it for them. Three of them might be enough to stand against a tavern full of soldiers, if the soldiers were sufficiently drunk.

Besides, she was ready to leave now. She would find it easier to fight her way out of the room with another musketeer on either side of her than she would on her own.

She wasn't quite quick enough for their liking.

The blonde poked her in the chest with her sword. "Drop the wine, thief, and give us a hand." She turned away again, muttering "gutter rat" under her breath in a disgusted tone.

Much as she disliked being called a gutter rat, Miriame was always very obliging when she had the point of a sword aimed at her heart. She took the wine out of her jacket, dropped it on the stone floor with a smash, and stood up groaning. "Do I have to?"

The looks on their faces were answer enough.

They turned to the door again and, quick as a flash, Miriame swiped another bottle of wine and tucked it inside her shirt. She was not leaving without the booty she had come for. Indeed, she probably would have holed up in there and waited until the uproar had died down if she hadn't noticed that the shorter musketeer was breathing heavily and holding up her sword arm as if it were weighted with lead.

She'd get back at them for that gutter rat comment, though. No one, but no one, called her that and got away with it. She had scrabbled her way out of the muck with all her teeth and claws. No chance remark from a stranger was going to put her back there.

In the time it had taken Miriame to steal a couple of onions, the uproar in the tavern had exploded into a full-scale riot. Her companions had evidently riled a few of the cardinal's guards good and proper. A roar of rage greeted their return, and a group of soldiers came after them with swords raised high and eyes bulging with fury.

With some effort, they fought their way through the crowds and out through the kitchen when the stamping of hooves and the sounds of the bugle announced the arrival of the guard to quell the riot.

Damn the fighting—she had no wish to be caught by the guards. Her years spent as a thief had made her more leery of being caught than most.

She raced toward the back door out of habit rather than fear. The guards were easy enough to escape—their horses could not climb stone walls or scurry over rooftops as she could. If one kept off the wide roadways where the horses had room to canter and maneuver and hem you in, one was safe from them.

In the street outside she stopped for a moment to plan the easiest escape route. Her two comrades from the tavern were beside her still, panting with fear, their eyes wide.

"Where to now?" one of them asked breathlessly.

They both turned their heads towards Miriame expectantly. She grinned to herself. She wouldn't leave the two poor fools to the mercies of the guards, but she wouldn't let them off freely either. Now was the time to get them back for calling her a gutter rat.

"Follow me," she called, as she raced over a stone wall and disappeared down the other side. They followed her, more agilely than she would have guessed.

Over walls, through alleys, even over a few rooftops, she led them at a punishing pace, keeping close enough to the guard to make them think they were still in danger. Finally when she wearied of the game and felt she had punished them enough for their rudeness, she stopped. "We should be safe enough now if we get inside."

The other two were panting heavily, doubled over with their hands on their knees to catch their breath.

The bugle sounded again, quite close, and the shorter

musketeer gave an anguished look at her feet, as if she couldn't bear to ask them to run another step.

"That's only for show," Miriame reassured her, feeling sorry for her. It was the other one, after all, who had called her the gutter rat. "They have no hope of catching us if we get off the street."

Her attic room was close by, but she didn't feel like volunteering the information. All she owned was in that chamber. She would not let two strangers into it so easily as that.

A whispered conference between the two others ascertained that the blonde musketeer's apartments were the closer. Feeling slightly shamefaced at the other woman's evident exhaustion, Miriame agreed to lead them safely there. She knew her way through the back alleys better than most.

They made their way there through the shadows, hugging the walls with their bodies and stepping softly on the cobblestones in their heavy boots. Miriame was accustomed to moving quietly, so as not to attract any unwanted attention to herself, but the other two were obviously novices. They must, she thought with a glimmer of amusement, rely on their uniforms and a fake moustache to disguise and protect them. She wondered how they had lasted more than a day in the barracks. Was she the only musketeer in the whole of Paris with a sound pair of eyes?

The apartments when they finally reached them were grander than any Miriame had ever seen. She acted as nonchalantly as she could, though her eyes were busy darting here and there, marveling at the woman who would spend her wealth on such useless fripperies as velvet cushions and finely worked tapestries for the walls. She had not even imagined such luxury could exist outside the walls of a king's palace. How pathetic her own hard-earned hoard seemed in the face of such riches as these.

She thought distractedly of the onions she had stolen, their papery skins rustling in her pockets. If she had such luxuries as these at her command, she would never bother to pilfer anything again.

She wandered over to the cabinet and gazed in admiration at the delicate crystal glasses inside. She hardly liked to touch them, they looked so fragile in their beauty, but the bottle of wine in her shirt called out to her. She was as dry and dusty as a highway in midsummer after her dash through the streets of Paris.

The bottle was soon uncorked. With careful hands she took a couple of glasses out of the cabinet, filled them, and passed them to her fellow musketeers, who had both collapsed, exhausted, on the sofas.

The shorter musketeer was sitting stiffly, as if she had a poker down her shirt. She was evidently quite uncomfortable with her situation. "Gerard Delamanse at your service," she said, accepting the glass of wine with an awkward nod.

The tall, blonde musketeer had kicked off her boots and was lying sprawled back on the sofa in comfort, though Miriame did not miss the watchful look in her eyes. "William Ruthgard, also at your service."

Lifting the bottle into the air, Miriame toasted them both and took a long drink. She couldn't bring herself to use a glass. They were too beautiful. What would she do if she broke one? "Since we are in a formal mood," she said, amused at their pretense, "let me introduce myself as Jean-Paul Metin. At your service, gentlemen." She wondered how long it would take either one of them to realize what to her seemed so blindingly obvious—that all three of them were playing the same part.

Her comrades were no more used to drinking than

they were at playing being men. After no more than a glass or two of the strong Rhenish wine, the shorter musketeer became visibly giggly. Her eyes were clearly fixed on the blonde as she nibbled absentmindedly on her bottom lip.

She twitched visibly under the attention. "What are you looking at?" she finally blurted out in a belligerent tone.

"Your moustache is coming off," the other replied with a shrug, not seeming to comprehend the implications of what she was saying. "You need to glue it back on again."

The blonde jumped to her feet on the instant, wobbling a little from the effect of too much wine. "Just what are you implying?"

Miriame drained the bottle in her hand dry. It was definitely time to rescue the conversation before blood, or worse, good wine, was spilt. "She's right, you know. You need better glue that doesn't lose its grip when you sweat. Personally I find that false moustaches are seldom worth the effort. They're damnably itchy, and it's so hard to get them to look natural. It's easier to pretend that you shave religiously every night and morning."

Both of them swung their heads around to her to cope with this new threat. "What do you mean by that?" the shorter musketeer growled, all trace of giggle gone from her voice. It was almost deep enough to pass for a young man's again.

Miriame grinned. "Your chest wrappings have come as loose as your comrade's moustache, and I've never yet seen a man with a chest like yours. Though now you mention it," and she stroked her chin with a thoughtful air, "there was a hugely fat innkeeper I knew once who could have come close. He had bigger breasts than most women I've ever seen. It made me quite jealous, I'm telling you."

The two of them looked at each other and then at Miriame, realization dawning slowly.

The short one was the first to break the silence. "You're a woman," she said to the other musketeer. She sounded as though she could not quite believe her own words. "And so," she said to Miriame, "are you."

"Guilty as charged." She looked ruefully down at the empty bottle of wine in her hand. She had been able to swipe only a single bottle. She looked hopefully up at the tall blonde. With as many fancy tapestries as the woman had, surely she could rustle up another bottle of wine from somewhere. "Do you have another bottle, or will I have to make do with ale?"

She soon realized that there was no point in waiting for an answer. The other two were staring at each other, talking nineteen to the dozen. She turned away from them and started to search through the sideboard. She had saved their backsides tonight—a bottle of wine was the least they could give her in return.

"Aha, success." She turned back to face them again, a fresh bottle of wine in one hand and a glass in the other. "Come, gentlemen, shall we make our introductions again?" she said, as she poured them both another generous measure. "Let me start. May I introduce myself not as Jean-Paul Metin but as Miriame Dardagny, born and raised in the back alleys of Paris, lately a pickpocket, recently turned musketeer in the hopes of making my fortune with rather less risk to my neck."

The blonde stretched out her legs in front of her. "Courtney Ruthgard at your service. I have a cousin named William of around my age. I borrowed his name to become a musketeer and avenge the wrong that one of them did to me and my family. God willing, he will sleep with the worms before too much longer and I shall sleep easy in my bed again."

Miriame could well understand the black hatred that was driving her. No wonder she looked like a hired ruffian about to strike. She felt the same way herself whenever she thought about Rebecca, and the man who had murdered her so evilly . . .

"Sophie Delamanse," the short one chimed in. "My twin brother, Gerard, was a musketeer before he died of the plague—the plague that I brought into the house. I loved him dearly and would have given my life for him, but I was the cause of his death. I decided to take his place, and win in his name the honor that should have been his."

Honor? Miriame shook her head in puzzlement. Hatred and a desire for revenge she could understand. She felt them herself, deeply and bitterly, for the man who had taken Rebecca away from her. But to risk her life for the sake of some notion of honor? The idea was quite foreign to her.

The wine was clearly going to Sophie's head again. With another giggle, she reached under her shirt and pulled free the wrappings that bound her chest, sighing with pleasure as her breasts swung free. "Ah, that feels better. I never dreamed how uncomfortable men's clothes could be until I had to wear them myself."

At her cue, Courtney pulled off the tattered remains of her moustache, tossed her hat aside and ran her hands through the strawberry blond hair that fell straight to her shoulders. "I detest wearing hats, but I look impossibly feminine without mine." Her usually somber face relaxed into a grin. "I'll forgo the moustache in future though. I would hate to have it fall off in my dinner."

Miriame was perched comfortably on the arm of a chair. She was perfectly at home in her clothes. "Breeches are far more practical than dresses when you live on the street. I haven't worn a dress for as long as I can remember— not since I first realized what can happen to young girls who find themselves on the streets." She couldn't imagine donning cumbersome skirts—they would hamper her movements far too much. Her breeches were her protection not only against the rain and the wind, but also against the evil that was in the world. She needed them to hide in, to hide her sex from the world. They were her talisman against harm. Without her breeches she would feel as naked as a newborn babe.

Sophie was staring drunkenly up at the ceiling. "So what now?"

Miriame rested her boots on the low table in front of her. The wine was starting to make her feel a little sleepy herself. "We have a drink, we rest our feet, and then you and I make our way home again once the guards have given up the chase."

"That is not what I meant."

"What did you mean then?"

"Well, we can hardly go on pretending that we don't know each other's deep, dark secret, can we? So, what do we do about it?"

Miriame raised her bottle. There wasn't much that could be done about it, to her mind. "You keep my secret close and I'll keep yours to my dying day. Should either of you betray me by so much as an incautious word, I throw the pair of you to the wolves. Agreed?"

"And that's all?"

"What more do you want?"

"We could make each other's lives far easier. Alone as we are now, we risk attracting unwanted attention from those who may want to befriend us. If we succeed in keeping our fellows at a safe distance, we may seem suspicious because of our solitary ways. Alone, we are vulnerable. Together, we can form a barrier against the rest of the world that our enemies will not be able to break."

Miriame raised her glass in a cynical salute. It was clear that this was the woman who joined the King's Musketeers for the sake of her honor, even if she was full of horse shit. "All for one, and one for all, and all that? How quaint."

Sophie glared at her. "I'm serious."

Miriame looked suspiciously at the wine in the bottom of her glass. She had long ago learned that no one made you an unselfish offer. There had to be some personal advantage for Sophie if the three of them banded together, though she wasn't sure she knew yet exactly what it was. "Why? What good will it do you?"

"How long can you be a musketeer and yet not be one?" Sophie asked. A wistful look passed over her face, as if she wished only to belong. "How long can you survive surrounded by people you cannot afford to trust or confide in?"

Miriame crossed her arms over her chest. Sophie had her head in the clouds. She was blind to how the people in the streets lived their lives. Each to his own and the devil take the hindmost was her way. If she had trusted in anyone else to save or protect her, she would be dead by now. "All my life so far."

"Are you not sick of it? Don't you ever long to have a friend to talk to?"

Loneliness—that was what was wrong with Sophie, Miriame suddenly realized. Sophie wanted a friend to confide in. Miriame wasn't sure whether she wanted to be that friend or not. She was used to her solitude. It fitted her easily. She looked after herself and no one else. She worried about no one and no one worried about her.

"How long will it take before your fellows notice that you never go swimming with them?" Courtney asked. "Or that you never strip down to wash off after a hard day's fighting? Won't they start to think you strange?" She wrinkled her nose. "Of course, most men wash infrequently enough that they may not notice."

She had managed perfectly well so far, particularly

seeing as she wasn't overfond of washing herself. "Each to his own. If I don't bother them, they won't bother me," Miriame said.

Sophie shook her head. "You may spit and curse along with the rest of them, but you'll never be able to piss in the corner of the courtyard like they do. Sooner or later, one way or another, they'll find you out."

Courtney screwed up her face in disgust. "Men are such pigs."

Miriame was silent for a moment, digesting their words. She had managed well in the barracks up until now, but there had been a few times she had been lucky, she had to admit. It was more difficult living in close quarters with a crowd of men and keeping to yourself than living on the streets where nobody bothered anyone else anyway—not if they wanted to live long and die in their beds.

She could see why Sophie and Courtney both thought it would be to their advantage to team up and band together. Now that she thought about it, it could well be to her advantage, too. It was worth considering more carefully. "So, what do you suggest we do about it?"

"We band together. Not just for one night, but for all time."

"We eat and drink together."

"We keep each other's secrets."

"We serve our King together."

"We look after each other's interests."

"Brothers-in-arms." They were getting increasingly excited, waving their glasses in the air and talking faster and faster, tripping over each other in their hurry to get their words out.

Miriame lifted her nearly empty bottle. It was difficult not to be infected with their enthusiasm, but she needed to keep a cool head. She would associate with them for as long as it suited her, but no more than that. She would not rely on them in any way, and it would be well for them not to rely on her. Self-sufficiency was critical to her peace of mind. She would not risk having her heart broken again as it had been when Rebecca had died in her arms. That memory haunted her still. She had not been able to protect Rebecca. Who was to say she would be able to protect Sophie and Courtney any better?

She would associate with them for now—it suited her needs to do so—but she would guard against becoming overfond of them. Friends were a weakness she couldn't afford.

She toasted them with her bottle. For now, they would be her companions, no more than that. "Fellow musketeers, sisters-in-arms, *vive la compagnie!*"

Chapter 3

Jean-Paul Metin, newly healed from his wound, rode along the streets of Paris towards the barracks, regretting with every step the glorious mare that had been stolen from him. His new bay gelding was decent enough in its own way, but it was nothing like the fine, high-mettled mare that Francine, his beautiful Francine, had given him. He would pay double its worth to have it back again, merely for the sake of the woman who had given it to him.

Dear, precious Francine. He had promised to pay her a visit as soon as he arrived in town and was accepted into the King's Guard under her recommendation. The captain of the musketeers would never be able to refuse him with such a woman as his sponsor. Indeed, he imagined that there were few people in the whole of France would dare to refuse any favor that Francine deigned to ask of them.

Joining the King's Guard had been a lifelong dream of his, but one that he thought he would never be able to attain. He had put it aside at the same time as he had grown too tall for his childhood pony and entered into man's estate.

His father was descended from minor gentry in the south of France, far removed from the court and with no hope or expectation of royal favor. Their family was obscure, with no great wealth to make a splash, and no close family connections with any of the great nobles of the land.

Had it not been for Francine, he would have been destined to remain a farmer, like his father, and his father's father, working the soil with his hands while his soul hungered for adventure and romance, gradually dying inside as his dreams withered in the baking sun of the stone-filled fields he had to tend.

Thanks to Francine, his younger brother could now inherit the farm—and with his blessing. Augustin had a bone-deep love for the land of his fathers that he himself had never felt. For Jean-Paul, the land had meant only countless hours of toil at the mercy of the elements, courting the favor of fickle nature, for little reward. Augustin would love and nurture the family acres as he never could have.

Francine had offered Jean-Paul the opportunity he had craved—the chance for excitement and adventure as a soldier. How galling it was to think how little he had justified her faith in him so far—robbed and wounded nearly unto death before he had so much as reached the barracks.

How worried she would be about him. As soon as he had recovered from his wounds enough to write, he had dashed off a brief note to tell her of his mischance, but he dared not add all the love and affection for her that he felt. His note was warm, but impersonal. It could have been from a mere acquaintance of hers. Nobody would ever guess from the contents that it was written by a man who was sick with love for her, a man who had spent endless hours in Francine's arms, drowned in utter bliss, worshipping her body, and sharing her bed.

How he wished with all his heart that she could have stayed in the country with him forever, but it was not to be. Louis XIV, the imperious Sun King, was his rival—and the King had summoned her back to him once more. She had wept on parting with Jean-Paul, but go she must. He could only follow after her and hope that in the byways of the royal chateau at Saint-Germain-en-Laye he would find some time to be alone with her once more, snatching minutes of joy instead of wallowing in their happiness for hours as had been their wont.

Once he was accepted into the King's Guard and had furnished himself with a uniform from the money he had borrowed at a ruinous rate from a crafty old money-lender in the Left Bank, he would pay her a visit. He would not present himself to Francine in the guise of a beggar, all his belongings down to his very boots stolen. Minor gentry though he was, he was too proud for that. He would present himself to her as a soldier, worthy of her respect—and of her love.

The captain of the musketeers was trading blows with one of his men in the practice yard. He raised his eyebrows but did not put up his sword when Jean-Paul dismounted and introduced himself with a few brief words. "Metin, Metin," the captain said, half to himself, as he parried a quick blow. "Now where have I heard that name before?"

"The Savage," said the man opposite him with a grunt, as he ducked the swinging blade aimed in his direction. "He's named Metin as well."

The captain smacked his head with his open palm and put up his sword. "Of course, I recall now. A young fellow with the finest black mare I've seen in a long time, and a dab hand with a knife. He'll be well worth his salt once he's had a few manners beaten into him."

Metin took a step backwards, startled out of the fine speech he had prepared. *A man with his name had just joined the musketeers? Riding a fine black mare just like the one that had been stolen from him?*

The captain turned his attention back to Metin. "So then, Metin the second, why should I have you then? What have you to offer me?"

Metin switched his mind back to the job at hand, his ears pink at the thought of being caught woolgathering. He drew his sword out of its scabbard and knelt in the ground at the captain's feet. "My sword and my loyalty," he said, offering the hilt.

The other man spat on the ground. "Pah. Any man can promise me loyalty and then run me through when my back is turned. Do you have anything of rather more practical use than a few gallant gestures?"

Metin flicked his sword into the air and caught it again by the hilt as he jumped to his feet. "I am no coward, to attack a man from behind—"

The captain silenced his protests with a wave of his hand. "Can you at least ride better than your namesake? He sits on his fine mare like a sack of potatoes. It's a waste of good horseflesh."

Metin mounted his horse in a swift motion and set it cantering around the practice yard. Riding was one thing he could do superbly. His horsemanship had been what had first attracted Francine. She had seen him practicing jumps in a field close to his father's manor, and had stopped to watch. He had noticed her interest in him and had performed his best for her—first in the field, and then in her bed . . .

Once his horse was in a steady canter, he got to his feet in the stirrups and then, with one swift leap, he stood in the saddle, balancing adroitly as the horse cantered around the yard.

A quick flip and his hands were on the saddle, his legs sticking straight up in the air. A somersault later and he was facing backwards. A quick jump and he had landed on the bare back of a mare that was drinking from the water trough in the corner. Taken by surprise, the animal reared up on her hind legs to shake him off, but he gripped her tightly with his knees and brought her to the ground again.

Only when he had the mare firmly in his control did he slide off and doff his hat, which had miraculously stayed on, to the captain. Breathing hard from his exertions, he realized that he had lost much of his suppleness and agility while recovering from his wound. Even such simple tricks as these taxed his still sore chest. "Yes, I can ride." He held his hand over his chest, trying not to let the pain show on his face. Judging by the dampness he could feel under his fingers, he feared he had torn the edges of his wound open once more.

The captain roared with laughter. "An accomplished acrobat and horse thief, I see. Can you fight as well as you ride, or do you prefer to run away on someone else's horse when the fighting gets too close?"

Metin felt his face burn with shame and rage at the insult. "I am no horse thief," he ground out between gritted teeth, his hand resting on the hilt of his sword, his fingers itching to draw the blade on the man he would call his captain. "Neither am I a coward. I will fight any man to the death who calls me one."

The captain dismissed him with a look of disdain. "Be off with you, you young hothead. You can prove your mettle on the battlefield some other time. Your riding has won you a place in the King's Guard—for now. As long as you ride toward the field and not away from it, I shall be happy enough. Come, Renouf," he said, as he gestured toward the man he had been sparring with moments before, "take Metin the second and show him the ropes."

Renouf shrugged. "Where to, Monsieur Acrobat?" he called.

Metin was tired and his chest ached, but his horse depended on him. He would see to his gelding's comfort before he saw to his own. "The stables."

Renouf nodded in approval and slouched away. Metin limped after him, reins in his hand.

The captain scratched his beard idly as he watched them go. "I haven't done so badly with these Metins. Metin the first is a magician with his knife. Metin the second is a trick rider. With a brace of Metins among us, we could carve up a regiment of Spaniards before breakfast."

There was a gentle tapping on the door. Francine sat up in her bed, instantly wide awake. By the faint glow she could see through a crack in the curtains around her bed, she guessed that it was early dawn.

She picked up the looking glass that she kept beside her bed for emergencies such as this, straining to see her reflection in the dim light. As far as she could see, she looked as pretty as ever. She patted her hair into place, arranged the Alençon lace ruffles of her nightgown fetchingly around her deep décolletage and smeared just the tiniest bit of rouge on her pale cheeks to give them a healthy glow. "Come in," she whispered, in a low, deliberately seductive voice.

The handle of the door was turning before she had finished speaking. The smile on Francine's face grew wide as the King of France padded into her bedchamber, wearing a fur-trimmed robe of silk brocade and matching slippers. The luxury-loving King lost no chance to adorn himself in costly attire, though tonight he wore but a plain nightgown of fine linen beneath his robe and a small nightcap on his head. At last, the moment she had been waiting for ever since she had returned to Paris from her exile in the country.

He stood at the side of her bed and looked down at her severely. "I hope you have duly repented of your foolishness?"

She held out her arms to him, averting her eyes from the patches of bald pate she could glimpse under his too small nightcap. She much preferred him with his black, curling wig on. Without his hair he looked shriveled and uncouth, not at all like the legendary Sun King in the royal portraits. "Your Majesty," she said, looking up at him from under her eyelashes coquettishly. "Dare I hope that you have forgiven me at last for my hasty words? Indeed, I did not mean them. I have regretted them so often while I have been banished from your side. I swear I did not mean to anger you with them. They were naught but a foolish jest."

King Louis XIV of France yawned rather inelegantly and picked up the jeweled candle snuffer. "We have forgiven you for the moment, Madame de Montespan." His voice was stiff and uncomfortable. "If you do not repeat your folly, naturally. Such conduct is unbecoming to a marquise. The King of France does not consort with ill-bred women with quick tempers and loose tongues and no respect for their monarch." He snuffed out the candle by the bed in one swift motion.

Francine's heart sank. He had not yet forgiven her, that much was clear. She would have to work on him with all her might were she ever to regain her position as favorite. Still, he was here with her at last, and that was what mattered now. She would win him to her side again, doing whatever she had to do. She would purchase a love potion from Madame Argueille, the witch, that very day to win him back, though it would cost her ten gold pieces or more, and put her soul in peril to truck with such agents of the devil.

"Did you miss me while I was away in the country?" she asked in the darkness, as he kicked off his slippers with a muffled grunt and clambered into bed beside her. She cuddled up to his chilled limbs, warming them with the heat in her own. "Did you miss your little Francine?"

He lay on his back with his arms behind his head, cold and unresponsive, ignoring her caresses. "My mind was much taken up with matters of state. I had little leisure in which to miss you."

"Matters of state?" She gave a light laugh and nuzzled her head in his neck like a playful kitten. "Sometimes I forget, your Majesty, that you are the King and have such weighty affairs to tend. Here I was, banished in the country, imagining all sorts of horrors in my exile—that you had forgotten your Francine, that you were whiling away your hours with another love. All the while you were tending to your duty with all due honor and respect. I will have to apologize for my wayward imagination."

The King unbent just a fraction. "I was tending to the matter of my sister-in-law, Henrietta, the Duchesse of Orleans. I mislike her correspondence with her brother, King Charles of England, and would have brought her into ways more fitting to the French Court."

Henrietta. Damn the woman. She had heard rumors even while in the country that the King was enamored of the English princess, his own brother's wife, and sought to make her his latest mistress. She did not like to hear her rival's name on her lover's tongue. "Surely the duchesse is only too pleased to do your Majesty's bidding?" she said, the tartness in her voice barely covered with a layer of honey. Heaven knew, she could not afford to give the King a taste of her temper just at the moment, much as she would like to.

She felt the King stiffen beside her—in all the wrong

places. "The duchesse is proving most obdurate. I am not pleased with her."

Good. She hoped the duchesse proved obdurate for a long while yet. Louis had not the patience for a long pursuit. He would as soon seek solace in someone else's arms—someone who would give him the attention and excitement that he craved. Someone like her. "Do not worry about your affairs of state now, your Majesty. Now is the time for rest—and for pleasure." She suited her actions to her words, reaching around to touch him in a way that had never before failed to arouse him.

He pushed her hand away. "Desist. I am not in the mood for taking my pleasure."

Then why on earth had he come to see her? The King never paid an idle visit in his life—everything he ever did was fraught with secret meanings.

He must have sensed her unspoken question. "I have heard a scurrilous rumor whispered in the court that the English princess is a witch and has unmanned me. People whisper that I cannot lie with a woman or give her pleasure any more."

Francine shrugged in the darkness. She doubted he had ever given any woman pleasure by lying with her in the past. What was new in that?

"It is foolish nonsense, but it offends us that they try to make a mockery of our royal personage. I will sleep in your bed tonight to still the wagging tongues whose noise affronts my ears. If you do not want to molder away in a nunnery for the rest of your days," he added, with an icy glare, "you will say nothing of what has passed between us this night."

At least he trusted that she would hold her tongue. That was a good start. If she could but get him to sleep in her bed regularly, it would be a short step to becoming the royal lover once more. Besides, even if she did not become his mistress again in fact, she would be so in reputation—and that was what mattered. "You can count on my silence, your Majesty."

He grunted in reply. "I am weary and would sleep." He turned over on his side and in just a few moments, her sovereign began to snore softly.

The sun was high in the sky when he finally awoke. Francine stifled a yawn. She had been wide awake ever since he came to her chamber, plotting how to regain his interest as he slept fitfully by her side, and the lack of sleep was starting to tell on her nerves. As soon as she felt him stirring, though, she turned to him with murmured words of love and welcome. However sleepy she might be, she needed to make him want to stay by her side.

He barely looked at her as he sat up and stretched and yawned, his foul breath pervading the air trapped in the curtains drawn around her bed. Without so much as a word to her, he clambered out of her bed and padded out of her chamber in his nightgown and slippers.

Francine rose from her bed and stood at the door of her chamber, watching him go down the corridor back to the royal apartments. Her standing as the mistress of *Le Roi Soleil*, the unofficial queen of his gilded, luxury-loving court, would be short-lived if the King did not make more of an effort. He did not even turn back to glance at her as he padded off.

Her only consolation was the look in the eyes of Count Colbert, the King's minister, a man with a fat, pale face like bread dough. He had been her sworn enemy from the moment she had first come to court as a lady-in-waiting for the Queen Marie Thérèse. His eyes bulged out of their sockets as he came strutting around the corner of the hall and saw her standing at the door to her bedchamber, and the King disappearing down the hallway.

"Monsieur Colbert," she said, acknowledging his presence with a brief nod.

He gave her a glare of furious irritation, to which she responded with a triumphant smile. The story would be all over the palace before sundown that the King had returned to her bed. If Colbert didn't spread the news, she would do so herself.

Madame de Montespan was feeling far from triumphant, though. Back in her chamber again, the door safely closed once more, she opened the casement window and drew back the curtains of her bed to let in the fresh, cold air. A light dusting of snow covered the ground, glistening in the sun of the cool, clear day.

Still in her nightgown, she sat down in front of her dressing table and stared at herself in her looking glass. Barely twenty-four, in the prime of her youth, and the King was already turning away from her. She stared at her reflection closely and touched the tip of her finger to her face. There was a wrinkle there, surely, that had not been there the night before.

She threw her pot of rouge on the dressing table with such force that it shattered into a thousand tiny fragments. A crystal bottle of perfume was caught in the fray. It tipped over, splintering the fragile top and sending waves of a strong flowery scent through the room. She swore and rang her bell violently to summon her maid, Berthe. "Clean it up," she hissed.

Berthe nodded silently and knelt on the floor, picking up each shard of crystal carefully between her thumb and forefinger.

Francine watched her in fuming silence. She was tired, disappointed, scared, and in a foul temper to end all foul tempers, and she didn't care who among her servants knew it. She had every right to be furious with the world.

Berthe picked up the last fragment and ran her hands over the carpet to make sure that it was all collected, wrapping the shards in her handkerchief to dispose of elsewhere. "Is there anything else I can do for you, Madame?"

Francine shrugged. What help were servants in such a crisis? She needed a witch. "Not unless you know a spell that will recall the King to me."

"He was here with you last night, Madame," Berthe quietly reminded her. "That is worth much."

Francine got to her feet and paced up and down the chamber. "It is not enough, Berthe. It is not enough. I did not race back to Paris as soon as he recalled me from my exile in the country for this." She stamped one slippered foot in exasperation. "I thought he had missed me. I thought he was ready to restore me to favor once more. Damn my foolish tongue. I should never have teased him so, however much he infuriates me."

Berthe seemed to choose her next words carefully. "He will return to you again, Madame. He always has before. No one else can please him as you do."

If only she could be sure that her maid spoke the truth, not just fair words to coax her out of her ill humor.

"No other mistress of his is prepared to go so far to please him."

Francine would do anything for him, anything, to keep him coming back to her bed. Sex was the one weapon she had to keep him in her thrall, and she would wield it to its best advantage, always seeking out new and exotic ways to arouse her royal lover.

Berthe was on her knees now, sweeping the grate. "He will surely realize that no other woman cares for him as you do. No man can resist a woman who loves him."

Care for the King? Francine snorted with impatience. She was not such a fool as that. Loving was for fools and servants. She cared for the King only as far as he served her ambition—no more. She had seen what loving him had done to his first mistress, Louise. Louise had loved him dearly, poor fool that she was, but the King had cast off Louise for her, who loved him not a jot.

Louise lived in a nunnery now. Francine shuddered. She would never retire to a nunnery. Never.

Heaven knows she was in no danger of loving the King so well that she would forsake the world when he rejected her. He did not appeal to her in any bodily way. His shoulders were narrow, his calves thin and spindly, his breath stank of the filthy cheese that he loved to eat, and he had rather less than the average man had to please a woman with. Neither was he a pleasant companion, in bed or out: he was suspicious and grasping, and cared more for gold and power than he did for his mistress or her pleasure.

"I love being his favorite mistress. That is all." Courtiers of both sexes bowed and scraped at her feet, hoping to win her notice, knowing that a word from her into the ear of the King might make their fortune, or send them to the Bastille. The men flattered her to her face, while the women whispered words of poisoned jealousy behind her back. She didn't know which gave her the more pleasure. She would bed a hundred filthy misers more disgusting than the King simply for the pleasure of being so courted and so envied.

Berthe was still kneeling by the fireplace. Francine snapped her fingers at the girl. "Come, leave the grate alone, and attend to my hair. I have to be in my best looks today."

The girl brushed the ash off her hands onto her apron and hurried to Francine's side. "Yes, Madame."

Francine seated herself in front of the dressing table once more, smoothing out the frown on her forehead with her fingertips. She could not afford to frown—it gave her wrinkles.

Her haste to return to the King's side and regain her position had been for naught. In her absence, the King had all but forgotten her. Last night was the first night he had come to her bed, and she had been back at court for six weeks and more.

The King's words that morning had made the reason for his neglect of her clear. He was obsessed with Henrietta, the Duchesse of Orleans, and had eyes for no other woman.

Henrietta, pah! Francine stuck her tongue out at her reflection, wishing she could dismiss her rival that easily. The woman had nothing that she didn't have herself, and better. The King only wanted her because she was forbidden to him by both church and state. She was his brother's wife. He ought never to touch her.

The King coveted what belonged to his brother, even down to his wife. He wanted to show himself to be above the law by making her his mistress, and having made his point clear, he would doubtless cast her off again.

In the meantime, Francine's position was not to be envied. Those courtiers who had always been her friends were deserting her in droves to seek a new object of their flattery, whose ear was closer to the King's than hers now was. Their desertion rankled as her crowd of hangers-on grew gradually fewer in number and of less importance.

Even more worrying were the sneers of those she had always hated and who hated her in return. Their knives were out and, being sharpened, ready for the kill. Chief amongst her enemies was the cardinal, a close friend of Colbert's. Now that the King was no longer in thrall to her, the cardinal would surely be seeking a way to discredit her for good, to have her banished from the court forever. She was sure he was working against her this very moment, poisoning the King against her with lies and innuendoes. She knew how the game was played—it was exactly what she would do if the situation was reversed.

She couldn't live if she were banished from the court. The court was her life—the only life she wanted. She would rather die than be exiled forever.

At least Count Colbert knew that the King had returned to her—if only for the night. Louis was right to trust in her silence. How she hoped no one would ever know that he had come to her chamber only to sleep.

If she could not have him, she would not be denied her other pleasures. She remembered with a fond smile the young man with whom she had spent such a pleasurable few months of her exile. What a contrast to the King. He was all a lover should be—a handsome face with chestnut brown curls that hung past his straight shoulders, white teeth and sweet breath when he kissed her, a firm back, hard thighs, and even harder in between them. Mmmmm. She felt herself grow aroused and wet just at the thought of him. She had not been so well pleasured in a long time as he had done. What had his name been again?

She racked her brain for a few moments. Metin, that was it. Jean-Paul Metin. He had sworn to follow her to Paris, though she had counseled him against it. In the end, she had written a letter to the captain of the King's Guard, asking that a post be given him. If he were to come to Paris, he would need a fitting occupation that would keep him busy enough so that he would not dance attendance on her all day.

She had thought about asking that Jean-Paul be made a Gentleman of the Royal Bedchamber, but having him around the court all the time would be tiresome and might irritate the King. All things considered, having him out of the way in the barracks most of the time would be far preferable.

She wondered if he had made use of his letter of introduction, or if he had stayed in the country on his farm and forgotten his lover from the court. He had sent her a pretty note a while ago about how he had been wounded in the heart but was now recovering apace. She hoped he was not trying to tell her that he no longer cared for her. That would be a bother. She had not worked off her fancy for him quite yet.

Berthe had finished her hair and Francine glanced at herself in the looking glass. For all her four-and-twenty years, she was a beautiful woman still. She would remind the court that Madame de Montespan was not yet ready to take her place among the ex-mistresses of the King.

And in the meantime . . . she took up a piece of paper and dipped her quill into her inkpot. Berthe curtsied and began to withdraw. "Don't go yet." It was high time she discovered what had happened to young Metin and whether or not she could make him dance to her tune once again. There was no one presently at court that she liked better.

The King was no longer interested in her. She would see if introducing a rival would pique his pride and rekindle the flame between them.

"Take this," she said to Berthe, handing her the letter, "and have it delivered to Metin of the King's Guard. Make sure that he gets it today."

The young man was naive and biddable and her note should bring him running. If she could not enchant the King once again, she would at least amuse herself in secret between Metin's strong young thighs.

Miriame gazed with mingled horror and astonishment at the young man leading his horse into the stables. She knew that man—she knew that face with the green eyes and the brown ringlets curling around his ears. It was the face of her doom.

How had he survived? God himself must have sent down a miracle from heaven to cure him. She would have staked her life that the wound on his chest was a mortal one—that he would have died before the week was out. Men just did not take such a blow to their chest and live.

Come to think of it, she *had* staked her life on his death. She had joined the musketeers under his name, riding his horse, jingling his money in her pockets, even wearing his boots. He would be sure to find her out as soon as he realized that she had stolen his identity. If nothing else, he could easily have her hanged as a horse thief.

She shut her eyes for a second, imagining the hangman's rope as it tightened about her neck, cutting off her air, slowly strangling her as her body twisted and jerked in its death throes. Unthinkingly, she gasped and put her hands to her neck to claw away the rope.

Her companion looked at her strangely. "Are you all right?"

Miriame's breath was shallow with panic. Her chest felt constricted, as though she could not breathe, as though the hangman's noose were already around her neck, choking off her life. There was no help for it. She would have to run. Without a word, she turned her back on her companion and walked away, almost stumbling in her hurry to be gone.

Snow crunched under her boots as she strode out of the yard. She would not risk taking the black mare with her, for all that she had grown very fond of the beast. The mare was the one thing that marked her without fail as a thief.

There were the letters, too, of course, but no one knew about them. She had not shown them to anyone—not even to the Captain. They would not betray her.

The rings on her fingers that she had taken from what she thought near to a corpse? She slid them off her fingers and into her pocket. She would take them to a pawnbroker and have them turned into money as soon as could be, or swap them for others that would not condemn her instantly.

She would run back to the slums and be safe.

The slums. She stopped dead in her tracks. Was she really going to run back to the slums? The very thought of them filled her with horror. She had grown used to a better life—she could not face going back to sleeping on a pile of rags on the floor, sharing lice with whatever derelicts flopped next to her. She wanted to keep the tiny apartment that served as her refuge from the world. She did not want to be cold, so cold, whenever the winter wind blew or the snow fell. She wanted to live in a chamber that did not leak, with a fire to warm her in the winter, and a window to open for a cooling breeze in the heat of summer. She wanted to earn a decent living as a soldier, not to pick up crumbs discarded by the rich. She was tired of stealing and sneaking. She wanted to fight, not beg. Was running away really safer than staying to brazen it out?

And she *was* a musketeer, unlike the real Metin. Who was to say that she had stolen his identity along with his horse? Who would her fellow soldiers believe anyway if it were ever to come to that—the comrade who had proved his worth among them already, or the newcomer?

She had friends and supporters in the barracks already, and Sophie and Courtney would support her to the last. Well, Sophie might not if she ever realized that Miriame had stolen the real Metin's money and horse, but Miriame would simply leave that bit of her story out in the telling. The brigands who had tried to murder the real Metin would come in handy as scapegoats for all the thievery of which she had been guilty.

She would sell the horse and buy a new one right away. Once the pretty black mare was gone, what could the real Metin prove? Metin was a common enough name. So was Jean-Paul. It was not impossible that there were two musketeers of the same name. Unlikely, to be sure, but not impossible. The name she had adopted alone would not be enough to hang her. If she took care, she would not give the black-hooded executioner any further reason to come after her with the fateful rope in his hands.

At least hanging was a quick death. Faster and cleaner than starving or freezing.

She turned on her heel and started to walk back toward the barracks. She would dispose of her horse this instant, and prepare herself to brazen out the lie she had adopted. She would not give up all she had won through her hard work. She would not go back to the slums to die by degrees. She was a soldier now, and a soldier she would stay.

She was heading cautiously towards the stables when a grimy lad from the streets ran up to her. "Are you the musketeer Metin?" he asked in a hoarse voice.

Miriame stared at him, not knowing what she might be admitting to. "What's it to you?"

The lad pointed back over his shoulder. "Them soldiers over there said you were. I have a message for the musketeer Metin."

She wasn't sure she liked the sound of this. She knew of no one who would be wanting to send her any message that she might want to hear. "What is it?"

The lad dug into a pocket in his tattered breeches and drew out a piece of paper. "It's a letter. A lady gave me three whole sous to bring it here to you."

A letter for her? She took it with a curious hand and broke open the seal. There was nothing but a few cryptic words written on it. "Tonight. Eight o'clock at the westernmost door of the palace. I shall count every minute until then." The note was not signed.

The lad was still waiting expectantly, hugging his ragged jacket to his chest with thin arms. She knew only too well how he felt, desperate for another sou or two to buy bread, yet too proud to beg for it. She dug in her pocket for a handful of precious francs and tossed them at the lad. "Buy yourself a warm coat or you'll freeze to death before the spring comes."

He snatched the coins out of the air and then ran as fast as he could, laughing with delight at her generosity, before she could change her mind and take them from him somehow.

She tucked the note into her pocket. She would think more on it before she ventured to decide whether or not to keep this odd appointment.

The bells tolled seven before she had remembered the strange note at all. The hours before then had been spent disposing of everything that could mark her as the thief who had stolen the real Metin's belongings. She had traded in the black mare at the horse market for a chestnut gelding with a sweet temper and an easy stride. The rings had been exchanged at the pawnbroker's for a handful of gold. The letters she had hidden behind the loose brick along with her growing pile of wealth—they might yet be worth something to her and she was loathe to get rid of them until she had to. She had kept nothing that could incriminate her—nothing but several sets of linen, a pair of breeches and a fine waistcoat, and the boots.

She could not get new boots made quickly, certainly not boots as fine as the ones she had taken from Metin. Besides, what harm was there in keeping the boots? No man could tell his apart from another's. She would never hang for a pair of boots.

Her mind freed from anxiety now that she had pawned the last of the jewelry and seen her new gelding bedded down for the night in the stables of the barracks, she stopped at a cook shop and bought a hot meat pasty. It burned her fingers as she walked along, nibbling at a tasty corner.

Should she keep the appointment? For all she knew, the note was meant for the real Metin and not for her at all. It could be a ruse to lure the real Metin out into the open so his would-be assassins could try their luck once more.

She shook her head at the idea. She didn't really think so. It would be unlike that evil man's usual way of operating. He was more likely to shadow his prey, jump on him from the dark with a quick flick of his knife, and then be gone again. Writing a note to his intended victim to lure him into a trap was a subtlety that would be beyond him.

More likely, the real Metin had friends in Paris who wished him well. After all, why would anyone write a note to someone he wished to harm?

Besides, Metin had only arrived this very day. The note could well be meant for her. She must know far more people in Paris than he did. Of course, she doubted that many of her acquaintances had ever learned to write . . .

Still, what had she to lose by keeping the appointment? Nothing, as far as she could see. If the note turned out to be meant for the other Metin, she would simply apologize for the mix-up and take her leave. She would keep her wits about her and take her knife with her in case of any trouble.

On the other hand, what had she to gain, either? She crammed the last bite of her meat pasty into her mouth and licked the rich gravy from her fingers. Maybe he had a wealthy uncle he had never met who wanted to make

him his heir. Maybe, maybe . . . her invention failed her.
She didn't know what she might stand to gain, but she
was prepared to find out.

Busy as he was with getting settled into the barracks, it
was not for some hours that Metin reflected on the
words he had heard the captain say as he walked his
gelding to the stables. "Metin the first is a magician with
a knife." The words haunted him, taunted him with their
unspoken meaning.

Had he joined the musketeers at last only to find his
would-be killer there before him, masquerading as himself? He shook his head as if to shake the idea away, but
it refused to leave him altogether.

He had been wounded by a man with a knife—that
much was clear by the marks left behind on his chest.
His recollection of the attack was very dim, but he
seemed to remember that there had been more than
one attacker. Two or three of them perhaps, if not more.
His black mare had been stolen, his papers had been
taken—the thieves had not left him so much as a change
of linen to call his own.

Then he arrived at the barracks this morning only to
hear of another man of the same name having joined
some scant weeks before him—and with a fine black
mare.

It had to be more than a coincidence. Thinking him
dead, the other man must have talked his way into the
musketeers using Francine's letter of recommendation.
The other Metin could be none other than the man who
had tried to kill him.

Either he was born under an unlucky star, or else some
one must bear him a very powerful grudge to set a hired
killer on him. He could not think that he had offended

anyone so deeply that they would wish him dead, but he supposed it was possible. It was a wise man who knew all those who would do him an ill turn if they could.

At any rate, he would keep a close and watchful eye on Metin the first. His life might well depend upon it. He would start that very evening—after he had paid a secret visit to his dear Francine, of course. The incomparable Madame de Montespan came first in his life, and always would.

Miriame stared in wonderment as her guide opened a door and showed her into an antechamber of incredible richness. A fire roared in the grate, thick rugs covered the floors, and the air was redolent with the scents of spices and mystery.

The servant, for such her guide evidently was, despite the fine gown she wore, bowed her head. "Madame will be with you shortly," she whispered, and she scuttled into the inner chamber and closed the door behind her.

Well, one of Miriame's questions had been answered. A woman, not a man, had made the appointment with her.

She paced along the wall, examining the chamber with a thief's eye. The tapestries were finely woven and beautiful, but too cumbersome to carry. The paintings were glorious to look at, but she doubted they would be easy to sell and would only fetch a fraction of their true worth. The intricately blown glass decanter full of wine was less easily traceable, but it was too fragile to be easily hidden on her person and what would she do with the wine it contained? Indeed, there was little she could even consider stealing. Unless, of course, she were to pocket a couple of the leather-bound volumes lying on the table. Books were hardly a great interest of hers, but they fetched a fair price. She could easily slip a couple of the smaller books inside her jacket, and no one would suspect a thing.

She strode over to the window and looked out into the darkness. She was in a place she did not know, in the very palace of the King himself—two good reasons not to consider robbery. She had mounted several flights of stairs on their way here from the small door on the western side—the window was too high to jump from if she were caught with stolen gold up her sleeves. Only the very brave or the very foolish would attempt to steal in such a perilous situation.

She opened one of the volumes and read, very slowly. Her fingers caressed the smooth vellum pages, itching with the desire to steal it. Some of the words were too long and complicated for her to puzzle out, but the story itself was fascinating, about an adventurer who traveled to the Levant and was made a slave of the Sultan. She wondered whether it was true or just a tale. Mayhap if she slipped it into her jacket now, she could even finish reading it before she took it to the fence to sell for her . . .

She heard a low, melodious laugh behind her and a woman's voice broke the silence. "You did not use to be such a bookworm, Jean-Paul, my sweet."

She snapped the book shut again and whirled around to face the speaker. A woman in a velvet dress of royal purple and embroidered satin slippers was standing by the door to the inner chamber. Her golden hair hung in ringlets to her bare shoulders, and here and there in the ringlets were scattered what were surely diamonds. Around her neck was a necklace of midnight blue sapphires, and her fingers were so covered with rings of every size and shape with every kind of stone in them that it was a wonder she could lift her hands at all.

With some effort, Miriame snapped her mouth shut

again, swept the hat from her head, and made a low bow. "Your servant, Madame."

At the sight of Miriame's face, the woman gave a squeak of fright and put one beringed hand to her mouth in a gesture of horror. "Who are you?"

"Jean-Paul Metin at your service, Madame. A musketeer in the service of the King of France."

"You are not the Jean-Paul I used to know. Come now, confess." Her voice, now that she had gotten over her shock, was cold and severe, a hundred years away from the purr with which Miriame had first been greeted. "You are a spy, I am sure of it. The cardinal or one of his minions has sent you to me to try to search out my secrets."

It was Miriame's turn to be confused. "I do not know any cardinal." She didn't even know so much as a parish priest. She had never been much for churchgoing, and the only priests she had happened across were so abominably stingy when it came to giving alms that she had never bothered to cultivate their acquaintance.

"Who is your paymaster then? The Comte de Colbert? Simon de Maupassant? It must be one of them."

She shook her head. This woman would clearly be an uncomfortable enemy to have—for all that she wore a gown and carried no obvious weapon. "I am in no one's pay, save the King's himself."

The woman looked visibly shaken. "The King has sent you to spy on me?" Her voice trembled and she twisted one of the rings on her fingers nervously. "Is Louis so tired of me that he must resort to having me spied on by strangers to come up with an excuse to put me aside?"

"No indeed, Madame. I am a soldier, not a spy." It was definitely time for Miriame to remove herself from this complicated affair as quickly and smoothly as she could. Something about it hinted of danger to come. She only wished she could snaffle that book before she left. "However, I think I have the answer to your confusion."

The woman looked up, unshed tears glinting in her bright blue eyes. Really, she was quite a beauty with her pale skin and her even features, Miriame thought dispassionately, and her rich dress only added to her charms. No doubt that beseeching look would cause most men to fall at her feet and swear eternal devotion to her. She smothered a smile. If the woman expected Miriame to be moved by her distress, she was sadly mistaken.

Miriame bowed. "I am Jean-Paul Metin of the King's Musketeers, but I am not the only one. Just today a new Jean-Paul Metin joined our guard, a young man of about my age or thereabouts. I didn't give it a thought until now—Jean-Paul is such a common name, and Metin is hardly a rarity either. A boy gave me a note and I opened it and read it, never considering that it might not have been meant for me. I must apologize most sincerely for my mistake and bid you farewell."

At her explanation, feeble as it sounded even to her own ears, the woman's face gradually cleared. "You are not a spy?"

"Certainly not, Madame."

"And you really are a musketeer?"

It still amazed Miriame, even after all these weeks, that she had been accepted into the King's Guard. She spread out her arms to show off her uniform. "I am."

"Then I must beg your pardon for my rudeness to you earlier." The woman's voice was all honey and warmth now, nothing like the ice and fury it had been just moments before. "I had thought you were sent by my enemies at court to ruin me. A woman in my position, you know,"—and she fluttered her fan weakly in front of her face as she peeped over the top of it—"I can never be too careful. My enemies are all around me, waiting for their chance to tear me down."

God in heaven, now the woman was trying to flirt with her. This was an unexpected—and rather unwelcome—development. Why, oh why, had she not ripped up that note and thrown it into the gutter while she had the chance? "Your enemies, Madame?" Miriame said, forcing a gallantry she was far from feeling. She supposed that while she was dressed like a musketeer, she had best act like one, too, so that none would see through her disguise. Never had she found it so difficult to act like a man. "Who could possibly wish you harm?"

She trilled a laugh that set Miriame's teeth on edge. "How foolish of me. If you are really who you say you are, you do not even know who I am."

"I must confess I do not, Madame. You have the advantage over me there."

Her smile was sweet enough to give Miriame's teeth the rot just looking at it. "My name is Françoise Athénaïs de Montespan—the Marquise de Montespan—but you may call me Francine."

Francine de Montespan? The mistress of Louis XIV? The real Jean-Paul Metin, the man whose identity she had stolen, was the secret lover of the Sun King's mistress? If his identity had been discovered by the King's men, it was no wonder Jean-Paul had been attacked in the street and left for dead. Things were starting to make a horrible kind of sense to her now. "I am honored to make your acquaintance, Madame Francine."

"I am pleased to have met you, Monsieur Metin, though you were not the Monsieur Metin I had been expecting." She heaved a sigh and touched her fingertips gently to Miriame's arm. "I must not keep you from your duties any longer, I suppose. Are they so very arduous then, the duties of a musketeer?"

If Jean-Paul's identity were known to the King already, or to the cardinal or whoever this Francine woman was so afraid of, then Miriame herself was in peril, too. She had inherited the danger along with the name she had stolen. "They keep me well occupied."

The fingertips pressed a little harder against her arm. "So well occupied that you have no leisure to visit your friends?"

Blast and botheration. Why could she not have stolen the identity of some nobody who had no enemies and had never cuckolded the most powerful king France had ever known? Of course, if the real Metin had not been such a fool, he would not have been wounded and she never would have been able to steal his identity. She supposed it served her fair and square for not looking into the matter more carefully before acting. "I know few people in Paris, Madame, so my duties do not seem so onerous to me. I have little call for leisure, so I do not miss it."

"But you must count me as one of your friends now, Monsieur Metin," she said. "Now that we have been introduced, I will take it quite amiss if you do not come to visit me again."

Of course, even if she had fully realized the danger Metin was in before she took over his identity, she would have done so anyway. He had been her chance to break out of the slums. She would risk death a thousand times for the chance of a decent life. Now, at least, she knew what she was dealing with and would be on her guard. "You are too kind to a poor soldier, and a stranger."

The marquise rapped Miriame's knuckles gently with the fan. "You are not a stranger now, Monsieur Metin. Or may I call you Jean-Paul?" She heaved a sigh, more with her bosom than with anything else.

Miriame admired her artistry. With such a gift as she

had for manipulating her audience, Madame de Montespan would never be in danger of starvation. "You do me
a great honor. I would be delighted if you would allow me
to call on you," she lied. The stuffy atmosphere, laden with
perfume and spices, was starting to give her a headache.
The marquise really ought to open her casement more
often to let in some fresh air. "But will your husband not
object if you were to receive a male caller, all alone?"

At the mention of her husband, the marquise's eyes
darkened. "The marquis is too busy with his own position
at court to keep an over-careful eye on his wife's friends,"
she said tartly. "You are not afraid of a mere courtier, are
you? The brave musketeer that you are?"

"And the King? Would he not be even more careful
with your virtue than your husband?"

She laughed gaily. "As long as you are discreet in your
visits, how would he ever know of them? I certainly shall
not court his anger by telling him. What the King does
not know will never hurt him. Besides," she added coyly,
"there is no harm in a simple visit. I am so lonely sometimes in the long, cold winter evenings when the court is
dull and tiresome. I thought mayhap we could play a
game of cards together, or you could read to me. Why
should the King mind if we are engaged in such innocent pursuits, even were he to discover your visits?"

Miriame held back a sigh. She could see no escape.
The marquise was quite determined. "I would be pleased
to play cards with you, Madame, whenever you might call
for me."

"Tomorrow night?" the marquise suggested, twisting a
small diamond ring from her middle finger and pressing
it into Miriame's hand. "At the same time? I will have
Berthe wait for you by the door as she did tonight to escort
you here."

Miriame closed her fingers over the ring in her hand,

her head swimming with astonishment. She had just been given a king's ransom for a mere promise to visit the marquise and play at cards.

Her disguise held some unexpected advantages. For such a pretty bauble she would visit in her musketeer's uniform, and bow and scrape and mouth foolish words that she didn't mean for a month altogether. "I will treasure this for your sake," she said, as she raised the jewel to her mouth and kissed it.

Just as long as the marquise did not try to kiss her, she thought all of a sudden, an uncomfortable feeling in the pit of her stomach. Ugh—she didn't care for the thought at all. Playing cards was tolerable enough, but kissing the woman was quite out of the question, even for another diamond ring.

She backed quickly towards the door of the chamber with her loot, kissing her fingertips and waving them at the marquise as she turned to leave.

Madame de Montespan fluttered her fan in front of her face. "Until tomorrow."

Miriame gave a smart salute in reply. "I shall count the moments until then."

The same maidservant led her through the maze of corridors back to the western gate. Miriame heard the door shut and the bolts click behind her as she strode off into the snow. She had had an exhausting day that had tired her in both body and spirit, and she was looking forward to the peace and privacy that her tiny chamber afforded her. Her own space, where she was safe from the rest of the world. How she treasured it. How glad she was that she had made the decision to stay and fight it out—not to run.

She had barely gone five steps when a threatening figure in a long swirling cloak, his face shadowed by a heavy hood, materialized out of the darkness in front of her. It pointed its sword at her, forcing her to stop dead in the street.

"What do you want?" she demanded. She was annoyed, but hardly scared, by such an open challenge. If her assailant had seriously wished to harm her, he would never have given her such a clear warning of his intentions, but would have jumped her without a word and tried to slit her throat before she had a chance to fight back. She had no fear of those who fought her openly, but a healthy fear of those who crept in the shadows, stalking their prey like an alley cat on the prowl.

"Draw your sword, you scoundrel," the figure demanded in a voice filled with fury. "Draw your sword and fight me like a man."

Chapter 4

She pushed the flat edge of the blade away with one gloved hand. "I am in no mood for jesting with strangers. Be off with you, and let me be."

"Draw your sword and fight me like a man," the figure repeated, "or I will carve out the very heart from your body and spit it on the tip of my blade."

He sounded terribly determined. She sighed in annoyance. "Who are you that I should fight with you?"

The figure threw back the hood of his cloak with a flourish. The moonlight glinted off the planes of his cheeks and shone silver on his shoulder-length hair.

She groaned. "You." Damn it all. She was in no mood for a confrontation with her namesake right now. She was carrying a jewel worth a small fortune in her pocket, and did not want to lose it in the fray. Besides, she had a headache. She was not even in the mood for admiring his spectacular good looks, which combined virile masculinity and grace. He was almost irresistible now that he was on his feet instead of lying wounded in his bed. His face, even in the moonlight, no longer had the pallor of death.

"Go away and call on me in the morning, if you must. I'm tired and hungry and in no mood for a confrontation," said Miriame.

Jean-Paul Metin glowered at her. Even in the dim moonlight the fury in his eyes would have made many a soldier quail. "I see you know who I am."

"Of course. You're the soldier the other men talk about," she said with a wry grin. "Why, one of the lieutenants was almost salivating as he described you. One can only wonder," she said in a curious voice, "exactly how he came by the detailed information that he was revealing with such glee."

Just as she had hoped, her taunting set him off into a furious rampage. Without another word, Jean-Paul attacked. His anger gave him more force, but less care. He swung his sword wildly around his head and charged at her. If just one of his powerful thrusts had connected, she would have been seriously hurt, if not dead on the instant.

She sidestepped him easily. "Just so. You fight like a girl. What do you do of an evening when you have finished with your soldiering? Do you sew your own shirts? Or maybe you sit over your embroidery gossiping with the other women, or stir the cooking pots, or bend over for your lord and master to take his pleasure . . ."

She had not thought he could get any angrier than he was before, but it seemed he could. She parried his blows with some difficulty. Luckily for her, they were less than accurate, but so strong that the force from each strike she deflected traveled up her sword arm in a thousand shivers.

Back and forward they battled, he attacking, she defending, until she began to tire. Her long day was beginning to tell on her strength.

She had given him enough of a game. He must have worked out the worst of his anger by now. She wanted to go home to bed.

His attack showed no sign of letting up. Time to play

another game. With a quick fumble at her buckle, she loosened her scabbard.

He charged her, his sword up high. Instead of parrying his blow with her sword as he was expecting, Miriame ducked out of the way and swung her long scabbard along the ground at the level of his knees.

He tripped over it and fell with a thud to the cobbles, groaned, and lay still.

Miriame hesitated. She had saved his life once, after all. There was no sense in her undoing her good work and killing him now. Besides, her greatest enemy wanted him dead. That was reason enough for her to keep him safe.

In a moment, he stirred and raised his head to glare at her. He only had the breath knocked out of him, nothing more. She sheathed her sword and took to her heels, sprinting away through the dark streets towards her home.

His angry curses followed her down the street. She looked back before she turned the corner. He had stumbled to his feet, but did not look steady. His steps were faltering, and he leaned heavily against a wall to hold himself upright.

For just a moment she thought of going back to help him, but decided against it. That would only make things worse. In the temper he was in, he could easily do her damage before she could explain that she was there to help him. She doubted he would accept her help, anyway.

Still, she didn't like to leave him incapacitated in the street, easy prey for anyone who might be lurking in the shadows. Knowing what she now did about his enemies, he was lucky to still be alive. Half of Paris would bay for his blood!

She doubled back quietly, going the long way around so she could creep up behind him without being noticed.

He was retracing her steps of earlier that evening,

right up to the wall of the palace. He knocked on the western door, just as she had done.

There was no answer.

He knocked again, louder.

Still no answer.

He hammered furiously against the door with the hilt of his sword, the thuds reverberating through the night like thunder.

Just as she thought the door would cave in under the force of his blows, the marquise's maidservant finally came to the door and opened it just a crack. "What do you want?" She was clearly not pleased to be disturbed at such a late hour.

"I must see Madame de Montespan."

She was not impressed. "I am afraid that my mistress has already retired for the night. It is too late for her to receive visitors."

The musketeer was not to be dismissed that easily. He slipped his foot into the door so it could not be shut in his face. "Tell her that Jean-Paul Metin, the man who loves her more than life itself, is here to see her. Tell her that every moment of my life spent away from her is like a lifetime. Tell her that my existence has no meaning without her. Tell her that I love her more than ever before and would cross mountains to be by her side."

The maidservant hesitated. Miriame saw Metin slip a piece of gold into her hand. "Wait here for a moment," the woman said, "and I will see if she will see you."

Metin strode up and down along the street, his shoulders huddled in his greatcoat, stamping his feet to keep warm. His movements were surer now, though he put his hand to his head every now and then as if it still hurt him badly. Other than that, he seemed mostly unharmed by his fall on the cobbles.

Miriame was glad of his quick recovery. She could leave now with a good conscience. Indeed, she should leave now, but curiosity made her stay. What would the charming marquise do with two Metins to amuse herself with? Choose one and let the other alone? Or play them both on her line at once and trust in the strength of her lure to land them both?

Miriame was freezing by the time the maidservant returned. She rubbed her hands along her arms and danced up and down whenever Metin was looking the other way, in an effort to warm herself but the air was so bitterly cold that her best efforts did not help much. She was as glad as Metin when the maidservant returned and opened the door again.

He rushed eagerly towards the door, evidently expecting to be welcomed with open arms. "How is my darling Francine? Has she missed me as much as I have missed her? Will she forgive the lateness of the hour and allow me to see her? I have been desolate without her."

"My mistress is indisposed," the maidservant said, in a whisper that carried through the dark of the night. "She cannot see you now but begs you to call upon her on the morrow. She will be receiving petitioners after the noon hour."

"Indisposed? My Francine is sick?" Metin tried to force his way through, but the chain held the door fast and he could not get in. "Let me see her at once, I beg of you."

"She is not ill—but a megrim has made her tired, and she wants to sleep. She prefers that you not bother her at this hour. It is too late for visitors."

"But . . ."

His protests were no use. The maidservant shut the door in his face and drew the bolts home.

He thumped on the door again, but there was no reply.

After a few moments of indecision, he strode off, muttering to himself. "She has a megrim when I come to visit her now, does she? When one of my colleagues has just come from her apartments? How is it that she is too indisposed to see me, but not too ill to see that vile imposter who has stolen my name? I will call him out in the morning, see if I don't . . ."

Miriame left him to his grumblings and made her way home through the frozen streets to her own apartments. She could almost find it in her heart to feel sorry for him, she thought, as she climbed the stairs to her attic room and warmed herself in front of the dying fire in her grate. She had stolen more from him than she had ever intended. His money, his horse, his clothes, his boots, his name, his papers—and now, even the woman he loved.

She would give the woman back gladly enough. She would give him the papers if he asked her politely—they were of no use to her after all. She might even give him his boots if he begged for them—she could afford to buy her own boots now.

As for his name, that was Miriame's now as much as it had ever been his. She would not give that up—not for anything.

She liked the new Jean-Paul Metin even better than the old, Francine decided, as she completed her toilette in the warm light of the noonday sun. The previous Metin, for all his masculine beauty, had been a bit of a bore at times—always prating on about his everlasting love for her and wanting her to give up her life at court to be his wife.

Silly boy. He knew she was already married. The King himself had chosen her a tame husband to cuckold so she could bear the royal children without a scandal. Louis would be furious if she were to leave her husband for another lover, particularly if he were a young nobody unfamiliar with the sophisicated intrigues of the court who might rant and rave and behave like a jealous fool. She would lose the King forever were she to make such a disastrous mistake.

Young Metin had not had the wit to see that a bucolic country life among the peasants and the pigs and the pumpkins was not the life for her. Ugh. She passed her hand over her brow to smooth out the wrinkle that had appeared there at the very thought. She would shrivel up and die in such a place.

He had only thought of love and lovemaking. She herself had thought plenty about lovemaking, but not at all about love. He was an amusing distraction to her, and he could be nothing else, beg though he might for the keys to her heart. She disliked being pressed for what was not in her power to give.

The new Metin, though, was quite different. She could feel it already. He would not ask so much of her, but neither would he give more than he took—at least not without a struggle.

The new Metin would not think that she was the grand passion of his life—he was too shrewd for that. Indeed, he would not fall in love at all—or not easily.

He was more like her. A cat, deceptively tame, but ready to claw or to pounce. Solitary. Concerned with his own thoughts and feelings, not with anyone else's. Ambitious. Ready to climb over the backs of his comrades to climb as high as he could reach, and higher. Determined. Prepared to hang onto his position with all his might, no matter the cost.

What a triumph it would be to bring such a man to heel. What a victory she would have when she had subdued

him, forced him to fall in love with her and to admit it
openly, and become the slave to her whim. She would
make him abase himself, make him vow utter submission
to her in everything he said and did. Her victory over him
must be absolute.

He would not be easy to capture. Harder by far than the
King himself, she feared. Louis XIV was a man of simple
tastes in women, despite the grandeur of his court and
palaces. He could be captivated by nothing more than a
pair of blue eyes and a heaving bosom, and the impression
that a woman found him the most fascinating man alive.

Metin had barely glanced at her bosom. She sensed
both his wariness and his imperviousness to her beauty.
He would have to be ensnared by more subtle lures. She
shivered a little with excitement. She had not been faced
with such an exciting and challenging task for a long
while.

Careless generosity to start with, she decided, to keep
him coming back to her. How his eyes had lit up at the
sight of the jewel she had given him. A few such pretty
baubles and she could guarantee that he would return
to her. That part at least was simple.

Then she would need plenty of wit and humor to keep
him entertained while he was here. He had seemed interested in her latest novel—maybe she would offer to
read a chapter aloud to him. The King, a magnanimous
patron of all the arts, had often commented on her soft,
melodious speaking voice and said that he liked to have
her read to him. She would see if the new Metin liked it
equally well.

A hint that she was lonely? Yes, but only a hint. Enough
to let him know that she valued his company, but not so
much that she seemed to complain. A man liked a woman
to be cheerful.

Then, at the very end, a rush of vulnerability. He

would have to save her from something or other—she would think of that when the time came. No man could resist being worshipped as a hero.

Then she would have this new Jean-Paul where she wanted him. She would make him acknowledge her as the victor. She would subjugate him. Then and only then would she toss him aside.

Velvet. Red velvet. Miriame eyed the gown suspiciously. She wasn't too sure about it. It was so . . . so feminine. Not her style at all. She didn't know why on earth she had ever agreed to wear it.

Sophie, already dressed in a gown the color of emeralds, and looking every inch the lady, held the red velvet up to the window. The sunshine lit it with a warm glow, making the fabric seem almost alive. "Try it on for me. Please! You cannot come to my wedding as a man in boots and breeches. My husband would not look twice at you dressed as a woman—it is only natural for a woman to want her friends with her on her wedding day, after all, and I do so want you both there with me. If you were dressed as a man, he would be suspicious of our close friendship. You would have to fight him, or confess your secret—confess that I am not the only woman who has dared to masquerade as a man and join the King's Guard. I do not want you to fight him on my wedding day."

Courtney hooked together the last row of fastenings on the bodice of her petticoat and hugged a gown of golden yellow to her chest. There was an emotion suspiciously like love in her eyes. "I would fight a hundred husbands for such an excuse to wear a gown again, even though it is only for this morning. How I detest these stinking breeches that men wear."

Miriame would rather fight a hundred musketeers than

wear a gown on the street. "I'm not afraid of fighting him."
Even looking at a gown made her feel vulnerable and
afraid. If she put it on, everyone would know she was a
woman. She had kept her sex hidden for so long, why
would she ever reveal it now? If Rebecca had pretended to
be a youth, she would still be alive today. Women were easy
prey. Safety lay in being a man, or being thought a man.

"Maybe not, but I am. He's bigger and stronger, but
you're sneakier, and you're both as stubborn as mules.
One of you would end up hurt, and I'd rather not have to
bandage my friend or my husband on my wedding day."

Courtney pulled the golden yellow gown over her
head and turned her back to Sophie. "Do up my buttons
for me, would you?"

Miriame watched in fascination. How impractical
gowns were! You could not even fasten them yourself,
but had to rely on someone else to do it for you.

"All right?" Sophie begged as she deftly did up the row
of buttons that ran the length of Courtney's bodice. "We
have to leave soon for the church."

Just this once wouldn't hurt, she supposed grudgingly.
Miriame slipped her arms out of her jacket and kicked
off her boots. After all, she *had* promised.

By the time Courtney's buttons were fastened, Miriame was standing on the rug, naked as the day she was
born. She shivered a little in the cold air as she held out
her arms in defeat. "Dress me up, then. I'm all yours."

A shift and bodice, petticoats, stockings, slippers, and
finally a gown—she had never realized how complicated
getting dressed was for a woman. Thank the Lord she
didn't have to go through this fuss every morning.

Courtney made a final adjustment to her skirts and
stepped back to admire her handiwork. "Not bad," she
said, her voice full of satisfaction. "Not bad at all. You
clean up pretty well for a gutter rat."

Miriame stuck her tongue out and made a rude gesture. She would get back at Courtney for that one of these days, just see if she didn't. Courtney knew how much she hated to be called a gutter rat and did it a-purpose to bait her.

Sophie gave a squeal of mock horror. "Ladies in velvet gowns don't do such vulgar things. My governess would have whipped me for less."

"Gutter rats don't have governesses to whip good manners into them," Miriame reminded her with a sarcastic raising of her eyebrow.

Sophie put her hand on her hip, ignoring the remark. "You do look splendid, Miriame."

Miriame looked down at the gown. "Well, can I see myself in the looking glass then?" she asked irritably.

Courtney shook her head. "Not yet. Your hair—it's all wrong. What shall we do with her hair?"

Sophie bit one of her fingernails. "I see what you mean, but we have no time for anything fancy. How about braiding it? Would that help? Or some ribbons?" She sounded doubtful.

Courtney was silent for a moment, her forehead creased in thought. "I know just the thing." She scuttled over to a trunk in the wardrobe and emerged in a moment with a bunch of tiny red flowers on green stems. "Ribbon rosebuds. We can simply weave them through her curls and leave it at that."

Sophie clapped her hands in delight. "Just the thing. Here, let me have a couple, and I'll do the back."

Miriame stood where she was, feeling disgruntled, as her two friends fussed with her hair. She didn't suppose they had any intention of asking her opinion. What if she didn't want flowers put in her hair? She didn't want to be made into a figure of fun for children to point to and laugh at in the street. "*Now* may I see myself in the glass?" she asked, when they both stepped back.

Courtney pursed her lips. "I think so."

Sophie nodded. "Much better."

Miriame walked over to the looking glass in the far corner of the chamber. At least she was pleasantly surprised by how comfortable the slippers were. Not as practical as her leather boots, but so soft and easy on the feet.

Courtney pulled back the draperies of silk that looped over the glass, and Miriame stood and stared at her reflection. She blinked once, and then again. She had never looked like this in her life before. She had never known she *could* look like this!

She looked like a woman. She really looked like a woman. She had none of the blue-eyed, pink-and-white prettiness of Madame de Montespan, but even so she looked better than she had expected. There was nothing masculine about her—nothing at all. She looked as if she had been born in a gown.

Even the ribbon rosebuds in her hair weren't as bad as she had feared. She touched one of them gently. They looked quite natural, even fashionable. Why, in a gown like this, she could pass as a lady of quality. No one would ever suspect her of being a gutter rat.

Sophie was starting to shuffle her feet impatiently, anxious to be on her way. "Shall we go then?" she asked at last.

Miriame turned to follow her friends out of the safety of the chamber and into the streets of Paris, heading for the church. The velvet of her gown swished around her legs as she walked. Despite the silk stockings tied around her thighs, her legs felt naked without her breeches.

She had never felt so much like a woman in her life—or so vulnerable, either.

* * *

Metin strode through the streets of Paris with a purposeful air, heading toward the royal chateau at Saint-Germain-en-Laye. He would see Francine this morning, at her public levee if he could see her no other way. Come what may, he was determined.

He must have offended her in some way. No other reason for her coolness toward him made sense. Never before had he ever been refused admittance to her chambers, however late the hour. Never before had she contrived to avoid him, though he had heard her send out her maid-servant with the excuse of a megrim a thousand times, preventing impertinent visitors from interrupting them.

He could not believe that she had grown cold toward him. If he had offended her, he would beg her pardon on his bended knee. If, however, she was truly sick and had refused him admittance to save him the worry of knowing . . .

He felt his heart constrict at the thought. He would not rest easy in his mind until he was assured of her good health.

The church bells rang joyously as a wedding party appeared on its steps. A musketeer of his own company, though he didn't recognize the face. He had met few of his comrades as yet. Besides, he wasn't in the mood for making male friends. He wanted only to be with his Francine.

He glanced idly at the bride. She and her blond attendant were both pretty enough, he supposed, though nothing compared with Francine. Still, he envied his fellow musketeer his happiness, wedding the woman of his heart. How he would love to wed his beloved. If only she would agree to elope with him and live with him forever in a cottage in the country, far from the King and his court. He would even turn farmer again for her sake . . .

A movement at the door of the church caught his eye and he raised his eyes slightly.

By God, but here was a woman to rival Francine, if such a thing were possible. Her hair was as black as the wing of a raven, falling in a riot of curls to her shoulders. A few red roses were scattered through her hair, looking as if nature had sprinkled them there in homage to her beauty. Her skin was the golden color of pale honey fresh from the hive, her lips were full and red, and her eyes . . .

He looked again at her eyes. They were so full and rich and deep, deep brown—the color of the rich soil of his home. He could stay and look at her eyes forever.

Her eyes met his and he could have sworn that he caught a glimpse of fear in them. Her face turned a shade paler and she put a hand against the wall behind her to steady herself. She shut her eyes, looking as though she were waiting for an axe to fall on her head.

He gazed at her in puzzlement. Now that he thought about it, her face did look vaguely familiar, but he was sure he had not met her before. He would not forget such beauty in a hurry. If he did not know her, why did she look as if she had seen a ghost at the sight of his face?

She opened her eyes again, those incomparable, deep eyes that held such a promise of mystery and desire in their depths. Relief seemed to flood through her body at his lack of recognition. Without once taking her eyes from his face, she moved back through the church doors and out of sight.

He could not think why she had seemed so scared of him. He racked his brains to dredge up any recollection of her face, but came up with a blank. He was sure he hadn't met her before. His face was not one that usually inspired fear in women—quite the opposite, in fact. He was vain enough to think that most women found his features pleasing. At any rate, quite a few of them had told him so, and he preferred to believe them rather than not.

He slowed his pace and cast an eye at the sun. He had set out early for Francine's morning levee, preferring to wait near the chateau instead of pacing endlessly up and down in his own chamber. Plenty of time remained before she would even start to receive her morning visitors. He would chase up this raven-haired beauty and discover just what it was about him that had so startled her.

The church was dark inside. The walls exuded coldness and damp and a sense of gloomy foreboding that even the colorful patterns of light cast by the stained glass in the windows failed to expel. Not even the familiar scent of incense wafting in the air could warm the interior. He shivered. Considering all the beautiful places in the world that God might adopt as His own house, he found it hard to believe that He had chosen such a dank and dreary dwelling as this church as His abode on earth.

He crossed himself to guard against such blasphemous thoughts, bowed his head before the statue of Our Lady, and wandered toward the altar, his eyes scanning this way and that, searching for the beautiful woman who had caught his eye.

A glimpse of red made him turn his head. Ah, there she was—at the front and over to the side, kneeling low in the pew, her head bent in prayer.

He entered the pew, sliding across to where she knelt, her face hidden in her hands. There was no mistaking that she was the same woman. The red rosebuds in her black hair gave her away.

He sat beside her for some minutes, unwilling to disturb her at her devotions, but she did not move. The silence between them grew more and more tense, until it was so thick he could almost feel it pressing in on him.

Her shoulder twitched. She knew he was there, waiting for her. She ignored him, and hoped that he would leave her alone, but he would not be put off that easily.

He reached out his hand and plucked a rosebud from her hair. "You must want something very much," he whispered into her ear, "to be asking God for it so sincerely, and at such length."

She did not move her head. "Go away. I am saying my prayers." Her breath turned into steam in the cold air.

He settled himself as comfortably as he could next to her on the pew. The wooden bench was hard enough, but the thin cushion on it gave him some relief.

She turned her head a little to see what he was doing, and he smiled at her in return. She put her head back into her hands. "Go away," she whispered out of the corner of her mouth. "I do not wish to be disturbed."

"There's no hurry. I shall wait until you have finished."

"I do not want to talk to you."

"It's a funny thing, isn't it, but that is exactly why I want to talk to you."

There was a quick movement and the next thing he knew, a knife had appeared in her hand. The point of it was aimed perilously close to his groin. "Whatever you are thinking of, don't try it. I am armed," she said.

He grinned. He could not imagine such a beauty sticking a knife into his side. "So I see."

She jabbed it a little closer until the point of it was tickling his very manhood. "I am not afraid to use it."

Had she been a man and his enemy, he would be in a cold sweat by now. As it was, he admired her spirit. "I do not doubt it. But would you emasculate me just because I find you beautiful and wish to make your acquaintance?"

"You think I am beautiful?" She sounded disbelieving and the hand holding the knife wavered a little.

He made a pained face. "I would find you infinitely

more beautiful if you would desist from pricking my parts with your knife."

She moved the knife a scant inch away, removing him from immediate danger of skewering.

He adjusted himself a little, making sure that everything was still in one piece. "Ah, that's better." His most immediate concern now out of the way, he looked into her face. "Yes, I find you very beautiful. You can hardly be surprised by it. You must look at yourself every day in the glass. You can hardly have failed to see your own beauty."

She shrugged. "No man has ever told me that I am beautiful before."

He could not believe that he was the first to appreciate her. All the men she knew must either be blind or too tongue-tied to speak to her at all. Or maybe, he thought with a smile, they had been concentrating too hard on her knife to be able to look at the rest of her. That was a distinct possibility. "Dare I hope that you will look kindly on me then, the first man brave enough to tell you so?"

"No."

He shook his head. "That is not the right answer. I have told you, in all sincerity, that I think you truly beautiful. Can you not show that you are witty as well and come up with a charming reply in your turn?"

She raised her head and looked him straight in the eye, almost as if she had decided she had nothing left to lose. "Certainly, if that is what you wish. I think you are very beautiful also."

He was strangely flattered at this compliment from a complete stranger and he felt his ears grow hot. "Men cannot be beautiful. Only women."

"Nonsense. You have fine curling hair down to your shoulders, and a complexion as fine as any woman could wish for. Your shoulders are broad and strong-looking, and you fill out your breeches," she looked down as she spoke, "more than adequately."

He could not be quite certain whether or not she was mocking him. "So why did you turn pale at the sight of my face?"

She shrugged. "You must be imagining things. I did no such thing."

"And why did you run into the church to avoid me?"

She turned her head away from him, shivering a little in the cold air. "I wished to say my prayers. May a woman not enter church without being accused of trying to avoid strangers in the street?"

"I am not a stranger to you, though. You have seen me before, I am sure of it."

"And what if I have?"

"I am curious to know more about you."

"There is nothing to tell." She rose to her feet and looked pointedly down at him. "If you will be so good as to move, Monsieur, so that I may depart?"

He rose to his feet, blocking her way. "Tell me your name before you go."

"Why do you ask?"

"So I may know who to look for."

She smiled at his words, but the smile did not reach her eyes. "My name is Miriame. Miriame Dardagny. But I warn you, you will never find me if I do not want to be found."

He had not finished with her yet. He reached out and touched a lock of her glorious black hair, curling it around his finger. "How can I make you want to be found?"

She hesitated and then looked up at him. She was tall for a woman, but still she had to tilt her head back slightly to look into his eyes. "I am not sure you can do that. Even if you could, why should I give away my secrets? Men never treasure what comes to them too easily."

He tugged gently on the lock of hair around his finger. "Tell me one of your secrets—a secret desire that you have. Give me some clue how I can make you want to be found."

"I will give you one clue," she said, staring straight into his eyes. "I do not like to feel trapped. If you try to coerce me into anything, you may not live to regret it."

At her rebuke, he moved out of the pew, freeing her to go where she would. "Then if I cannot come to you, will you come to me instead?" he asked, following her down the aisle toward the back of the church.

They had almost reached the door of the church when she answered him. "I will be here in the church a se'nnight from now. You may find me here if you so wish."

"I have your word on that?"

She shook her head. "No, I do not give you my word. You will have to come here and take your chance that I am worthy of your trust." She pushed open the door of the church and walked out into the sunshine. "Fare thee well. Do not follow me or I will know for certain that you are not worthy of my trust and I shall not return."

How had she guessed that he had been planning to follow her, just for a short distance, to see what direction she was headed in? With such a threat as that, he would not risk even so much as looking in her direction. He bowed low. "It shall be as you desire, Mademoiselle. Your wish is my command."

A low laugh was the last he heard from her as she walked away.

Francine. He had almost forgotten about Francine as he had talked with the mysterious stranger. He felt a momentary pang of guilt at trifling away the moments he could have spent at Francine's side. Still, he could not totally neglect his affairs for the sake of the marquise, for all that he adored her and would give his life for her.

He had a sneaking suspicion that the mysterious Miriame knew more than she was willing to tell him. Perhaps she had even witnessed the attack on him in the street. Where else could she have seen him before? Why else would she threaten him and hide herself away? He would keep the meeting with her in a se'nnight's time, and hope to find out more.

He strode out of the door of the church, took the steps two at a time, and hurried down the street. For now, he was on his way to visit Francine. Mysterious strangers would have to wait.

Miriame walked back to Courtney's apartments in a daze. Jean-Paul Metin, her sworn enemy, had told her she was beautiful. Last night he had tried to murder her in the street. This morning he had told her she was beautiful.

She had not changed in herself so much in the few hours between night and morning. All that had changed was his perception of her.

Perception was a more powerful force than she had realized before now. She had always hidden her sex underneath her rags, expecting that no one guess at her ruse, until hiding her sex had become second nature to her.

Now, for the first time she understood how powerful it was to reveal her true nature.

Metin thought she was beautiful. He had told her so, and had even seemed surprised that she had doubted his sincerity.

She looked at herself in Courtney's looking glass one last time, smoothing the red velvet dress over her waist and hips. She did not know what to think. She was still getting used to the idea of looking like a woman.

Courtney had already taken off her green dress and hung it away in the wardrobe. She came up behind Miriame and grinned at her in the glass. "Don't tell me that we have converted you not only to wearing a dress, but actually liking it?"

"Am I beautiful?" said Miriame. She hadn't meant the question to slip out quite so baldly, but an answer was important to her. Was it possible, was it conceivable that Metin was telling the truth? Did he find her attractive?

Courtney put her head on one side and thought about it for a moment. "You don't have the kind of beauty that is most fashionable right now: white skin, pink cheeks, golden curls, and a sweet simper to show your good nature."

Miriame tried not to let the disappointment show in her face. How foolish she had been to think it was possible, even for a moment. She looked nothing like that. Metin could not possibly think she was beautiful.

"You have a different sort of beauty altogether," Courtney went on. "Darker, more mysterious, quite exotic. You make the merely fashionable look ordinary. You have so much more character. A touch of spice, and more than a hint of danger. If I were a man, I would think you were more exciting than a whole chamber full of fashionable porcelain dolls."

"Are you serious?"

"Never more so." She gave another grin. "As I said before, for a gutter rat, you clean up pretty good."

Miriame was about to make another rude gesture but she stopped herself just in time. "Can I borrow this dress if I decide I want to look like a woman again?"

Courtney hugged her. "I knew it. You like wearing a dress and looking like a woman after all. You are not a complete musketeer—you have a woman's heart and soul buried under that jacket and breeches of yours." She hurried to her wardrobe, pulled out more dresses in a profusion of colors: burnt gold, deep green, and a blue the color of midnight, and piled them into Miriame's arms. "These will suit you very well."

Miriame stood open-mouthed at Courtney's generosity. "What shall I do with them?"

Courtney hugged her. "Take them with you. Wear them when you can. Learn how to feel like a woman again."

She gathered the dresses to her chest, tears misting her eyes. She didn't know whether she liked looking like a woman or not, but Metin seemed to like it well enough that she did.

Much to her surprise, she, in her turn, liked Metin well enough. That was enough for her to try wearing a dress another time.

Francine had once described to him a morning levee in her chamber: the crowds of people chattering, talking, laughing, even brawling on occasion, the smells of perfume and candle wax, the light and glitter and color, the very romance of it all.

Now that he was here at one of them, he failed to see any romance in it at all. Indeed, he wondered that Francine could bear it at all, let alone have to put up with it every day that she spent at court. The very thought was enough to give him the shudders.

The outer chamber was hot and crowded and so noisy that he could hardly hear himself think. He pushed through the crowds of painted and perfumed courtiers with growing impatience, making his way to the front. How false and unreal they all were, wearing close-cropped, curled black or white wigs that fell to their shoulders, white painted faces with red painted spots on their cheeks, and they minced on high-heeled shoes. Not a one of them would last a whole day as a soldier, or as a laborer back on the farm where he grew up. They were more like lifesize playthings than real people.

Finally the door to the inner chamber opened, and there was a surge toward the inner sanctum. He found himself squeezed in the middle of the crowd, his ears ringing from the excited, high-pitched chatter that assaulted him on all sides. The noise and the crush was more than could be borne. He employed his elbows with good effect until he had cleared enough space around him to at least breathe.

A couple of burly footmen stood at the entrance to Francine's chamber to control the flow of the crowd and prevent a riot. Just as Metin had struggled and pushed his way to the door, they stopped the flow. "Chamber's full now," one of them grunted. "You'll have to come back tomorrow."

Metin was having none of it. He forced his way past the footmen, quelling them with a furious glare. Nothing and nobody was going to prevent him from seeing Francine this morning.

The footmen evidently saw the determination in his face. They let him by with hardly a grumble, revenging themselves on those who tried to follow after him by shoving them viciously back, out of the way of the now-closing doors.

There she was at last, his Francine, reclining in her magnificent bed, her head resting on a mound of lace-trimmed pillows. Her blond curls were spread out around her head like a halo, and around her white shoulders was a shawl of sky blue, the same color as her eyes. In one hand she held a cup of that fashionable delicacy, hot chocolate. As he watched, she took a dainty sip of her chocolate from a silver spoon and ran her tongue over her red lips to catch the last drops.

He shuddered with desire at the very sight of her. How long it had been since he had held her in his arms, since he had spent the night making love to her in every way he knew.

He forced his way through the crowd to her and dropped to his knees by the side of her bed. "Francine, my love," he cried, seizing her hand and bringing it to his lips with all the passion he felt for her in the very depths of his heart.

Overcome with emotions—joy at seeing her once again mixed with relief at finding her well and happy—he could not give voice to all that he wanted to say or pour out his love. He could only clasp her hand to his heart and gaze at her with infinite tenderness. "Francine, my adored one."

Chapter 5

Francine snatched her hand away from his grasp with
a sinking feeling in her heart. Damn and blast the man.
He had displayed a woeful lack of sense, not to mention
a complete and utter lack of manners.

His idiotic display could not have come at a worse moment. She had just put on a thoroughly believable show
for one of the cardinal's cronies, carrying on about how
much she had missed the court while languishing in
exile and how glad she was to be back and reinstated as
the King's mistress once again—and the first Metin had
to turn up to spoil it all. How could she possibly pose as
a neglected woman, living only for the notice of her glorious King, if her old lovers were to appear out of the
blue and disgrace her with their tactlessness?

The second Metin would never have caused such a
scene. He was far too clever for such nonsense. He
would have understood the situation at a glance and
strategically retired from the field. He would not have
stayed to be dismissed. What a pity this Metin did not
have such sense, for all his beauty.

How could she have remained infatuated with him for
two months while she had been in the country? She
hardly knew how she had managed it. Seeing him again
now, amidst the tumult of a court levee, she saw clearly

that he had no fashion, no style, no grace, no presence. His hair was undressed, his face unpainted. True, he had a fine pair of legs, but then again, so did her footmen, and she would never even consider inviting either of them into her bed.

How desperate for company she must have been during her exile to be satisfied with such a lout.

She saw the cardinal's crony smirking and whispering to a group who huddled around him. One of them threw a glance in her direction, and they all laughed.

She would not tolerate such disrespect. This Metin would have to be sacrificed to her dignity. "Who are you, pray, that you accost me in such a familiar manner?" she said to him in her frostiest tone of voice. "I do not think I know you."

His face grew pale and he simply stared at her. "You do not know me, Madame?"

She could almost feel sorry for the desolation she saw writ on his face, but she had to be cruel to be kind. He had to find out sooner or later that she would not live among the pigs and pumpkins and peasants for him. "I certainly have no wish to know you. You are rude and unmannerly, to intrude thus upon my morning levee with your wild talk."

He dropped her hand and rose to his feet, his face composed, but pale as death. "I must apologize for my rudeness, Madame. I thought I knew you, but you turned out not to be the woman I thought you were." His voice shook a little. "I see now that you are someone else entirely. Please forgive my intrusion."

Pah. He would get over it soon enough, she thought, as he strode to the door. He was young. Indeed, he ought to be grateful to her. She had just helped him to grow out of his innocence and naiveté. Never again would he take the words of a woman at face value, and he would be more careful in the future on whom he bestowed his heart.

She had done him a service by bruising his young heart a little. Far from blaming her for her fickleness, Jean-Paul Metin ought to thank her for the care she had taken of him.

She turned back with a ready smile to the group of courtiers who surrounded her, and shrugged. "One has all sorts of admirers that one never knew about before," she said with a winning smile. "I suppose I should feel flattered. Though how the poor fellow thought he could ever compete with the King . . ." She let the last sentence trail off. No harm in reminding her audience at every turn that she was Louis XIV's mistress once more.

There was a smattering of sycophantic laughter. Francine sat in the middle of it, propped on her pillows, perfectly at ease with herself and with her conscience.

Jean-Paul Metin strode along the cobblestones toward the barracks, kicking a loose stone savagely in front of him. Francine, his beautiful Francine, had played him for a fool. He had not thought it possible that someone so beautiful could be so false. How could a woman with the face of an angel from heaven above possess the soul of a very devil, as black and as rotten as Satan himself?

He had loved her, adored her, worshipped her, and all the while she was laughing up her sleeve at him.

She had never loved him at all. That thought gave him more pain than anything else. If she had felt so much as a tiny fraction of the love he felt for her, she could never have cast him off so cruelly, humiliated him so publicly, as she had this morning. He had felt like an unmannerly boor, rudely daring to put his uncouth paws on her beautiful person without an invitation. She had deliberately made him feel that way.

He had wanted to pour his heart and soul out to her, he had made his feelings as clear as he could and she had denied him in front of the whole court. She had destroyed all meaning in the love they had shared. He was left with nothing. Nothing. Even in his memory, she had played him false—she had never loved him.

Miriame knocked heavily on the door to the western gate with her gloved hand, wondering whether she should stay to be let in, or run while she had the chance.

Berthe must have been waiting for her. She opened it on the instant and showed her inside. "Come in. My mistress is expecting you."

Miriame followed her with leaden steps, already wishing she had chosen to run away. She knew full well she was playing with fire. She only hoped the rewards would be worth the danger.

The marquise was sitting in her antechamber, a piece of fine embroidery in her hand, as if she were posing for one of her innumerable portraits. She rose to greet Miriame with a smile. "Ah, my dear friend, so you came to see me after all."

Miriame bowed. "Indeed, Madame Marquise. Did I not make a promise that I would be here?"

The marquise gave an arch look as she sat back down again on one end of a long sofa. "Not all men keep their promises." She patted the cushion beside her and gave Miriame an inviting smile. "Especially not their promises to women."

Miriame ignored the unspoken request to sit beside the marquise. "You cannot hold it against all men that certain of their number are rascals."

The marquise pouted a little when Miriame chose to sit on a high-backed chair on the other side of the chamber, well out of the way of her talons. "Indeed, I would never dream of it. I trust you. You are my friend, come to succor me in my loneliness. For that I owe you my thanks."

"I must apologize that I have only a very short time to spend with you tonight," Miriame said. "I would never have come at all, save for my promise." *And the hopes of another jewel or two to add to my growing hoard,* she thought to herself. *It would be as well not to kill the golden goose as long as it continued to provide the odd golden egg.*

"You are weary of me already?"

"I have been ordered on a mission that must take me out of Paris tonight. I should have been on my way hours ago."

"A mission?" The marquise's eyes lit up with excitement, scenting a new piece of gossip like a greyhound scenting a rabbit. "Tell me more."

"It is a *secret* mission," Miriame said, her voice as grave as she could make it. She hoped the marquise would believe her story. "I would not dream of putting you in danger by breathing the least hint about it. I should not even have told you as much as this, but I will be gone for some days. I would not have you think I had forgotten you."

Francine's bottom lip quivered. "Am I to miss you before I have even got to know you, my new friend?"

Miriame stood up again and bowed in Francine's direction. "I am sorry for the necessity of leaving you, but duty calls. Fare thee well, Marquise. May God keep you in His grace until we meet again."

Francine rose from her seat to bid her farewell. "Take this, my brave soldier, to speed you on your way," she said, pressing a small bag into Miriame's hands. "Come back to me when you return. I will not rest in peace until I know you are safe."

Miriame bowed over her hand and backed out of the chamber. She felt very pleased with herself. Not only had she been rewarded with a bag of gold, but she had also come up with a very good reason for avoiding the lusty marquise for some weeks.

She could always pretend that the secret mission had been delayed, that she had been in danger of her life, that she had been imprisoned and only just escaped, or a thousand other lies that the marquise would have to swallow. Being a soldier was proving to be an excellent excuse to cover a multitude of sins.

Sophie and Courtney were waiting for her at the gate of the city. She put her spurs to her new gelding to urge him on. He suited her well enough, but he lacked the fire of the black mare and would lag behind if she did not keep encouraging him. Enough of a moon showed through the clouds to let them make good speed without endangering their horses.

She had not lied to the marquise about her mission. She was, indeed, on her way to England. Sophie, Courtney, and she were on a mission to save the world or some such nonsense. She had not listened well to Sophie's explanations as to why honor and duty demanded that they ride as fast as they could to warn the English king about a supposed plot against the life of his sister.

She didn't care about royalty and their struggles. Neither did she give a toss about honor and duty or secret missions. But Sophie had mentioned a magic phrase—one thousand gold *pistoles* to share among the three of them for a job well done—and she had agreed on the instant. One thousand gold *pistoles*—she could hardly imagine such wealth. Even a third of it would more than double her savings so far. She would go further than England, she would go to the far-off Americas and more, to earn such a princely sum.

How she wished that Rebecca were here to share her wealth with her. Poor Rebecca. She had not been able to protect her sister when she needed it most, and now Rebecca was dead. No amount of hoarded gold would save her now.

She blinked furiously, glad of the darkness that hid her tear-filled eyes from her friends. She would not like them to see her weakness. The fastest route to an early death was letting others guess your vulnerabilities. Weaknesses were best kept to oneself.

Nothing would bring her sister back to her, but Miriame had promised Rebecca on her deathbed that she would look after herself. She would honor that promise.

The night was breaking into dawn before Sophie would let them stop to rest. Miriame was dog tired but determined not to show it. The events of the past few days had exhausted her beyond what she could bear.

She flopped onto the bed at the inn next to Courtney with a sigh of relief. What was Metin doing at the moment, she wondered, as she drifted off to sleep. Was he lying in his bed in the early dawn wondering the same about her? Or were his thoughts still fixated on the marquise, *la belle* Francine?

Foolish of him, if so. She doubted he would get far with the marquise. Oh, no doubt the woman had welcomed him into her bed with great alacrity—he was impossibly handsome, after all—but she would never let him into her heart. She was far too selfish for that. The marquise was not a serious rival for Metin's affections. She would weary of him soon enough and turn him away. Then he might have the leisure to think of a new woman, of a new love . . .

Maybe it was just as well that Sophie had called on her assistance for this mission to England. She realized the danger of thinking about Metin too long. She must not forget that he was a soldier and her enemy. Without meaning to, she had done him a great wrong, and could not even repent of her sin. But a single theft had proved so profitable, she would do it all over again tomorrow.

Still, he had called her beautiful—and meant it. God in heaven only knew what she would do about his interest in her, but she didn't want to give him up just yet. She wanted to get to know him just a little better, to talk to him, just be near him. She would even wear a dress for him, though being seen in one in public was more dangerous than she liked.

Jean-Paul Metin. She had chosen her name well. She liked the name, it rolled off her tongue easily. She liked the man it belonged to even better. She was already looking forward to their next meeting. There was a smile on her face as she drifted off to sleep.

A sharp jab in the ribs and Miriame was awake in an instant, though she didn't want to be. She gave a sleepy grumble and turned over. She had been having the most marvelous dream and was thoroughly annoyed at being woken.

"Get up. We have visitors," Sophie hissed into her ear as she shook the still-sleeping Courtney.

Her dream was gone, dissolved by the light of day. She rose reluctantly to her feet, stumbled sleepily over to the casement window and looked out into the yard to see who had come a-visiting.

Sophie's new husband, the Count Lamotte, was in the courtyard holding a sweating horse. With him were two other men.

She felt her blood run cold. Rebecca's killer was here, the cold-voiced killer, in the very courtyard of the inn, with him.

Sophie had not been speaking idly or exaggerating

the difficulties that lay in their way when she had said their mission was dangerous and they might be pursued. She doubted that Sophie's husband meant them any harm, but his being in the company of the killer with the cultured voice made her squirm.

She had no doubt that their lives were in danger—all three of them—whether or no Sophie's husband intended them harm. Whoever had sent the killer after them meant business. Clearly, they were not supposed to come back alive. Even if the Count did try to save his wife, chances are the other two would murder him along with the rest, if they could. She doubted that Rebecca's killer would prove squeamish about adding another body to the pile of those he had already murdered.

Her first thought was to run, to get as far away from him as fast as possible and to hide, but she dismissed it instantly. That would not work. He had their scent. There would be no escape.

Neither would she run away and leave her companions behind. They might not know it, but never had they needed her protection more than they did at this moment. Sophie and Courtney had been gently reared—they knew nothing about life on the street. They fought like gentlemen, and would expect others to follow the same rules as they did.

Miriame was under no such illusion. Rebecca's killer would give them no quarter, and would ruthlessly exploit every weakness he could find. They would prove no match for his street cunning. He would kill them as easily he would slaughter a babe in arms, or a barely grown girl who refused to lift her skirts for him.

She had no choice. Little as she liked it, she would have to take on her sister's murderer, gutter rat to gutter rat. She would revenge herself on him now, and protect her friends, or she would die.

Miriame was no longer the frightened girl who had watched in terrified silence as he had forced himself on her sister, and then slit her throat as calmly as if he had been slicing himself a piece of cheese. She had better weapons than her fists. She knew how to fight. It was time she tried out her new skills on her old enemy.

If she died at his hands, so be it. She would have tried her best and would have died in a cause worth fighting for. Few women could boast as much.

If she lived, so much the better. The specter from her past that haunted each waking hour would at last be laid to rest. She would rest easier in her bed knowing that that particular piece of vermin was dead and moldering in his grave.

She turned back to Sophie and Courtney, her face set. "Climb out of the window and escape that way. I shall deal with the three of them, and at least delay them long enough for you to get well away."

Courtney started to protest, but Miriame hushed her. Her mind was made up and she would brook no argument. "I have an old score to settle with one of them. This is my fight. I will have it no other way. Now make haste. Time is a-wasting." She gestured to the high-set window which looked down into the stableyard. "Go! I'll keep them busy for as long as I can. Our horses are rested and theirs are not, so they will be hard put to it to catch you again, once you get away."

With one leg over the windowsill, Sophie turned back to Miriame. "Be careful of yourself. Keep the door locked and do not open it to them on any pretext. You shall be safe enough with the door locked—they cannot come at you then. But if it *should* come to a fight," she added, as though it were an afterthought, "do not hurt the Count. I am sure he means us no harm."

Miriame nodded. Sophie was as careful of her new-wedded husband as of a new-hatched chick. "I will delay him if I can, but I will take care not to hurt him unless I cannot help it. He is safe from me. My quarrel is with his companion."

"Thank you." Sophie's face was white and set as she raised her hand to wave goodbye. "Until we meet again in Paris."

Courtney jammed her hat down over her ears. "Au revoir, Madame Thief. Until Paris."

Miriame forced a grin at the solemn farewells. "Don't worry about me. I'll come to no harm with the thought of all those golden *pistoles* waiting for me to claim my share." She wished she felt a fraction of the confidence they showed in her. She was well aware of the difficulty of her self-appointed task. Still, she had the glimmerings of a plan that might, just might, save her.

If she made it back to Paris alive, she would be luckier than she deserved.

Barely had the other two dropped out of the window when Miriame heard the tramp of boots up the stairs and a gruff voice shouted through the door at her, "Open up in there."

She would have to make all three of them as impatient and as angry as possible for her plan to work. Impatient men were careless men, and angry men were even more so. Besides, the longer she delayed them, the greater the chance for Sophie and Courtney to escape. If she were to fail and become the victim instead of the victor, every moment she could win for them gave them an extra chance, however small, of life.

She put on a bored voice. "Who might you be that I should open my door for you?"

"It doesn't matter who I am. Open the door or I'll break you into pieces."

It was obviously the Count, not too happy to think of

his newly wedded wife in a bedchamber with another man. Miriame would have laughed if her peril had not been so great. "Temper, temper. Surely you gentlemen will not mind waiting until I put on my boots."

She made a few shuffling noises as if putting on her boots, and then taking them off, and putting them on again. Finally, when she felt she had played that card for all it was worth, she stomped around on the floor with noisy satisfaction. "Ah, that's better. Now just let me put on my jacket."

"Open up in the name of the King, you fool." Not the Count this time, or Rebecca's killer, but the third man. Time to make him angry, too.

"You *do* like saying that, don't you?" Miriame said, choosing her words to be as offensive as she possibly could. "Does it make you feel important? I suppose a toad like you must puff himself up somehow." She heaved an exaggerated sigh. "Still, I'm afraid you'll have to wait until I have attended to my hair before I let you in. A gentleman must never be seen without his hair dressed."

It worked even better than she had expected. She had evidently touched a sore point. He was positively growling with rage through the door. "I shall kill you for that, you little weasel."

Time to insult the Count again. She needed at least two of them to rush at the door in a rage to have any hope of success. "You'll have to wait a moment longer, I'm afraid, for the killing to start. Just let me button up my breeches, and I shall be right with you."

That hit the right note. There was a sudden stampede of feet as one or two of them rushed at the door to batter it down.

She had to judge it just right, not too soon and not too late. Just as the assault on the door began, she unlocked it and whipped it open with all the speed she could muster.

Sophie's husband was taken by surprise, lost his balance and fell. The third man, a huge man with no neck and legs like tree stumps, tripped over him and tumbled to the floor.

Knife in her hand, Miriame sidestepped them before they had hit the floor. Rebecca's killer, not as angry or impatient as his fellows, was still on his feet.

He saw the knife in Miriame's hand and went to draw his own with a snarl.

But Miriame was fast, faster even than he was, and he had not expected such an attack.

Before his weapon was half out of its scabbard, Miriame had grabbed him by the hair, bent his head back, and sliced her knife over his exposed throat.

For a moment it looked as if nothing had happened. Had her knife been too blunt? Had her careful planning been wasted? Was he even now about to turn on her with a roar and cut her down where she stood? Then there was a gush of red as his lifeblood spurted out to puddle on the floor.

"That was for Rebecca," Miriame hissed into his ear.

She saw his eyes grow wide for a second, as if he struggled to remember the particular sin that had doomed him now, and then they glassed over into insensibility.

She shook him gently, but there was no response. His whole body had become limp; and there was no strength left in him, not even enough strength to keep up the flow of blood from the wound in his throat. He was dead. Rebecca's killer was dead.

She had expected to feel relief, even a measure of triumph. Instead all she felt was emptiness, as if all her thoughts and feelings had disappeared into nothingness.

The dead man's corpse was leaning against her, her body the only thing keeping it upright. With a shiver of disgust, she pushed it away from her. It fell through the door and into the room with the two others, who were even now just struggling to their feet. For their sins, they could keep him company a while longer.

She pulled the door to and locked it, ignoring the howls of protest that came from the other side of the door. She had done what she could—killed her enemy and delayed the others, though it was only a matter of time until they climbed out the window. The rest was up to Sophie and Courtney. She could do no more.

Her hands were covered with blood—his blood. She gave a grimace as she wiped them as best she could on the floorboards. She had to get out—she had killed a man here. The place stank of blood and death and horror.

She ran down the stairs and into the kitchen with shaking legs. "I've a bet on with the gentlemen upstairs that they won't get out of that chamber inside an hour," she said and she tossed the landlord a gold coin. "Whatever they say, don't set them free before then, my dear fellow. And if they climb out the window and come looking for me, tell them I rode south."

The landlord winked as he pocketed the coin. "As you wish, Monsieur."

"The loser of the bet pays the reckoning, so make sure you get what we owe you from their pockets before they leave," she added, forcing a grin. She had no time for explanations if he were to become suspicious.

He tipped his hat. "Thank you, Monsieur. I'll be sure to do that."

That business taken care of, Miriame ran to the stables. She thought for the briefest moment of catching up with Sophie and Courtney, before deciding against it. She had to make a fast escape and hide herself well. England would have to wait for another day.

She mounted her gelding, feeling wearier than she had for many a day, and galloped back toward Paris. She had killed a man in cold blood, slit his throat for no reason but that he did not deserve to live.

The pounding of the horse's hooves distracted her from the griping in her stomach until she was well away. Suddenly she stopped, swung down, and led the horse to a hidden clearing, where she was violently sick again and again, until there was nothing left in her stomach but bile, and even then she could not stop.

Evening had fallen before the clenching of her stomach and the shivering of her limbs quieted down. She remounted her horse and begin the long, weary ride back to Paris.

Francine raised her eyebrows in surprise. The cardinal himself at her levee? What did he want? She knew full well that he would rather destroy her than pay court with the rest of her hangers-on. He had never made a secret of his dislike, and she had in turn always cordially hated him.

He could not threaten her position now, not even with the trio of his pretty nieces that he paraded around in front of the King at every opportunity. They had wasted every chance they had ever had of capturing the attention of the great Louis XIV and now it was too late for them. Too late for them, and for every other young would-be consort who sought to usurp her place at the King's side.

The King had returned to her bed—and last night it had not just been to sleep. She was the King's mistress again, in deed as well as in reputation. No cardinal could ruin her now.

She gave him a triumphant smile. "Ah, Cardinal. You have chosen to join the throngs of those who would ask a favor of me, have you?" She knew full well that hinting at such a reason for his visit would infuriate him. "Come now, don't be shy. Tell me what I can do for you today."

The cardinal limped over and sat down heavily in an ornate gilded armchair beside her bed, tucking his sweeping red robes around him. "I was hoping for some amusement, Madame, that is all."

"Amusement?"

"Yes." His smile was very like the gaping jaws of a snake. "I hear you had a moment's entertainment yester morn—some young man falling at your feet and vowing everlasting love to you, I believe?"

Damn the rumors for spreading so fast. She hoped the King had heard none of them. He was bound to be less than amused. "I don't know why the footmen let him in," she replied. "Some young fool who knows no better, I suppose, trying to get my attention by shocking me with his bad breeding."

"I suppose the footmen were used to letting the young fellow—Jean-Paul Metin, was it not?—into your bedchamber from times gone by," the cardinal suggested with a malicious sneer. "It was a natural mistake for them to make. You cannot expect even royal servants to have such a prodigious memory as to be able to recall which of your lovers are to be admitted and when."

So that was his game. He sought to discredit her with the king by spreading rumors of her infidelity, did he? "You are mistaken, Cardinal," she said, in a voice of warning. "And no friend of mine would make such an outrageous claim against me."

The cardinal sniffed. "I am flattered, Madame. I had no idea you counted me among your friends. Though I must not break the ninth commandment, at certain times it is more politic not to speak the truth. I trust you will forgive me."

She stared at him angrily, furious that he had the gall to insult her so piously in her own bedchamber.

"I wonder if young Jean-Paul will prove more forgiving than his mistress?" the cardinal continued. "I heard tell that he has certain letters in his possession, letters that could well prove awkward for the lady concerned if they were ever to be found, and the King should see them."

Francine felt her face grow pale beneath her rouge. It was true—in the first flush of her infatuation, she had written Metin a dozen or more indiscreet letters. What a fool she was to slip up like that. She had thought that her distance from the court meant a measure of safety, less need for secrecy than before.

Evidently the influence of the court reached far and wide, and the reach of the powerful cardinal even more so.

"Embarrassing letters?" she said, forcing a laugh. "How glad I am that I never write any." He may as well know now that she had no intention of being caught in such a trap. Her discretion was well known. Let him know right now that she would deny all knowledge of the letters, were they ever to appear.

She wondered how on earth he had found out about them. Did he even now have them in his possession? Were his words a warning, a veiled threat not to interfere with his interests at court and risk ruination?

He gave a smile that made her flesh creep as he leaned towards her. "Lie to me all you want, you painted whore," he said in a whisper. "We will see if you can convince the King."

She watched him limp out of her chamber with hatred in her heart for his vile, misshapen body and even more twisted mind. She would have to recall Metin—the first Metin—just until she knew what had happened to the letters. If he still had them, she would have to wheedle them

out of him somehow. If he had lost them, or heaven forbid, sold them, she would at least know how to prepare
herself for the worst.

She couldn't imagine his ever selling her letters to the
cardinal, no matter how much he was offered for them.
The old man was a fool if he was counting on that. Metin
was too idealistic to do such a thing. However she had hurt
him, he would not stoop to such behavior. It was naive of
him, to be sure, not to take advantage of the tool her carelessness had put into his hands, but at least his innocence
worked to her advantage for once.

Visit Francine? Metin screwed up the note in his hand
and threw it viciously into the corner of his chamber.
Once upon a time, not so very long ago, such a summons would have set his heart to beating faster. He
would have rushed to obey his mistress, hungering for
an affectionate look or a kind word from her.

Not any more. He was beyond such foolishness now. He
would not race to her side to be mocked and laughed at.
He was not a toy she could discard with disdain one morning and then pick up again the next day when it suited
her.

He winced at the mere remembrance of the shame
she had made him feel. If she had been a man, he would
have called her out for such an insult. As it was, he could
only suffer in silence. But to return voluntarily for more
pain? He shook his head. He would not be a fool twice.

Then again, perhaps she was truly sorry for the scene
in her chamber. Maybe she had an explanation for it
that would take the sting out of her words—an explanation that would end with them both laughing over the
mistake. Did he not owe her at least the chance to explain it to him? Ought he to condemn her unheard?

He doubted there was anything she could do or say that would take away the sting of their last meeting. She had not been kind.

He had once thought her perfect in every way: a fragile, gentle woman taken advantage of by the King and his minions. Not so. Born to nobility, she clearly enjoyed the trappings of power that she had, at least as long the King's favor should last. She had opened his eyes for him to her selfishness.

But for the sake of the love he had borne her, he would go to see her to hear what explanation she might offer to appease him, but he would not hurry to her side. For the first time ever, she would have to wait upon *his* pleasure.

In the meantime, he would make it his business to find out more about the dark-haired beauty from the church. Miriame. It was an unusual name. It suited her. She was not like any other woman he had ever met.

Just as well that Francine had shown him her true colors. He could talk with Miriame all he liked now without feeling as though he were betraying Francine.

He smiled to himself as he thought of Miriame's red lips and the smoothness of her skin. He would like to sit by her side and pluck the red rosebuds out of her hair one by one.

She was so dark and mysterious that she fired his imagination. She would not fall into his hands like an overripe fruit, as Francine had done. He wondered how many hands Francine had dropped into before his own. The thought made him shudder with distaste.

Miriame would not be so easy to pick. He would have to lay siege to her, undermine her defenses, defeat the guardians of her honor, and carry her off at last.

How unlike the pink-and-white Francine was his dark-haired, black-eyed Miriame to look at. How much he hoped she would be unlike Francine in every other way as well.

He was sick of lies and deceit. All he wanted was the truth.

The cardinal stared at the man in front of him. "Where is André?" he demanded.

"Dead."

This was news indeed—unwelcome news. The man was a villain and a fool, but a useful enough tool to one who knew how to wield him. "Who killed him?"

The man shrugged. "No idea. The King sent him out on a mission and he never came back. Someone knifed him in a tavern just out of the city."

"Damn the bastard who killed him. I was looking forward to that pleasure myself."

The man in front of him twitched uneasily. "So, do you want me, then?"

The cardinal leaned back in his chair and gazed up at the man standing in front of him. "Why did André lie to me?"

The man's face paled. "Lie? About what?"

He shut his eyes. "Protesting your innocence won't help you, you know. Why did André lie to me about Francine's lover—the one with the letters you were supposed to find for me and didn't? Why did André claim he was dead?"

"He *is* dead. I stuck the knife in him myself."

The cardinal linked his fingers together and spoke in a soft, slow voice. "Are you calling me a liar?"

The man's face was green with fear. "No, your Excellency. But—"

"Good. I'm glad you have that much sense at least. Unfortunately for us both, André has gotten himself killed, so I cannot take out my anger on him."

The man nodded, barely able to stand on his feet with fear.

"I want those letters, and I want them now. I do not care what happens to the fellow—he may live or die as you please—but I want those letters. You will get them for me." He waved a bejeweled hand at the man in front of him. "You can only pray that you are a better thief than you are a killer. You knifed the man yourself? Pah!" He spat on the floor with disgust. "Now go. I do not want to see you again without those letters in your hand. If I do, it will be the worse for you."

Miriame made up a story—an illness so severe she could not move out of her bed—to explain her absence from the barracks. Her excuse was accepted without question.

She wasn't surprised. She still felt sick to the stomach whenever she thought about the rich red blood bubbling from the throat of Rebecca's murderer. The sickness in her stomach showed on her face. Her cheeks were paler than usual, a green-tinged pale, the unhealthy pallor of a worm that lives underground, never seeing the light of the sun.

She felt little better than such a worm. She had killed a man in cold blood. It was not an easy matter to forget. Neither was it an easy matter to forgive herself.

Her first day back on the practice yard, she scratched her opponent with the point of her sword and a drop of blood stained his cheek. At the sight of the blood, and the faintest whiff of its metallic scent, she began to sweat and shake uncontrollably, and she fell to her knees in front of everyone becoming violently ill.

She was furious with herself when her stomach stopped churning and she had recovered her composure once again. How could she be a soldier if she was afraid of the sight of blood? She would have to overcome her squeamishness somehow.

Even worse than her sudden sensitivity was the way that Jean-Paul Metin followed her around. Wherever she went, whatever she did, he was there.

When she fought in the practice yard, he showed up to watch her. When she ate in the officer's mess, he was no more than a couple of places away from her at the table. When she went out one evening with a gaggle of her fellows, he joined them without an invitation and sat next to her on a stool in the tavern to swill his ale in her company.

That last was too much for her. Could she never escape his company—not even away from the barracks? She did not want to be with him when she was dressed as a man. While she was a man, he was her enemy, and he would have to remain her enemy. She could not afford to let him find out the truth.

She fidgeted on her stool, growing increasingly irritated at his silent scrutiny. Finally she could take it no longer. She stared back at him aggressively and banged her mug of ale on to the table with a thump. "What do you want with me?" She had had just enough ale to loosen her tongue and make her less cautious than usual—and she was in the mood for picking a fight.

He shrugged, not letting up his study of her face for a moment. "I am interested in you. You have something that belongs to me."

Not any more she didn't. She'd made sure of that. She had kept nothing that could ever be traced back to him. "I do?"

"My name."

The conversations around her seemed to recede into the distance as she dealt with this new threat. "Would you like it back?" she asked, forcing out a laugh.

He ignored her question. "Who gave you the name you carry?"

He was treading on dangerous ground. She did not like being questioned, particularly about things she had no intention of answering honestly. She gave him a look as if she thought he was dim-witted. "My father, naturally. Who else did you think gave it to me?"

"And what was your father's name?"

"Why do you ask?"

He looked steadily at her. "I do not think that anyone gave my name to you. I think you took it—stole it, rather. From me."

He had lost little time coming to such a conclusion, but she would brazen it out for all that. She had too much to lose to walk away now. "Prove it."

He shrugged. "I cannot."

"Then why follow me around with your tongue hanging out? As if you were a hungry puppy and I was a juicy piece of meat you wanted to sink your . . . teeth into."

His eyes narrowed in anger at her taunting and his hand crept to the hilt of his sword. "You flatter yourself."

"Do I?"

"I could kill you here and now," he said, without raising his voice. "It would be no more than you deserve."

She grinned back at him. "You could try."

"What makes you so sure that I wouldn't succeed?"

She flicked her knife out of her boot and held it casually against his side, the tip of it pressing a warning against his ribs. "This."

He didn't move a muscle. "The captain said that you were quick with your knife."

The compliment pleased her, though she was determined not to show it. "I am."

"So was the man who robbed me and left me for dead on the streets not so long ago."

"It's a hard world out there. We all survive as best we can."

"By robbing strangers in the street?"

"Perhaps, if there is no other way."

"And murder?"

"Murder? I try not to resort to that. It's too messy and complicated." She closed her eyes for a moment and saw again the blood spurting from the man whose throat she had cut. Her heart began to race and she started to feel her stomach turn over.

In that instant, Metin had snatched the knife from her hand and pressed it against her side in his turn.

Her belly tightened. She was going to be violently sick again. She could feel it.

With a muttered groan she rose to her feet and stumbled out of the tavern. She only just made it to a bare patch of ground before she fell to her knees and retched over and over again into the dust.

Jean-Paul Metin followed his namesake out of the tavern and stood by as he emptied his guts onto the ground.

The boy was right ill, there was no doubt about it. Again and again he retched until his stomach was empty. Finally he sat back on his heels. "That feels better," he said, with a weak attempt at a grin.

Even in the pale glow of the moonlight, Jean-Paul could see that the other man's face was a sickly green. "You're not well."

He shook his head. "Too much ale, that's all."

Too much ale? That excuse wouldn't wash with him. Jean-Paul had watched him all day—he knew to a drop how much he had drunk. "You didn't even finish your first mug."

Metin held his belly with his hands as he struggled to his feet. "It was stronger than usual."

He leaned against the wall, watching the other Jean-

Paul. For all his weak stomach, he was a tough bastard. A real fighter. He couldn't help feeling a sneaking sense of admiration for his opponent. "You're not going to confess to stealing my name, are you?"

The young man shook his head. "No."

"Or anything else of mine?"

"No."

"Why did you try to kill me?"

"I didn't."

"I know you didn't kill me, or I would not be standing here right now. Why did you try?"

"I didn't. If I had wanted to kill you, you would be dead by now. I put my knife to your side right now only as a warning to keep away from me."

Jean-Paul shook his head. "I was not talking about just now in the tavern. Why did you try to kill me some weeks ago now, when I first rode into Paris?"

"I didn't. I don't murder strangers."

He raised his eyebrows in disbelief. "You have never tried to kill anyone?"

The young man shook his head, his face pale. "The only person I have ever tried to kill is dead. Very dead."

"You killed him?"

He nodded, his face positively green again. He clutched his belly as if he wanted to be sick again.

"Who was he?"

"I do not know his name."

"Then why did you kill him? Was he attacking you? Or were his pockets stuffed full of more gold than mine were?"

"I do not know his name, but I know his deeds. He deserved death many times over."

"For what reason?"

Metin looked up. His eyes were the most amazingly rich brown Jean-Paul had ever seen, framed with dark eyelashes as long as a girl's. He'd never noticed before how handsome his namesake was. "I had a sister once . . ." Jean-Paul could have sworn that a drop of moisture fell from his eye. The vicious little bastard had feelings, it seems. "He did not treat her well."

"You would kill a man for ill-treating your sister?"

"What better reason?"

"But you did not try to kill me?"

"No."

"And Francine? What is she to you? Have you stolen her heart from me, as you stole my name?" He was surprised to find how much he still cared what Madame de Montespan did. The fine lady behaved no better than a common strumpet and he should not care what sorry bastard she had replaced him with, but he did.

"Her heart?" The young man gave an ugly laugh. "What would I want with her heart, even suppose she were to have one?"

"You are not Francine's lover, then?"

He laughed again. "No—nor am I likely ever to be. I do not care overmuch for her. Neither would she care for me, I suspect, were she ever to know what I am."

So, Francine had not cast him off for someone who had stolen his name. Jean-Paul could be grateful for that at least. He was still convinced that the young Metin had a hand in his downfall and perhaps even tried to kill him. He didn't know what other secrets the young man was hiding, but ill as he was, Jean-Paul couldn't leave him on the street. "Come. Let's go get some better ale than the piss they were serving inside." He jerked his thumb back at the tavern. "It was enough to make anyone ill."

The young man wiped his face on his sleeve. "I'm fine." His voice had turned sulky and he made no move to follow Jean-Paul.

Surprisingly, Jean-Paul felt almost sorry for him. "You don't want another drink?"

"No, I don't."

Still he hesitated. "I can hardly leave you here in the street, puking your guts out like a girl."

The young man turned on him with a snarl. "I didn't ask for your help and I don't want it. Get out of my way, and stay out."

Jean-Paul shrugged. Their short truce was over. He strode off into the night, ignoring the curses ringing in his ears. Damn the ungrateful bastard. He would not bother to hold out the hand of tolerance again. Next time the lad got in his way, he would kill the little whelp, damn him.

Miriame watched him go in silence. He seemed to be sure she had stolen his name. She could never convince him otherwise—and there was little point in trying. As long as he could not prove her theft, what could he do about it? No magistrate would listen to him on such slender evidence as he could muster against her.

The moon was full and the night still. She could hear little save the faint sounds of revelry from the tavern she had left and the clump-clump-clump of Jean-Paul's heavy boots on the cobblestones as he strode off into the night.

She breathed deeply of the cool night air. If she shut her eyes, she could almost imagine herself in a romantic scene, parting from her lover, her handsome soldier. He had been so close to her. She had needed only to reach out her hand to him and she would have been able to touch him. She had needed only to tilt her head back, raise her eyes to his and invite him to kiss her lips . . .

She stumbled over a cobblestone and opened her eyes again. He had been so close, and yet so far. Who was she trying to fool? The real Jean-Paul Metin knew her only as his comrade—and as a thief. She would have to wait until the morrow, when she could don one of Courtney's gowns once more, and get his attention as a woman. He would never look at her without anger in his eyes as long as she was a man. Nor would he look at her with desire.

An evil taste remained in her mouth from her bout of sickness. She spat on the road beside her. Even if she was wearing a dress, he would not have wanted to kiss her in the state she was in.

She wanted to kiss him, though. Oh, how she wanted it. She wanted to feel the touch of his lips on her own, his rough hands caressing the smooth skin of her breasts, the press of his body against hers.

Miriame wanted him to desire her and only her. She wanted him never to think of that painted and powdered Madame de Montespan again. She wanted him to take *her* as his own.

She was a fool, she knew, but how she wanted him to see her as a woman again.

Chapter 6

Miriame shivered as Jean-Paul Metin slid into the pew next to her. How she had wished and prayed that he would be there. Until she felt his presence next to her, she had not dared to hope that he would come.

"You didn't fail me after all, Mademoiselle Miriame." His soft voice sent shivers up her spine. "I did not know whether you would be here or not. God must have seen fit to answer my pleas and brought you here to be with me."

Miriame smoothed down the red velvet of her dress—the very one that she had worn to their first accidental meeting—and tried to keep the exultation out of her voice. "Do not read too much into it. I felt the need to say my prayers again, that is all."

He took her hand in his and held it to his chest. "You are lying."

His hands were as rough and tender as she had imagined them to be. "Yes, I am."

"Why did you come here? Tell me the truth."

She would not answer that just yet, though she knew he knew the answer already. Why would she have come here if not to see him again? "Why did you?"

"To see you again."

She smiled. "Why did you want to see me again?"

"You are very beautiful."

She felt a shiver travel from the nape of her neck all the way down her spine. She liked being called beautiful by him. "That is the only reason?"

"I wanted to talk with you as well . . . because you mystify me, because you keep secrets from me that I want to discover."

"Ah." She drew her skirts around herself, as if to hide away. "That is a warning to me never to tell you my secrets or I will instantly cease to be fascinating."

He shook his head. "I wanted to be near you, too."

"You do?"

"You make my heart beat faster when I am with you. I can think of nothing else but you."

"I did not know I have such power over you."

He took her hand and placed it on his heart. Through the thin linen of his shirt she could feel the beating of his heart. He closed his jacket over her hand, imprisoning it inside. "Do you feel my heart beating?"

She could feel the warmth of his skin under the palm of her hand. "Yes."

"It beats just for you."

She tried to draw her hand away, but he kept it there with his, trapped in his shirt. "What nonsense. Give me back my hand."

"What if I do not want to? What will you do then?"

"Do you not remember what I said to you when last we met? I do not like to be coerced. I do not like to be trapped. Now give me back my hand."

He let it go. She did not take it away, but caressed him softly through the linen of his shirt.

He groaned a little at her touch. "You do not want your hand back after all?"

She smiled at him. "I do not mind if it stays there a

little longer, as long as I can take it away again when I have a mind to."

"You are a contrary woman. I am almost afraid to tell you that you can leave it there for as long as you like, in case that puts it into your head to take it away."

"Indeed." She gave him one last caress and put her hand back in her lap. "I see you are a man of your word. I am glad of it. I would hate to have to get out my knife again to convince you that I am in earnest."

He touched one of her cheeks lightly with the tip of his finger. "You are a woman. I am not afraid of your knife."

She closed her eyes, concentrating on the sensation of his fingers brushing over her face. She had never known that such a simple touch could make her yearn for more. "More fool you."

"You would never hurt a fly."

His confidence in her was touching—but ill-founded. "You would not sound so sure of yourself if you knew that I have killed a man with that knife."

"You? No, I do not believe it."

"Do I surprise you?"

"I am surprised you would claim to have done such a thing. Murder is not a laughing matter—especially not for a woman."

"I assure you, it is no idle boast." She opened her eyes again. "Do I shock you?"

"It shocks me that you would speak of such a thing. To kill a man with a knife? I cannot believe it of any woman, least of all you. You are so beautiful."

"Men can be such fools not to think a woman capable of murder." She could not help but smile at the startled look on his face. "Would it sit better with you if I had used poison? Would killing a man in his sleep be more suited to my sex or to my beauty?"

He was starting to believe her. She could tell by the look of dawning suspicion in his eyes as he gazed at her. "Why did you kill him?"

Miriame still did not like to think of the body, lying on the floor, dead. Her stomach turned over and she fought to control her rising nausea. "He had been sent to kill me. I merely got in first."

"Why had he been trying to kill you?"

"It's a long story. Besides, he was an evil man. He deserved to die."

"He deserved to die a thousand deaths for trying to harm you. What could be worse than trying to hurt you, my beautiful Miriame?"

She was struck with a sudden flash of inspiration. If she told Jean-Paul the truth now, she could deflect his suspicion away from her so she didn't have to fight him every time they met as fellow musketeers. Revealing a small part of the truth might well be enough. Perhaps he would never realize that she had not told him the whole story. "Well, for a start," she said, hesitating slightly, "he tried to kill you once, too."

Metin looked at the young woman in front of him with new eyes. What did she know about him? "What do you mean, he tried to kill me, too?"

"You asked me once before why I had turned so white when you saw me on the church steps," she almost gabbled in her hurry to get her story out. "I thought you were a ghost come to haunt me and I ran inside to get away. I was hoping that God and his angels would protect me if I was within the walls of the church."

So she had known more about the attack on him than she had confessed before. It was all very strange. "Go on."

"The man I am talking about, I saw him—he knifed you and left you for dead on the streets." Miriame leaned forward and touched him on the chest, drawing a line with her finger almost exactly where his scar was. "Right here, if I remember well."

He shuddered from her touch, though it was a touch of pity and not of affection. "How do you know this?"

"I was watching from the shadows. There were five or six of them. They pulled you off your horse and one of them knifed you. I saw his face and recognized him from before."

"So you killed him? Because he attacked a stranger?"

"Not then." She shook her head. "There were six of them and only one of me. If I had gone to your aid then, they would've killed me, too. They left you in the street, no doubt expecting that you would bleed to death."

"And the man who stabbed me? Who was he?"

"I do not know his name. I had the bad luck to come across him a few days ago. He did a great evil once, an evil that I could never forget or forgive. I saw a chance to repay him, and I took it. I slit his throat with my knife and watched his life's blood bubble away onto the floor." She shuddered and bent her head, looking young and lost, so unlike the self-possessed beauty he had seen when he strode into the church. "I am not sorry that he is dead. I will never be sorry for that, but I had never killed a man before. There was so much blood. It makes me ill to think on it."

He put his arm around her shoulder, hugging her to his body. She looked like she needed the warmth of his presence.

Miriame swallowed convulsively. "I have not told another soul what I have done. It was horrible. There was so much blood."

They sat there in silence for a moment until her

shudders stopped and she raised her head again. The silvery marks of tears remained on her cheeks, but her face was pale and composed.

He stood up and offered her his arm. Poor woman, to have been driven to murder. He could not guess at the depths of her despair for her to have even considered such a desperate act, let alone to have carried it out. "Come walk with me in the park. The sunshine will chase away your gloomy horrors."

He was not revolted by what she had done. Quite the contrary. She had summoned up the courage to defend herself against the villain. How proud he was that she had been the victor. She was truly brave.

They descended the church steps slowly and strolled to the park that ran along the river. The fresh air put some color back into her cheeks and she walked with a spring in her step.

Metin was silent, thinking over what she had told him. She had killed the man a few days ago. He had been speaking with his young namesake only yesternight. His conclusion was inescapable. The boy could not have been the one who had tried to kill *him*.

He stopped walking and turned to face her. "I do not wish to upset you further, but can you tell me what he looked like? This man who tried to kill me?"

She squared her shoulders and swallowed hard before answering. "Not in the first flush of youth, mayhap in his thirties. A bit taller than me, and thin as a rake. Straight brown hair, light brown, that hung over his eyes. A face like a weasel, and a personality to match. He spoke like a gentleman born and bred, but he was no such thing. The meanest beggar on the street was more of a gentleman than ever he could be."

Definitely not a description of the lad who had stolen his name. *He* was not a one to inspire such hatred as he could hear in her voice. "And the others? You said there were five or six. What did they look like?"

"I did not see any of them as clearly as I saw that man, but I did not recognize any of them. Why do you ask?"

"Was one of their party a young man, scarcely more than a boy, a slight fellow with a delicate face and long black curls to his shoulders?"

She creased her forehead in thought. "No, I am sure none of them would fit such a description. They were all older than that for a start, and none of them had a face I would describe as delicate. They looked battered and beaten, like the gutter rats they were."

Jean-Paul took her by the hands and looked deep into her eyes. He hated to make her relive the moment, but he was glad that she had done so for his sake. "Thank you, Miriame. You have relieved my mind of a horrible suspicion I have been harboring. You have set my mind at rest and I am grateful to you."

Again, he silently admired her eyes, a most unusual shade of brown, the color of rich earth. With a sudden start, he realized that he had seen those eyes before. An exact copy, if he was not mistaken. "Do you have a brother?" he asked, trying to keep his voice as casual as he could.

She shook her head emphatically. "No."

Her answer came too quickly for his liking—barely before he had finished the question. "Odd," he said, touching his finger to her cheek. "I would have sworn I know a man who has just your eyes."

"I shall be sure to ask for them back, if ever I come across him." Her words were said jestingly, but he sensed that she was troubled by his remarks. She turned her head away and refused to look at him.

She claimed she had killed the man who knifed him because he deserved to die—though she wouldn't say why.

The lad with her eyes claimed he had killed the man who had hurt his sister.

He would stake his life on it that there was only one body.

So which of them was the killer? Miriame Dardagny—or her brother, the young musketeer with the knife who had stolen his name?

He did not need to ask which of them was the thief.

Jean-Paul—the real Jean-Paul—paced up and down the richly furnished chamber, cursing under his breath. Francine had called him and he had answered her summons—eventually. Was she punishing him for not jumping at her bidding by making him wait for her now? It would be just like her to be so petty.

He coughed. The damned incense she burned everywhere made him feel lightheaded and irritated his throat.

Just as he was about to stamp out again, her summons be damned, Francine appeared at the door, looking like an angel in a pretty gown of pale green. "Ah, Jean-Paul," she cried, holding out her hands to him with every evidence of delight. "How delightful it is to see you again."

He bowed stiffly. "So you have remembered my name this evening, Madame. I am honored."

"Come now, Jean-Paul, do not be angry. You know how things are at court. I cannot take the same notice of you that I could do in the country. The King would be angered and I would lose his favor again." She fanned herself rapidly with the peacock feather fan in her hand. "That would never do."

How could he ever have imagined that she loved him, this painted porcelain doll who simpered at him so sweetly and so falsely. "The King's favor means more to you than mine does?"

"Of course it does, you silly boy. How could it be otherwise? Louis the Fourteenth is my sovereign—and yours. Without his favor I am nothing at court. As the King's mistress I am courted by all. Would you have me give that up?"

"Then my love meant nothing to you."

She pouted prettily. "You are sweet, but your love could not give me silk gowns and Brussels lace or an apartment in the royal palace."

How could he ever have found her fascinating? Though of noble birth, Madame de Montespan was no more than a self-centered, mercenary whore, selling her body to the King for sparkling baubles and the illusion of power. "So the King did not compel you to return as you claimed?"

She laughed, the sound of water tinkling merrily over the rocks in a stream. "He compelled me to go away when I displeased him. As soon as he allowed me to return, I came back with wings on my heels. He had no need to compel me."

"You lied to me."

"You were so in love with me I had not the heart to tell you the truth." She sighed and a tear trembled on her lower lashes. "It would have hurt you more than I could bear. I was fond of you. I could not bear to see you suffer."

"Indeed. You publicly humiliated me instead."

"I did not want to lose the King's favor again. He might have exiled me forever." She lifted an imploring face towards him. "You must see how it is—"

"Yes. I see." He turned his back on her. "Fare thee well, Madame. I hope the King's attention is worth selling your soul for."

"Wait. Before you go . . ."

He stopped with his back toward her still. "What do you want?" This, he knew, would be the real reason she had called him back. She wanted something from him. Why else would she bother to speak to him?

"The letters I wrote to you . . ." Her voice trailed off into nothing.

He turned to face her again. "What about them?"

"Could you please give them back to me?" she wheedled. "It was foolish of me to write them to you. I would not have the King find out about them. He would be furious. You wouldn't want the King to be angry with me—or you."

She wanted her letters back. That was the reason for this whole charade. "I'm sorry, Madame. I no longer have them."

"Where are they?" Her voice had lost some of its softness. "Did you destroy them?"

"Nothing so dramatic. I was robbed one night in the street and the letters, along with everything else I had, were stolen from me."

Her face turned pale all of a sudden. "Who took them?"

He shrugged. "I have no way of knowing. I was more concerned at the time with the wound in my chest. They stabbed me before they robbed me."

"You must not lie!" She snapped her fan shut with a vicious flick of her wrist and fixed him with an evil glare. "Swear you didn't sell them to the cardinal's men!"

"Sell my letters? What kind of a man do you think I am?"

She shrugged. "I need those letters. If the cardinal gets them before I do, he will give them to the King and I shall be ruined. They will pack me off to a nunnery. I would rather die."

Scheming little fraud though she was, he didn't want

to see her ruined. Her unhappiness would solve nothing. "It is possible that I will find the culprit. If I know who robbed me," he said slowly. "And if he still has the letters, I will find them and bring them back to you."

A light of hope sparkled in her eyes. "Do you swear it?"

"On my honor."

She took his hands and stood on tiptoe to kiss him on the cheek. "You are a good man, Jean-Paul, and better to me than I deserve. I thank you. I will not forget what I owe you if you can do me this favor."

He stood stiffly, trying to remain unmoved at feeling her hair brush his cheek and her breasts press up against his chest. "I have no wish for a reward, Madame. I offered to help you only because it was the honorable thing to do."

"You have earned one anyway by giving me hope." She looped a gold chain from around her neck and pressed it into his hands. "Give this to the woman who will love you as you deserve. Mayhap she will love you all the better for such a gift." She smiled at him and held out her hand. "Friends again?"

He took her white fingers and pressed them against his lips. He would never trust her, but he would no longer hold a grudge, either. He understood her now as he never had before. She was only a woman but determined to make her way in the world despite formidable obstacles, as he was determined to make his way. They had chosen different paths, that was all. "Friends again," he agreed.

He left her chamber in a thoughtful mood. She had sacrificed her fondness for him to the caprices of the King. At least she had been fond of him once. That took away something of the sting of her betrayal.

She had taken nothing but what he had thrown lavishly at her feet, begging her to accept. Jean-Paul would never forget that lesson—she had taught him well—but he could at last forgive her for teaching him.

The young man who had stolen his name was waiting at the western door. Miriame's brother, if he guessed aright, with all Miriame's courage and daring, but none of her beauty and sweetness.

Jean-Paul glared at him, shut the door behind him with a bang and stood with his back to it, feet apart. "What are you doing here?"

He shrugged. "The marquise asked to see me and I am here at her command. What is it to you, anyway?"

Jean-Paul did not know who he wanted to protect from whom. The lad was a thief and a scoundrel. Francine should be warned against him. Then again, he was very young and must be even more green and inexperienced than Jean-Paul had once been himself. What hope did he have if the diabolically charming Madame de Montespan were to work her wiles against him? His conscience smote him at the thought of leaving this one to walk unwarned into such a snare. "What would Francine want with you?"

The other Jean-Paul gave a cheeky grin. "That is for me to know and you to guess."

"Francine is not the woman for you."

"I am sure you are right."

"She is using you to further her own ends."

"I have no doubt of it."

"She wants the King and no one else."

The boy's grin widened. "Ah, that is where our opinions differ. I would have said she wants the King in her public bed so she can queen it over the rest of the court. But in her private bed she wants someone who can give her what the King does not. She wants a real man."

"She wants you? You think she wants you?"

"Only for the moment, but that is fine with me."

Jean-Paul clenched his fists together in an effort to keep his temper in check. "You told me you were not her lover. You swore as much."

"I'm not." The young man shrugged one slim shoulder. "Not yet. She likes the chase as much as the capture."

"So you intend to be her lover. You are a nothing, a nobody."

"I shall be her lover only if she catches me. She'll appreciate me more if she has to work hard to get me. No one appreciates the ripe fruit that falls into their lap at the first shake of the tree. I would have thought you'd found that out already."

The taunting made Jean-Paul see red, as it always did. "You're a scoundrel. I will warn her against you."

"I wouldn't bother if I were you. She'd probably be quite excited about it and even more determined to catch me. Besides, she'll think you are jealous of me for replacing you in her affections, fickle as they are, and will mock you behind your back for your fondness."

Jean-Paul fought his rising temper. How did a mere boy manage to bait him so successfully every time? He could hardly see him now without wanting to tear him apart from limb to limb. "I should kill you, you know."

"I thought we had already tried that before. It ended with my knife at your side."

"No, it began with your knife at my side and ended with *my* knife at *your* side. Then you puked your guts out like a girl."

"Details, details. Now please be so kind as to move your carcass out of the way so I can dally with the marquise."

"Do you really want to waste your time with such a woman?"

The young man put his head on one side and thought for a moment. "Not particularly. But she pays well."

How had he taken so long to see the resemblance between his mysterious Miriame and her brother, the false Metin? Their eyes were exactly the same color. Their skin had the same golden tint, their curly hair was the same jet black, though Miriame wore it around her ears in glorious disarray and her brother kept it tied with a piece of leather at the nape of his neck. They were even about the same height. "I met your sister today."

That made his ears prick up. "My sister? I wasn't aware I had one."

"Miriame. Miriame Dardagny. About your height, dark hair, eyes the same color as yours. A very beautiful woman, despite her marked resemblance to you." The more he saw this other Jean-Paul, the more resemblance he saw to Miriame. It was not just the way they looked, but the way they walked, the way they spoke, the way they had of raising one eyebrow in disbelief. Heaven knows, they were alike enough to have sprung from the same seed as twins.

"She sounds like just the sort of woman I'd like to meet. Please, introduce us some time. But not right now, if you please. The marquise is waiting for me."

"Miriame saw the men who knifed me some five or six weeks back."

"How nice for her. Did she enjoy the entertainment?"

"She told me she killed the man who knifed me."

"Ah. She has a vicious streak, this supposed sister of mine."

"It would seem so."

"I'm not surprised. Most women do." The young man looked pointedly at the door. "You must excuse me. The Marquise is waiting. Please let me pass."

Jean-Paul had to warn him, if only for Miriame's sake.

He was her brother and no doubt she loved the rascal well enough; she had certainly tried to cover up the evidence of his thievery. And he was a likeable rogue for all that. "You do not know what you are getting yourself into. Francine will eat you before breakfast."

"I think not. I am tougher and more indigestible than you might expect. Now move."

Jean-Paul could see no other way out unless he was to fight the other man. For his pretty sister's sake, he was loath to do so. Besides, thief though he was, there was something about the young man that Jean-Paul couldn't quite put his finger on. Something that made him want rather to befriend him than tear him to pieces. He would leave Francine to do the tearing for him. She was better at it than ever he could be. Without another word he moved to one side.

The young man turned back when he was partway through the door, a malicious smile on his face as if he were delighting in Jean-Paul's confusion. "Make no mistake, Monsieur. Do not underestimate my sister. Miriame is even tougher than I," and he was gone.

Miriame leaned against the door, breathing hard. She had been careless, and Metin was not a fool. He had seen the resemblance between her in breeches and her in a skirt and had decided they were related. Brother and sister. His guess was closer to the truth than she liked, but if she could keep him in such a mind, then all would be well. Obviously he would just have to never see them together.

In the meantime, she had the marquise to deal with.

"Ah, Jean-Paul, my friend, you have arrived at last." Madame de Montespan welcomed her with open arms. Bother. She had almost been hoping that her tardiness would have put the marquise's perfect nose out of joint. "I am glad to see you. Was your mission successful?"

Miriame sidestepped the embrace as gracefully as she could. "My mission?"

"Ah, I see I must not talk about it. You soldiers, with your secrets. I am sure we women would not know where to turn to without you to guard our borders. We would be overrun with bloodthirsty Spaniards in no time at all."

Miriame raised an eyebrow and smiled a secret smile. "Perhaps."

The marquise sank gracefully down on the sofa and gathered her billowing, lustrous skirts close to her. "I am glad to see you are back in Paris again, safe and sound after your adventures."

"I am glad to be back, too, and in such fine company as yours."

The marquise fluttered her fan in front of her face. "How can you bear to be a soldier? Are you not terribly frightened in battles when you have to face your fearsome enemies?"

"It is a soldier's duty to be brave."

"But to be so brave as to fight another man unto the death?" She shuddered delicately, and patted the seat beside her invitingly. "Come sit down beside me on the sofa and tell me—have you ever killed a man?"

Miriame perched herself on the edge of the sofa, as far away from the predatory Francine as she could get. "None who did not deserve to die."

"You are so brave to face the enemy for the sake of your womenfolk." She sighed in admiration. "Have you never been wounded?"

"Never badly."

"Mon Dieu!" the marquise cried. "Tell me where that I may shower it with the kisses and healing prayers of a friend."

Miriame obligingly pushed up one sleeve and showed the marquise the scar she had received when she had fallen over on the cobbles as a child and cut her arm through to the bone.

The marquise's fan fluttered even faster. "Oh, you poor thing." She took Miriame's arm in her hand and touched the scar with featherlight kisses from the top to the bottom. "Was it a Spaniard who did this to you?" she asked, looking up at Miriame through her eyelashes. "He must have been very fearsome to get so close to you and wound you so."

"A huge Spaniard with eyes the color of coals and a beard as black as night," Miriame agreed, reclaiming her arm and pushing her sleeve down again. "But I had my revenge. I chopped him up into little pieces and flung them to the crows. He did not live to boast of his deeds."

The marquise gave another thrilled shudder. "Tell me some more stories about the battles you have fought. Tell me about how bravely you struggled against the enemies of France and won in the end. Oh, do tell me everything. I am quite dying of longing to hear your stories."

Miriame obliged, telling one bloodcurdling tale after another of heroic bravery. She would rather tell stories than have any more scars kissed, that was for certain.

At one point, during a particularly bloodthirsty part, she felt Francine's hand creep into hers, as if she were frightened. Miriame was not fooled—it would take more to frighten the redoubtable Madame de Montespan than a tale of terror. The time had come for a strategic rearguard action.

"Then he thrust his sword at me, like so." She leaped off the sofa again and matched her actions to her words, mimicking the thrust and parry of swordplay as she continued with her story. It took more energy to amuse the marquise this way—but she felt much safer than she had while sitting on the sofa by her side. She was far less in danger of being pawed to death.

Francine clapped her hands in delight as Miriame capered and pranced in front of her. "Oh, Jean-Paul, how very brave of you! I swear you must be the bravest musketeer in the whole company."

Miriame's powers of invention finally ran out, as did her breath. After a succession of imaginary battles, she sank back to the sofa again and gulped the glass of wine that Francine had poured for her. "Thank you, Madame," she said hoarsely. "Fighting is thirsty work."

"You made the battles come alive for me." Francine's eyes were wide with wonder. "It was as though I had regiments of troops storming through my chamber as you spoke. I was quite frightened at the tales you told."

If Francine had been truly frightened, then Miriame would eat her hat—cock feather and all.

"Shall I read you a story, now?" Francine offered. "I could read you the romance that you picked up the very first time you came to see me in my chamber. You were quite engrossed in it when I arrived, as I remember. I was almost jealous of the book, the way it held your attention so closely. Maybe if we share it together . . ."

"I would be honored, Marquise, if you would read to me." Anything to keep the marquise's mouth engaged— Miriame hoped to avoid an attempt at a kiss.

The marquise picked up the book from the low table and began to read aloud.

Miriame was soon lost in the rhythm of the words, imagining herself traveling with the hero on his ship, looking out to sea, rolling with the motion of the waves, as he returned to his beloved France and the woman he loved above all others.

The marquise's voice grew softer, and then faded away. She let the book fall on to her lap with a sigh. "I wonder what his love must have been feeling, looking forward to seeing him again after all that time."

Miriame was recalled back to reality with a thump. "She had most likely lost interest in him long ago."

"Do you truly think so?"

"Of course. What woman would pine away for her lover over the seas when she had twenty more ready to take his place in her bed? Not all at once, of course." She was in the mood to be surly—she had liked the marquise's reading far more than she liked her flirtatious conversation.

"It seems that you think women are fickle and inconstant lovers, who are never true to the ones they love?"

Miriame looked into the marquise's wounded blue eyes. Really, the woman should be on the stage. She had missed her true calling as an actress. "Yes, I do believe they are."

Madame de Montespan sighed and dropped her eyes. "You do not have a very high opinion of my sex, I fear."

"But they are no worse than men."

"I am glad you do not single out women for your displeasure. But I am sure you would be like the hero of this romance—true and steadfast to the woman he loved, come what may, however many years had passed before he could be with her."

"You flatter me, Madame. I cannot claim that I would be any better than the common run of men—true when it suited me to be so, false when truth or fidelity no longer served my purpose."

The marquise sighed again and shook her head. "You are too young to be so cynical. I dare swear that you have never been in love or you would never talk this way." She raised her head and fluttered her eyelashes at Miriame. "Come, tell me truly, Jean-Paul. Have you ever known what it is to be in love?"

"I am not sure even what love is, let alone know if I have ever been in love before."

"You would know it if you had ever felt that way." She gave him a longing glance. "Love hits you all of a sudden, like a thunderbolt falling from a blue sky. You are powerless against its force. You can do nothing but submit to the feelings that overpower you.

"The one you love becomes the object of all your thoughts. You cannot eat or drink without thinking of him. You cannot breathe without thinking that he might be breathing the same air as you. You count each moment until you see him again, until your beloved is in your presence.

"Then, when he is there, shame and shyness hold your tongue hostage. A thousand times the words to describe how you feel for him are on the tip of your tongue, longing to escape, but always they elude you. You can say nothing, do nothing, but drink in the magic of his presence and hope he, too, feels the same intoxication that has robbed you of your senses."

Miriame moved uneasily on the sofa. The marquise was remarkably eloquent. "Thank heavens I have been spared such misery as you describe. I shall take care to continue to avoid it in the future. Loving someone cannot be worth the bother and the pain it causes."

The marquise took Miriame's hand in hers and patted it softly. "Stay in the same mind for as long as you can, my dear Jean-Paul." She wiped a solitary tear from her eye. "Indeed, there is nothing can match the pain of loving someone who does not, who cannot, return the feeling."

"My dear Madame de Montespan, I shall heed your advice." She rose from the sofa and bowed to take her leave. "Duty calls me and I must unwillingly bid you *au revoir* for now."

"You will come to see me again?" the marquise asked,

her eyes bright, the tears vanished now. She unpinned a
gold brooch in the shape of a horseshoe from her dress
and pressed it into Miriame's hand. "Take this, to remember me by. It will bring you luck, as it has brought me."

Miriame closed her fingers over the present. The diamonds set into the brooch cut into her palm. "Thank
you, marquise. You are too generous to a poor soldier."

"Think nothing of it, my dear man." She gave a soft,
sweet smile. "Keep it, for my sake."

Jean-Paul clasped Miriame's hand in his as they
walked along the banks of the river. For several weeks
they had been meeting in secret whenever they could.
He would have given all his time to her, but she was wary
and shy, and would not meet him as often as he urged
her to.

He could not invite her back to his chamber, and she
had never invited him to call on her at her home. No
doubt she was afraid of his meeting her brother there.
He did not press the point.

So they met in the church where he had first seen her
and spent their stolen hours walking along the river
bank. The murmur of the water and the song of the
birds gave them at least an illusion of privacy.

Ducks quacked to each other as they waddled along the
path looking for food in the thin grass of winter. They
came curiously up to his toes, but he had nothing to feed
them with. After a while, they waddled away again into the
icy water, looking disconsolate. He watched them idly, the
winter sun glinting off their blue and green plumage. How
blessed he was to be in Miriame's company. Each precious
hour with her gave him more and more pleasure.

He picked a sprig of an early flowering shrub, tempted
out unseasonably early by the warmth of the late winter

sun, and tucked it into her hair. The dark pink of the blossom stood out richly against her dark hair. How could he ever have preferred the sickly pink-and-white complexion of the false marquise to Miriame's honeyed gold? But everything had changed. Now it was only the dark hair and golden brown skin of his beautiful Miriame that he desired. "You should warn your brother to stay away from the marquise. Madame de Montespan is a female to be reckoned with."

He felt her grip on his hand tighten for a moment, but she did not deny that she had a brother. The young scapegrace must have told her that he had already given that secret away. "Why is that?"

"He will be sorry if he does not. She will play him false, as she once played me."

She smiled a little at his words. "My brother's marquise used to be your paramour?"

"Yes," he said shortly. "When I was younger and more foolish than I am now."

"She cast you off, did she?" By the mischievous look in her eyes, the wench was enjoying teasing him.

"Yes, she did. Once I had served my purpose she tossed me aside and went straight back to the King."

"You are jealous of his successor, then?" Her voice was tart.

He shook his head, marveling that he was not jealous in the slightest. Madame de Montespan had brought him to Paris, and then freed him to find a woman who was more worthy of his love. Despite all her petty cruelty, she had done him good in the end. "I am not jealous of any man, least of all your brother. I felt it my duty to warn him for your sake."

"For my sake?"

"Rascal though he, he is your brother. I would not see him used and cast out as I was."

She smiled indulgently at him. "Why don't you warn him yourself?"

"I tried to once, but he laughed off my concerns. He does not know her as I know her."

She shook her head. "My brother's *amours* are his own affair. I doubt he would listen to me any more than he did to you."

He held her hand up to his heart and held her gaze with his own. "You are his sister. He would have to at least give you a hearing."

"You are his comrade. Will he not give you a similar courtesy?"

Metin thought of all the times in the last few days that he had tried to collar the slippery young fellow. The other Jean-Paul had been avoiding him on purpose, slipping away out of sight as soon as he came near. "No, he will not."

She did not seem to realize the seriousness of the situation. "You have tried to warn him. Will that not do to salve your conscience?"

No, it would not do. Jean-Paul had tried to befriend the lad for his sister's sake, but he had responded mockingly to all overtures of friendship. Jean-Paul did not trust him, but neither did he want to see another heart broken as his own had once been. He looked deep into Miriame's remarkable eyes. How could a sweet, pure soul like hers understand the dangers that a woman like Francine held for the innocent? "A broken heart is not so easily mended."

"I would not fear for my brother on that score. He has no heart. Certainly none for the marquise."

"You sound very sure of that."

"I am quite certain." She gave a low laugh. "My brother will never give her his heart. He may be young, but he is not so foolish as that. He does not even like her and will never fall in love with her. You may be quite sure that he is using her for his own ends."

He pressed her hand to his chest so she could feel the beating of his heart. He had no wish to spoil any more of their afternoon by talking of such things. "And you, sweet Miriame, are you as cold-hearted and unloving as your brother? Do you have a heart to give away?"

She looked at him then, her eyes soft and warm. "Once I might have said yes to your question, but now— I am not sure that I do."

Was she beginning to feel for him the same way that he felt for her? He hardly dared to breathe the hope even to himself.

He had seen her so few times, but already he felt as though he knew her well. She was beautiful and brave, and loyal, too, even though her loyalty was wasted on her scapegrace brother. Her honesty could not be questioned, and her purity was in no doubt.

Ah, how he would like to help her to discard some of that purity that she wore around herself like a protective cloak. She was as skittish at his touch as an unbroken filly, first seeming to demand his attention, but moving away in alarm when he was too hasty. One moment she would look at him with lips that begged to be kissed, and the next moment she would turn her head away, as if to refuse him before he even asked.

She shivered a little beside him as they walked.

He reached out and touched his finger to her cheeks. "Are you cold?"

"A little," Miriame admitted.

He put his arm around her shoulders and pulled her closer to him. Her body tensed up against his and then relaxed a little into his warmth as they walked along. He savored the small victory. Her capitulation would be all the sweeter for the time she had made him wait.

She was no lightskirt to be toyed with for a day or two and then cast aside. Such a woman demanded more respect than that. He would make her his mistress, set her up in her own apartments, pay her to keep herself for him alone. Once he had won her favors, he would never share them. He was not a wealthy man, but he would treat her well. She would have no cause to complain of him.

Neither would he have cause to complain of her, he was quite certain. Indeed, if he could win Miriame for his own, he would count himself the luckiest of men.

"What do you mean the brooch is a fake?" Miriame demanded sharply of the old man hunched over his shop counter in front of her. "It is real, I would swear to it, as I am a soldier." She thumped her fist down on the counter and glared at him. "Do not try to cozen me, you old fraud, or it shall be the worse for you."

The old man looked up at her with shrewd eyes set into his sunken face. "Storm all you want, Monsieur Musketeer, and it won't change a thing. The brooch is finely made, I warrant you, and might fool one who knows little of these matters, but it cannot fool me. I will give you five francs for it for the sake of the workmanship. It is not worth a sou more. Take it to whoever else you may, they will say the same thing."

Miriame gathered the horseshoe brooch into her gloved fist again and stamped out. She would not be tricked by such a blatant lie.

Two hours later she was back again. She tossed the brooch on the counter with a furious glare and held out her gloved hand. "Five francs, you said?" None of the other pawnshops she had been to had offered her more than three.

The old man gave a wheezy chuckle and counted out

five francs into the palm of her hand. "What did I tell you? Nothing but a cunning fake."

Miriame thrust the coins into her pocket and left. Five measly francs for a tedious evening fending off the marquise's advances? Five francs? Had the brooch been real, it would have fetched five hundred or more. Bah! She had been bought with nothing more than a shiny but worthless bauble.

Still, she had to admit Madame de Montespan had tricked her cleverly. The marquise had asked her to keep it for her sake. Miriame could not now go and tax her with the worthlessness of the gift, thus giving away the fact that she had tried to sell it.

How cheaply the marquise bought her favors, with copper burnished to look like gold and a few bits of cheap paste. She wondered if Jean-Paul had been cozened so shamelessly as she had been.

The real Metin had at least been able to join the King's Guard for his efforts. That had cost the marquise little more than the trouble to write a letter. A convenient way of rewarding his service to her with something of immense value to him and nothing at all to her.

She had to admire Madame de Montespan. She had not met anyone for a long while who could get the better of her with such barefaced boldness and shameless ingenuity.

What was more, the woman who had tricked her wore a gown, not breeches. She had been cozened by a seemingly fragile female, who did not hide her sex, but used it to her advantage.

She could see that there was much merit in being a woman in certain circumstances.

There was no longer, however, any merit in pretending to be the marquise's lover. Five francs for an entire evening? She would say goodbye to that entanglement with some relief. The real Metin, too, would no doubt be pleased with the news. She would have to be sure to take all the credit for her so-callled brother's decision, and claim a suitable reward.

Miriame looked up at Jean-Paul through her lashes as they walked once more, together but not touching, along their favorite path on the river bank, and gave him a half smile. It was one of the marquise's favorite tricks, one that she thought might be worth adopting. She hoped she could use it with rather more effect on Jean-Paul than the marquise had had on her.

She wanted Jean-Paul to want her. She wanted to drive him as mad with desire for her as she was for him. She could barely eat or sleep for wanting to see him again when they were parted. She was infatuated with him, she knew, but she could not help it. "My brother has promised me he will give up his evenings with the marquise."

He smiled back down at her, though his green eyes still looked troubled. "Do you believe him?"

"He swore to me that he would." She linked her arm into his and pressed against his side, his very nearness making her heart beat faster. "I do believe him."

He stroked her cheek with tenderness, sending a shudder of desire coursing through her body. "You believe everything your brother swears to?"

God in heaven, how she wanted this man. How she wanted him to take off her gown, smooth his hands over her bare skin, touch his mouth to her breasts, spread open her legs and . . . she felt herself blushing at the sensual nature of her thoughts. Just as well he could not read her desires. "No. I am not that foolish. But sometimes I believe him, when I think he is telling me the truth."

His eyes searched hers, those green eyes of his that

made her think of cats in the night. "He might not be telling the truth."

"I think he will be pleased to be rid of her. For all your fears that she would break his heart, he does not care for her overmuch."

"I am glad to hear it." His smile at last reached his eyes, clearing them of the clouds that had darkened them momentarily.

"So you will not tease him any more about it?" She leaned in toward him until the tips of her breasts just grazed his arm and felt her nipples harden and tighten in response.

"Has he been complaining of me?"

She had to hide her smile in his shoulder. "He swears that you follow him wherever he goes, that he cannot escape you for more than two minutes together."

"I do not trust him." He sat down on the bank and took her hands in his. "Miriame, if I ask you a question, will you tell me the truth?"

"It depends on the question," she said flippantly, while inside her heart was sinking. She had known she could not put this moment off forever. Foolish woman that she was, she had fallen in love with the man she had robbed.

"Your brother . . ." His voice faded away to silence.

"What about him?"

"I do not want to hurt you, Miriame, but your brother—he . . . he is a thief."

She bowed her head. She could hardly deny it.

"Why did he do it, Miriame? Why did you let him do it? I cannot believe you encourage him. He robbed me of my horse and my clothes when I lay near death in a freezing gutter. He took my letters and joined the King's Musketeers in my name." It was a statement, not a question.

She sighed. There was no point in denying her guilt. She could only try to make it easier for herself. "You have no proof of that. You cannot have him hanged for your suspicion."

"You have known of this before now, I gather? You knew all along that your brother was a thief?"

She nodded her head, not wanting to speak. She could not bear to tell him the truth. Not now. She was not ready to lose him.

"Why? Why did you not tell me?"

She let her hair fall over her eyes so he could not see her face. "He did it for my sake."

"For you?"

Tears prickled on the back of her eyelids and she fought to keep them at bay. "I was starving." She had not admitted so much in a long time.

He looked at her as if her words made no sense. "You didn't tell me that."

"My brother and I are all that is left of my family. Before he stole from you and became a musketeer we never had enough to eat. He earns fistfuls of money now. I have wanted for little since he has turned soldier.

"You cannot know what it is like to be poor on the streets of Paris. I was hungry, so hungry that my stomach hurts even now to think on it. I was dressed in rags. I had no shoes for my feet, but had to walk barefoot in the snow. He was no better than I."

"What of your parents? Where were they?"

"My parents?" She shook her head. "I never knew my father. My mother died of a wasting fever when I was scarcely more than a child, but my brother cared for me—and stole food when he could not earn it to fill our bellies. Without him, I would perished miserably."

"Then your brother has long been a thief—" he broke off.

"Perhaps you thought I was a lady because of my fine gown." She sighed. "It takes more than a fine gown to make a lady out of a gutter rat. We found your body lying in the street—the men who tried to kill you had not even bothered to rob you. You had a purse full of gold. It was as if God had opened the heavens and showered manna down on us."

"You are all alone in the world save for your brother?"

"I am." She lifted her head and looked straight at him. Let him dare despise her now, and she would bid him farewell with a light heart. He would not deserve her love.

Jean-Paul sat in silence, his head in his hands. Finally he raised his head and looked at her. "Believe me, miscreant though he is, I have no wish to see your brother hanged."

The clearness of his eyes told her that he spoke truly. She felt her heart begin to lighten from the worst of her fears. "Then what will you do with him?"

"I will have to ask that rapscallion, I suppose, for your hand, though I would as soon horsewhip him."

Miriame felt her breath stop in her lungs. "You what?"

"You are alone in the world and need someone to look after you. I would be that man if you will have me."

"You cannot be serious." Of all things, she had not been expecting this.

"I am. Perfectly serious."

"But I have just told you that I have nothing. No dowry, no prospects, no relatives even barring the brother who stole all he owns from you. How can you want to marry me?"

He took her hands in his. "Miriame, there is no other woman that I love. Not the marquise—"

She shrugged. "She is lovely, and rich, and has a fine position at court. You would never want for anything if you were to wed such a one. Of course, she has a husband already, but why should such a trifle as that put you off? No doubt she would slip him poison in his morning chocolate if the stakes were worth the risk."

"I would have nothing that was worth having. I would not have truth or love or honor. These are worth more than all the marquise's jewels together."

She smiled to herself. Most things were worth more than the marquise's jewels. She had just had a lesson in that herself. Still, her conscience smote her. She had hardly been truthful with him herself. "Can you be sure what you would get with me?"

He captured her chin in his hands, forcing her head up to meet his gaze. "Tell me truly, Miriame. Tell me without fear, knowing that I will not ever harm you or yours, whatever the answer you give me now. Do you love me?"

How should she answer that question? With the truth, or no? "Yes, I do."

He looked as satisfied as a cat that had got into the cream. "Then with you, I will at least get love. While you loved me I would at least not need fear poison in my chocolate."

She might love him truly, but what was love? Was it the desire for his body that she felt within her every time he was near? Was it the way she craved his presence when he had gone? Such foolish fancies were a shaky foundation on which to enter into marriage. They would not last. She could not risk putting her life in his hands. She had too much to lose. "I do not know what to say."

"Say yes. Just that one word, and you need say nothing more. I will look after you from that moment on. You need worry about nothing."

He had odd notions about what would appeal to a woman. To be looked after and not have to worry about anything? Once, she might have wed him just for good food to eat and fine clothes to wear, but not any longer. She was above that now. She had made her own way in the world. She had no need of a man to look after her. He would try to put her in a cage and suffocate her, forbid her being what she most longed to be—the mistress of her own destiny. "I will think on it."

His face was desolate. "Can you give me no hope?"

She touched her hand to his cheek, refusing to give in to the pity she felt for him. One day, one day soon, she promised herself, she would tell him that she and her so-called brother were one and the same person. Then he could decide whether he still loved her. "Maybe, when you know me better, you will ask me again. Until then, I cannot answer you."

"That is all you can say to me?"

"That is all."

"I swear that, whatever secrets you are hiding from me, I will love you nonetheless."

"If I were you, I would wait until you know them before you make rash promises."

He held her by the shoulders, forcing her to look up at his face. "That was not an idle boast. You are a remarkable woman, Miriame Dardagny, whatever secrets you have. I love you, and I always will."

She thought of the boots she was wearing, boots that she had taken from his body as he lay on his deathbed. Would he be able to forgive her once he knew how deeply she had trespassed against him? "May God keep you of that mind." She rose from the bank and brushed off the wisps of grass that clung to her dress. "Fare thee well."

He stayed her with one hand. "Wait. You have made no promises to me."

Promises? What use were promises? They were merely empty words, but she would not make him one regardless. She had deceived him enough already. "And I will make none."

His hand clasping hers did not let go as he leaped lightly to his feet. "I will not let you forget me so easily."

She looked up at him as he towered over her, blocking out her sun. "Can you stop me?" she asked, one finger gently tracing the lines of the scowl that marred his forehead.

"Yes. I can. With this." He lowered his head to hers and claimed her mouth in a kiss.

Expecting fierceness and rage, she received only warmth and tenderness. Expecting a bruising attempt to dominate her and force her into submission, she received instead a gentle persuasion, a sweetness with only a hint of the passion he held back so carefully.

Her resistance was no match for his soft caresses. They would not harm her. She opened her mouth under his, opening herself to him.

She had never known a kiss could be so beguiling. He tasted her as if she had been a fragile blossom in early spring and he was the bee who came, ever so gently, to steal her nectar.

He made her feel cherished, loved, protected, and filled with wonderment that he would want to take her to his heart. His kiss made her feel warm and wanted. She clung to him as if he were her savior, as if he would protect her from all that threatened her. If only he would go on kissing her like this forever . . .

His kiss deepened then, slowly demanding more of her. The more he asked of her, the more she wanted to give him, and the more she wanted in return. Shivers of delight skittered down her spine as he pressed her body against his. She could feel him, all of him, against her. His body was hard and strong, like a fine marble pillar that stood its ground and would not move for aught.

The passion in his kiss tormented her with its sensual

promise of more to come. He held her in his arms and made her respond to the seeking of his mouth. She could not refuse his asking. She had no will to refuse him anything. He was her lover, the man she wanted to cleave to until death swept her out of his arms.

She moaned and clung to him, kissing with a fierce intensity that she no longer wanted to control. Let him feel how much she loved him and wanted him. Her kisses, at least, did not lie.

He broke their kiss, and she whimpered softly, bereft. "You will not forget me now?"

Miriame shook her head. She could not forget him now, were she to try for a thousand years. His kisses had branded her soul forever.

He took a gold chain from under his doublet and looped it around her neck. "The person who bestowed this upon me told me I should give it away to the woman who would love me as I deserve."

She put her fingers to the gold and touched it reverently, loving it not for its exquisite workmanship or its value, but for the sake of the man who gave it to her with such sweet words. "I have not deserved it yet."

Jean-Paul brought her fingers to his lips and kissed them one by one. "You will, my love. You will."

Chapter 7

Miriame made her way home again in a daze. Jean-Paul Metin, the most handsome of musketeers, had kissed her until she was almost fainting from desire. How could she tell him the truth now? Maybe she could kill off her imaginary brother and wear only gowns from now on. Then Jean-Paul would never have to know the truth about her. He could continue to love her and she would bask in that love forever, until the stars fell from the skies.

He had even asked her to marry him. Of all things, that was the most unexpected. If she were to invent a fatal accident for her brother, she could marry her Jean-Paul and he need never know how she had tricked him.

He had kissed her until she was breathless with wanting him. How could she *not* tell him the truth now? He knew she was a gutter rat, that she had been brought up in poverty and knew nothing else. He knew she had no money, nothing that would tempt a lesser man to marry her, and yet he had offered to wed her. How could she repay his generosity and his faith in her by making him live a lie?

Miriame had to tell him. She had to tell him that she was a thief, that she wore breeches and lived as a man. She had to tell him that she had no brother—that she was her own brother. If he still wanted her after her confessions, only then could she possibly accept his love. If he cast her off when he realized she was not the sweet innocent he thought her to be, well, so be it. She would live. She would challenge him to a duel and whip his sorry hide for his foolishness, maybe, but she would live.

She would have to choose her moment well to tell him the truth. A moment of calm and peace. A moment when she would be able to explain all that he meant to her and how happy his company made her.

First of all though, she had to do as she had promised and break with the marquise. That, at least, would be an unadulterated pleasure.

Jean-Paul watched the figure of the lad as he walked toward the western door to a rendezvous with the marquis. So, the wretch had lied to his sister along with everyone else, had he? He was not surprised—indeed, he had suspected as much. He had waited in the nearby street for confirmation of his suspicions for two long, cold hours. The only thing that surprised him was how such a thieving rakehell could have such a beautiful woman as Miriame for a sister. They had both grown up in the gutter, but Miriame was as untouched and unspoiled as a rosebud in the spring. All the dirt had fallen to her brother's part.

The boy needed someone to take him in hand before he ruined his life. He supposed as Miriame's husband-to-be he would have to volunteer for the thankless task—one almost guaranteed to fail. Still, if he were serious about wedding Miriame, looking after her brother would become his duty, and one that he must not shirk.

He had not meant to ask Miriame to marry him. The words had slipped out before he had fully realized what he was saying, but now that the offer was made, he did not want to retract it, even if he could. Her life had been so hard and full of suffering, but she was so dignified despite her situation that nothing else but marrying her had seemed possible. He would not insult her by asking her to become his mistress. He could not bear to lose her. He would make her his, before the eyes of God and man, and they would cleave together as one.

Then he would deal with her wayward brother. With the memory of Miriame's kisses burning sweetly on his lips, he had no desire to teach the false Metin the lesson he so sorely needed. The pup had to know, though, that his sister had a protector now. He would not let him lie to her again, if he could help it.

Jean-Paul stepped up behind him just as he was about to knock on the door, and placed his hand heavily on his shoulder. "You told your sister you were giving up the marquise, did you not?"

At least he had the grace to blush at being caught in his lie, though in the fading light of early evening Jean-Paul almost missed the telltale color that struck the young man's cheekbones. "I have to tell her so, do I not? I cannot vanish without a word of farewell. Madame de Montespan has some friends left in high places."

A feeble excuse for one last visit, and one Jean-Paul would have made himself not so very long ago. "Metin— ah, one day I shall know your real name—you must be wary. She will ensnare you again so you will not want to leave."

"Ensnare me?" The young man shrugged off his hand and had the ill grace to laugh in his face. "You're a fool if you think so. It would take more than she has to ensnare me. Come, let me pass."

Jean-Paul turned his collar up against the light drizzle that had begun to fall and looked him right in the face.

He would not back down in this challenge he had made, or any hope he had ever had of leading Miriame's brother into a different path would be irretrievably lost. "You would be wise not to make an enemy of me."

Metin stared back at him, one eyebrow raised, quite unimpressed with his threats. "As you would be of me. And, more to the point, you would be wise not to make an enemy of the marquise. She is expecting me and will not be happy with the man who makes me late. Again."

Jean-Paul drew his weapon and pushed the lad back with the tip of his sword so he could not get past. "Have you no shame, lying to your sister and to me?"

"What is my sister to you?" There was an odd look in his eyes, as if he cared passionately about the answer to his question.

"Your sister is a fine woman, and I love her dearly." He gritted his teeth. "How she came to have such a brother as you is beyond me, but for her sake I will not run you through."

A flash of anger sparked through Metin's eyes. "How very tolerant of you. And does my sister love you as well, or is your love yet again unrequited? Perhaps you have only chosen another Francine for yourself." He grinned wickedly as he danced just out of reach of Jean-Paul's lunge. "Do you want another woman to make use of you for as long as it pleases her to do so, and then turn you out into the cold?"

Jean-Paul could feel his face darken with rage at the mention of Francine. That painted whore was not fit to be mentioned in the same breath as his Miriame. "If she does not love me now, she will one day, I swear it. I love her more than I love my own life."

His avowal seemed to amuse Metin. "Then I suppose for her sake I will not run you through, either, much as you deserve it for delaying me."

How could this stripling drive him wild with anger every time? He would not hurt him, but he would teach him not to mock his sister, or the love that Jean-Paul felt for her. With a roar of fury fueled by frustration and love, he charged.

Miriame met his rush with a deliberate calm that she knew would just anger him more. It was wicked, she knew, but she could not refrain from teasing him when he was in such an aggravating mood. He thought she was a rascal and a scapegrace, did he? She would show him one of these days that there was more to her than a pretty, dark-haired girl in a red dress. She *was* a gutter rat—and a fighter and a soldier, too. She had robbed more men than she could remember, and she had even killed a man, who had richly deserved his violent end. She could hold her own against any musketeer who wanted to cross swords with her. She was who she was, and she would make no apologies for herself. If he really wanted her, he was welcome to try and catch her—but he would have to take the bad along with the good. More fool he if he had fallen in love with the pretty side of her and not seen what was hidden below the surface.

After a few furious rushes that she easily deflected, he made a deliberate effort to calm down again.

His eyes now burned bright with determination rather than with rage. She saw in him the look of the fanatic who would not let this battle go, whatever it cost him to carry it through to the end.

She doubted he would hurt her—but he would force her to submit if he could, and acknowledge him as the victor in their battle of wills. She steeled herself to meet his onslaught.

His next pass was not as fierce, but neither did it fall so wildly. Miriame had to dodge out of the way, elusive as the eels she used to catch on a bent hook baited with a piece of rotten meat. She was thankful now for the hours that Renouf had spent training her. She could tell she was about to need every lesson she had ever learned.

Jean-Paul harnessed his anger until he had it contained within himself where it could not get away and overwhelm him. He would never get the better of the lad if he were to unleash his rage. Only coolness and a clear head would allow him to win. "Will you give up the marquise?" he said, as he came at her again.

"Why should I give her up on your say-so?" his opponent taunted him, trying to rile him once more. "You are nothing but one of her discarded lovers, after all."

With a effort, he damped down the anger he felt at the pointed reminder of Madame de Montespan's faithlessness. His anger was not at Miriame's brother but at Francine, for the way she had made a fool out of him, for the way she had made manipulated him so cleverly. She had pulled the strings, and he had danced for her like a marionette

Jean-Paul stepped back to take a breath and collect his wits.

He had loved her, but it was the love of an inexperienced young man who thinks everything is as it seems on the surface and who is flattered into a feeling he would never otherwise have dreamed of. He had fallen in love with the illusion she had created of herself, not with the real Francine. The real Francine was not worth loving—she had no heart to return the love she was given.

Still, his pride was hurt that Francine had turned him out in favor of Miriame's rakehell brother. His amorality was a match for hers, that was true, but why else did she prefer a callow youth to a man like himself? Damn it all, false Metin was scarcely more than a boy—too young even to grow a beard.

Francine had appealed to his vanity when she had first made love to him. Now his vanity was hurt that she chose to make love to another, and to one, moreover, who was his inferior in every way. Including in a fight. He would prove that once and for all, right here and now.

He parried one of Metin's blows successfully and thrust back at him so that the lad had to sidestep clumsily to avoid his blade. "Think you that you will last any longer by her side?" he taunted in his turn. "You have nothing to offer her that she wants. She will soon tire of showering gifts on one who cannot give her anything in return."

"Quite likely," the youth replied, his breath beginning to come faster as he started to tire. "The difference between us is that I shall be pleased to go when the time comes, while you were tossed out of doors like a dog with the mange, begging and whimpering for a reprieve. That must have hurt your pride, did it not, Monsieur Musketeer?"

He would hurt more than Metin's pride if the lad did not cease taunting him. "I will not give you the opportunity to be tossed out. You promised your sister that you would leave Francine. I am here to hold you to that promise."

Metin's laughed in his face. "You will be a busy man indeed, if you think of trying to protect Miriame's honor as you protect Francine's. There is not so much difference between them as you might think."

By God, but that was too much for him to take. He would teach the stripling a lesson that would stay with him for a very long time.

He flicked his sword and scored a long shallow cut down his opponent's arm. First blood to him.

Metin swore at the sight of his blood dripping onto the cobblestones and lunged at him furiously.

He easily parried the blow. "It would be wiser for you not to insult your sister in my presence."

"What do you know of my sister? That she is pretty? She may be ten times the whore that your precious Francine is and you would never know."

Jean-Paul had been patient up to now, but enough was enough. It was time to end this farce. He attacked Metin with thrust after thrust until his back was against the wall. He gave his sword another expert flick, and the lad's weapon clattered uselessly to the cobbles. "Give me one good reason not to kill you," he said, the point of his sword resting on his opponent's throat.

The youth stared at him, quite unafraid. Despite everything, Jean-Paul had to admire his nerve. He must be made of steel to face death so calmly. "Francine would be most put out if I do not visit her this evening," he said lightly.

It was almost as if he was daring Jean-Paul to do his worst. "What care I for her disappointment? She will find herself another man to gull before your body is cold."

"True enough, but then again my sister is fond of me," he said carelessly. "She could never wed my murderer."

Maybe so, but Jean-Paul would not admit it. "Your sister has too much sense to grieve long over a scapegrace such as you."

The youth was not impressed. "Kill me and you'll find out how wrong you are——" He broke off all of a sudden. "Watch out behind you." His voice was a low, urgent whisper, a far cry from the mocking laugh of mere moments before.

"You cannot fool me with that simple trick . . ." he began, but the look in the his opponents's eyes silenced him before he had finished the thought. He had never seen fear before—but he saw it now.

With a muffled curse he whirled around, his sword crossed over his body in a defensive position. He could only hope that the boy would not stab him the instant his back was turned.

Not a moment too soon. Before he had the time to blink, three men were upon him, swords drawn.

He had been fighting for some while and he was growing weary. This fight was different, though. He and the false Metin had been fighting for dominance, for control, for pride. He knew at the first rush by his new attackers that this time he was fighting for his life.

Three of them against one of him, and he was already tired. He didn't like his odds. If he could not win, he would at least sell his life as dearly as he could and take company with him into death.

Out of the corner of his eye he saw Miriame's brother stoop and pick up his sword from the cobbles. His heart sank lower. He doubted the lad would be able to resist joining the battle against him—he had no sense of honor or fair play that would prevent him from finishing off a weakened enemy. And what better way did he have of ensuring that Jean-Paul was kept out of the way? Miriame would never know what part her brother had played in his downfall.

The odds were now worse than ever. Four against one. Their advantage was insurmountable. He could not possibly win through.

He concentrated on the swords in front of him, avoiding injury where he could rather than risking his life in an attack. If he once started to bleed, he would lose his strength quickly and the fight would be over before it had even begun.

The air was thick with sweat and fear. His sweat. His

fear. He wet his lips with his tongue, tasting the salt of effort on his face. His shirt stuck to his back with a clammy wetness. Four against one. Impossible odds. He could not even run.

His back was against the wall now—the same wall he had pinned Miriame's brother to only minutes ago. Minutes? It seemed like a whole lifetime ago.

Jean-Paul prayed that he would carry the news of his murder to her and let her know that he had died bravely. She at least would mourn his passing, weep at the death of the man who loved her better than anyone else had. He could not hope for anything more.

He battled on, more out of desperation than anything else. He would not give up his life just because all seemed lost. Heaven knew that he could not expect to be rescued—miracles did not happen to men like him. He would perish in the filfth of the street, not even knowing who wanted him dead, or why.

Miriame clutched the hilt and hefted the sword in her hand. She knew those men. She had seen them before—when they had tried to end Jean-Paul's life some weeks ago.

She had not come to his aid then until he was nearly dead. She would do better this time. He would not survive such another wound.

His three assailants were pressing him hard but he held his own. She paused for a moment to admire his sword strokes. He was as agile as a cat. They could not get past his defenses, but neither could he take the risk of attacking them, and leaving himself vulnerable from another quarter. They knew that, and were wearing him down bit by bit until they could close in for the kill with the least danger to themselves.

There was little point in joining the fray by his side. Two against three was no guarantee of success. No—she would have to disable one of them immediately. Cowards that they were, two against two should have them turning tail and running.

She and Metin had been fighting just moments before—his attackers would not suspect she would come to his aid. She had surprise on her side.

Carefully she crept around behind them, taking care they did not notice her. She chose the biggest of them. She had no wish to kill again, but there were ways of disabling a man without killing him. Besides, Jean-Paul needed to know who his enemies were and what they wanted from him. Being attacked in the street twice in nearly as many months was more than coincidence. Somebody badly wanted him dead.

She swung a vicious blow at the legs of the tallest attacker. He half turned towards her with a look of surprise on his face and then fell to the cobbles with a groan.

Jean-Paul wiped the sweat out of his eyes. The light had grown so dim he saw little but the blades in front of him, flashing in the moonlight. "Goodbye, Miriame," he whispered into the night. He doubted that he could hold out much longer.

One of his attackers suddenly fell to the cobbles with a cry of pain. He lifted his eyes and saw Miriame's brother, his sword bloodied, attacking them from behind.

His heart leaped with the sudden arrival of hope. His opponent had come to his aid after all, despite their quarrel, and was making his presence felt.

Jean-Paul fought on with redoubled vigor, seeing at last a chance for life.

By God, the lad had repaid all that he had ever stolen

from him with interest. He had saved Jean-Paul's life when he thought all hope was gone.

The man on the ground groaned and writhed in pain, unable to get to his feet. He fought one of them while the false Metin entertained the other, pressing them both back into the middle of the street where they could maneuver more easily. He fought well—striking as quickly as an adder, getting under the other's guard with a sneak attack whenever he could.

Faced with such odds as this, the two remaining men did not keep going for long. After trading a few more blows and finding out that victory was not as assured as they had hoped, they took to their heels and ran, leaving their wounded companion behind.

Jean-Paul Metin leaned over and rested his hands on his knees, panting with effort. "I owe you my life."

Miriame's brother knelt at the side of the wounded man. "Indeed you do. Twice over."

"Don't kill him," Jean-Paul said quickly, fearing a fatal revenge. "I want to question him first."

The lad raised a white face towards him. "Much as he deserves it, I was not going to murder a wounded man in cold blood." His voice was full of disgust at the idea. "I am disarming him—and patching up his leg so he does not faint from lack of blood before he can answer you."

The wounded man spat on the ground by the boy's feet. "The devil take me if I answer a question of yours. You've damn near killed me, the pair of you."

Jean-Paul crouched down by the man's head. "No doubt he will take you in good time." He pulled out his dagger and held it uncomfortably close to the man's neck and watched as his eyes bulged out with fear. "But your time may come a little earlier than you expect if you don't start talking. Quickly."

"You said as you wasn't going to kill me." The wounded man's voice rose to a high-pitched whine and his fingers scrabbled at the ground as if to lift himself up and away from the dagger by the sheer force of his fear.

"My companion here seems to be squeamish at the thought of slitting your throat as you lie here in the mud. Unluckily for you, I am made of sterner stuff and have no such qualms."

The stranger still had a little bravado left, despite his wound. "The cardinal will have you hanged for this. Or strangled in your bed, no one the wiser."

"Ah, now we are getting somewhere." At least he hoped he was. So the cardinal wanted to kill him. For the life of him, he couldn't see why. "The cardinal is behind this?"

The man closed his mouth and shut his eyes in a silent sulk.

He scratched the man's neck with his dagger. The man's eyes flew wide open again. "The cardinal is paying us to get rid of you," he said hastily. "He wants some letters you've got and then he wants you dead."

"What letters?"

"How should I know? I didn't ask, he didn't tell me." The wounded man gabbled in his haste to get the words out. "I swear, I don't know."

"You are a liar." He dug the dagger point in and drew blood.

"We took the wrong ones off of you the last time and he was mad fair to bursting. Said if we didn't get the right ones this time, we'd swing for it, the lot of us."

Now they were getting somewhere. "The last time?"

The realization of what he had just confessed hit the man and his face went gray.

"You tried to kill me before. Why is that?" Jean-Paul pressed the knife to the man's neck once again. "I should kill you but I'm feeling kind. Tell me the whole story, all of it, nice and slow and you might, just might, live to see the sun rise."

The man on the ground collapsed as if all the fight had suddenly gone out of him. "The cardinal sent us to get the letters you carried," he confessed. "He didn't care what happened to you after that so long as you didn't give him any trouble about it. We jumped you on the street, half a dozen of us, just to make sure you didn't get away. He had promised us a right royal sum of money for it all—more than enough for us all to share. We could have stayed stinking drunk for a month of Sundays and have some left over to go a-whoring. But we got the wrong letters and you didn't die when you were supposed to, damn your eyes, and we haven't been paid so much as a sou."

"Lucky for me, not so lucky for you. And did you also rob me of everything I owned, down to the boots off my feet, as I lay in the gutter?"

"Not me. André threatened to send us to the gallows himself if we was found robbing you of aught but the letters. He didn't want us to be caught with anything inscrim—inscrim—"

"Incriminating."

"That's the word. But we got the wrong letters so the cardinal sent us out again to have another go. Only André is dead and Henri has disappeared and Lavar was taken up a moon ago for killing a whore so there were only the three of us left. And your goddamned friend has crippled me and the others, pox on them, have left me here to die." He spat on the ground again. "God rot their souls, the yellow-bellied sons of whores. I hope the cardinal throws them to the dogs for what they've done to me."

"So the cardinal would have killed me for my letters."

The man nodded.

Jean-Paul got to his feet. He had as much information as the man could give him—and as much as he needed to protect himself.

Miriame moved to his side and poked the man on the cobbles with the toe of her boot. She almost regretted not killing the filthy lout. Almost. "Then the cardinal is more of a fool that I gave him credit for. And I give you leave to tell him so, with my regards."

"It's a man with a death wish who'd be a-telling him that," the wounded man muttered. "I'm too fond of my skin to be heard saying words like that."

"Then just tell him he's got the wrong man."

The man stared. "I aren't that daft. Jean-Paul Metin of the King's Musketeers was the one we were to rob. We ain't got the wrong one, for sure."

She gave a mocking bow. "Please, let me introduce myself. I am Jean-Paul Metin of the King's Musketeers and so is this gentleman. And I have the letters you want. Pity for you that I shall go home and burn them so they cause no further trouble to me or my friend here. The cardinal will never get them now, even if he murders us both."

"What did you do that for?" Jean-Paul asked, as they left the man groaning in the street. "They'll be after both of us now."

Miriame's brother shook his head. "Now that we know what they're after, the cardinal will give it up as a lost cause. His only hope of getting the letters was to take them by surprise. Now that you know what he wants, it's an easy matter to destroy them. As I said, I have them."

Jean-Paul had known that Miriame's brother was the thief all along, but it seemed churlish to charge him with it now. "Yes, of course," was all he said.

They walked along in silence for some yards. "Have you

changed your mind about going to see the marquise?" he said at last. "Is there something about risking your life that puts your mind off making love to her?"

The lad shook his head. "My mind was never on that in the first place."

The false Metin was cocky enough still. "If you knew what kind of a woman she was—" Jean-Paul began.

He wasn't allowed to finish. "I do know what kind of a woman she is. I am in no danger from her, I assure you."

"You have lied to me so many times before. How can I believe you now?"

Metin stopped in the middle of the street, his eyes blazing with impatience. "Damn and blast you, but I am sick to death of being accused. In this matter at least I am innocent."

"Prove it to me."

The lad shrugged off his jacket. "Very well. I had thought of telling you at a better time, but I cannot wait." As he spoke, he began to unbutton his shirt, fixing Jean-Paul with a determined eye. "If you so much as breathe a word of this to anyone, I will hunt you down and kill you myself and deliver your corpse to the cardinal's men."

Jean-Paul put his hand over his heart. "I will not betray your confidence. For Miriame's sake."

The lad slid his knife out of his boot. "That will be just as well for you," he said, punctuating each word with a flick of his blade. "Believe you me, you will rue the day you betray my secret to the world." Then he held the dagger up high and ripped through his undergarments with one long cut.

Jean-Paul stood and stared. His mouth gaped open. He could not speak for shock. His head swam as he tried to grasp the reality of what he could see in front of him. There was no doubting it. His eyes could not lie.

It was not a young man who stood in front of him, chest bare to the world, but a woman.

Chapter 8

Miriame had to stifle a laugh at the look on Jean-Paul Metin's face. He looked as stunned as a pike, his eyes wide and staring just like the dead fish lying stiffly on the fishseller's stall.

She had not meant to tell him in the street like this, but she could take no more of his absurd accusations, and she was tired of having to defend herself every time they met. She had no wish to hide beneath her breeches any longer. It was better that he know the full truth at last, whatever he thought of her for her masquerade.

She shook her pert breasts at him to emphasize her point. The air was freezing cold on her exposed skin, making her nipples tighten into hard peaks, and he stared at them as if he could not tear his eyes away. "I am not interested in making love to the marquise," she said clearly, so there could be no more misunderstandings. "I have never been interested in making love to her. She is not exactly my type. Do you believe me now?"

He wiped his hand over his brow and went back to staring at her breasts. "Ah, yes, I suppose I do." His voice came out as hardly more than a croak.

"Good." She pulled the two halves of her shirt together and began to button them. "Now that we've cleared that up, I can put my evidence away again before I get frostbite."

"Who are you?" He raised his eyes to her face again and was looking at her as if seeing her for the first time.

Miriame flung her jacket over her shoulders to stop herself from shivering. Her skin still felt like ice. "Can we talk more in front of a warm fire and a glass of wine? I'm tired, it's dark, and I'm getting cold."

"A tavern?"

She raised her eyebrows at his stupidity. "Do you think I am going to discuss my sex in a place where anyone might hear? Have you not got a bottle of wine in your apartments, and a landlady who can make you a fire? Then we can talk in private without fear of being overheard."

He hesitated. "If you think it fitting for a woman in your situation to visit me there—"

She barked out a short laugh. "I've masqueraded as a man for a long time. Do you think I have never visited a fellow soldier in his apartments before? For God's sake don't turn prudish on me now."

He looked at her strangely. "So you have been pretending all along. From the day you joined the Musketeers, no doubt."

She shrugged. "From childhood, actually."

"You do not have a brother?"

She shook her head.

He still looked disbelieving. "You have never had a brother?"

"No, I never did."

"It has been you all along." He sounded as though he could hardly believe it himself. "Just you all along."

"Just me."

"I will not hurt you if we go to my chambers," he said. "I only thought that you might not feel quite comfortable—"

"I know full well you won't hurt me. I have just saved your life, remember?" She slid her knife out of her boot again, tossed it in a glittering arc in the dark of the night, caught it again and slid it back into her boot in one easy movement. "Besides, my friend here"—she patted her boot—"is the very best assurance of my safety."

He made no reply and strode off down the road, jerking his head at her as an indication for her to follow him. She fell into step beside him, stretching her legs to match his long strides. God, but now that the danger was past and her secret was out, she was bone weary. She hoped he did not live far away.

Jean-Paul did not speak to her and his face was set as if in stone. She sneaked a peek at him as they strode along, but his expression did not change. He still looked stunned, but a new emotion had been added to those already carved on his face. His disbelief had been replaced with fury. He looked as angry as she had ever seen him before.

His apartments were modest enough, though larger than hers. In silence Jean-Paul lit a taper at the embers of the fire and stuck it into the stand on the mantelpiece. Miriame looked around her in the flickering half-light that it shed, curious to see how he lived.

A rough-hewn bed covered with warm, homespun woolen blankets stood up against the wall in one corner, and a straight-backed wooden chair stood in front of the fireplace. Miriame thought of the luxury of the velvets and tapestries of Courtney's apartments with a sigh. She had been spoiled lately, no doubt about it. Jean-Paul's rooms simply could not compare.

The chamber was warmer than the weather outside, but it was still chilly, and she was no longer warm from the effort of fighting, or of matching Jean-Paul's long strides. She hugged her arms around herself to stop herself from shivering.

Jean-Paul still did not look at her. He knelt in front of the embers of the fireplace and coaxed them into life again with a few strong breaths and well-placed sticks of wood. When the sticks were burning merrily, he added larger logs.

Miriame sat forward in her chair and held out her hands to the welcome warmth. The domesticity of the scene was unfamiliar, but comforting—Jean-Paul squatting in front of her at his task, the firelight flickering on his face and the candlelight shining from above on his golden-brown hair. She shivered as she watched his deft fingers pile on the last logs of wood, but this time it was not from the cold.

If only he would turn his head and look at her. If only he would speak to her, telling her that he forgave her, that whatever she had done to him, he did not care.

Her heart was beating so loudly she was afraid that he would hear it. She knew only too well that the time for telling the truth, the whole truth, had finally arrived.

How little she knew of this man, despite all that had happened.

She had once gambled her life on his death. Now she was gambling her livelihood, if not her life again, on his forgiveness—a much more chancy thing. She had told him her secret—something she had sworn never to reveal to any man. If he was mean in spirit, she would not last much longer as a musketeer. A word in the ear of the captain and she would be dismissed and disgraced, if not hanged for horse theft.

The fire was beginning to send out real heat now, making her face flushed and warming the room to the very corners. Jean-Paul got up off his heels and sat on the end of the bed. There was no other chair in the room. He still did not look at her. "Who are you?" His words were abrupt and his tone less than friendly.

She sighed. They were hardly the words of forgiveness she longed to hear, but she supposed they were a start. "Miriame Dardagny, also known as Jean-Paul Metin, musketeer in the King's Guards."

"*I* am Jean-Paul Metin. How did you come to steal my name?"

"No doubt you have guessed already. I saw the men following you as you rode through Paris. I crept after, hoping that something I could sell or pawn would come my way. I'd found no one else to rob that night and I was cold and hungry. They pulled you off your horse, took your letters, stabbed you, and melted away into the darkness."

His lip curled with disgust. "And you came to rob my corpse."

She felt a surge of anger at his disdain. He had never known want, hunger, cold as she had known it. What gave him the right to judge her? "I thought you were dead. Your money and your clothes were no use to you anymore." Her voice was hard. "Better they should keep me from starving or freezing to death on the streets than be buried with you. Besides, if I hadn't taken them, the next person who came across your body would have."

"But I was not dead. You robbed me anyway." He put his head in his hands as if he could no longer bear the weight of it. "I suppose I am lucky that you did not stab me once more to make sure I would not trouble you."

It troubled her that he thought she had no heart. She *did* have feelings, just like every other woman—she just didn't give in to them very often. She could not afford to. "You were still breathing, but only just. I couldn't bear to leave you lying there to die so I bandaged you with a strip from my shirt, dumped your body on the back of your horse, and carted you off to a tavern."

"And then stole everything I owned."

She ignored his ingratitude. He did not realize the depths of fear she had had to conquer in order to rescue him, or that in saving his life she had endangered her own. "Rumor had it that the landlady had a heart buried in her breast somewhere, unlike most of them. I gave her money and asked her to look after you until you died and then see you were fittingly buried. You were dying. I could do no more for you."

He shifted uneasily on the bed at her description, but he did not look up. "How came you to steal my name?"

"I read the letters you carried with you."

He raised his head at that and looked her straight in the eye, surprise written all over his face. "You read them yourself? You can read?"

She was nettled at his tone. "I was not always a beggar and a thief," she said, holding his gaze squarely with her own. "My mother taught me to read when I was small and I can remember much of what she taught me. I could read enough of your letters to know that you had an introduction to the musketeers."

"Then you turned soldier after reading my letters. Why?" He looked suspicious, as if she were not telling him everything.

"I was sick of being cold and hungry, of risking my neck every day to steal enough food to keep myself alive. I was already used to dressing as a boy—it was safer that none on the streets knew my real sex. Finding you was like a gift from heaven. I could not turn down such a chance to make a decent life for myself. I decided to be a soldier."

"But you could not fight."

She shrugged. "Maybe not with a sword, but I have always carried a knife. I should not have lived long on the street if I did not."

For a moment his expression softened into pity. She looked away.

Unbidden memories clawed at her mind. She did not want to remember just how bad it had been. She stared into the fire, concentrating on the flickering red of the flames consuming the wood. "Think of your very worst nightmare, magnify your fear and disgust a thousand times, and you still wouldn't know what living on the streets was like. It was worse than you could imagine." She did not want his pity—just his understanding.

"And the gown? Did you steal that as well?" His face was as hard as granite again. "Were you laughing inside as I poured out my foolish heart to you?"

Did he think she stole for fun or for the sake of her vanity? "I would not bother stealing a gown to wear. It was lent to me by a friend."

He shook his head incredulously. "I cannot believe that, after all the lies you have told me and all the thefts of which you have been guilty."

She had lied and stolen plenty, right enough, but she didn't need him to add more sins to her tally—particularly when she was innocent for once. "You saw me first on the steps of a church, among a wedding party, did you not?"

"Yes, but what has that to do with—"

"My comrade was to be married and wanted the two of us to be with her. I had no gown to wear. Neither, as it happens, did the bride. We both had to borrow one from the third of our party, who had gowns enough to spare." Miriame grinned at the memory of Courtney's closet, full of silks and satins. "She was the only one of us foolish enough to prefer gowns to breeches. Then you saw me at the church and did not recognize me as the musketeer you wanted to fight. You saw me as a woman, and I decided I did not mind wearing a gown quite so much after all. My friend was glad to lend it to me."

"Your friends . . ." He shook his head in wonderment

this time. "Please do not tell me that they are men-women as well. Soldiers? Musketeers?"

She would not confirm his suspicions. "What if they are? Surely you did not think that I am the only woman with enough spirit to carry off such a trick?"

He had no answer to give her. "What will I do with you?" was all he said, as he gazed at her.

Miriame took off her hat and tossed it beside her on the floor. She undid the leather lace that kept her hair tied at the nape of her neck, shook out her curls to loosen them and combed through them with her fingers. Now was her chance to force him to see her as a woman—as a desirable woman—not just as a woman who had deceived him. She would use every trick she knew to stop him from betraying her, to make him want her as she wanted him. "What do you want to do with me?"

He scratched his chin as he looked at her. "I wish I knew."

It was increasingly warm in front of the fire. She slid her jacket off her shoulders and reached into her shirt to pull out the remnants of her breast wrappers.

She looked at the strips of linen ruefully. They were cut through all the way—utterly ruined in her haste to prove herself. Not a single piece was long enough to salvage. She would have to get more.

She tossed them into the fire and watched them hiss and splutter on the flames.

He waved away the acrid smoke that rose from them as they smoldered in the flames. "What are you burning?"

She turned to face him. "My wrappers."

He blinked. "Are you going to give up being a musketeer and return to being a woman once more?"

He did not know what he was asking of her. She shook her head. "I have no way of earning my living as a woman. As a woman I would starve."

"I offered to marry you once."

"You did not know me then. Besides," she looked around at the chamber he occupied, "you cannot afford to keep a wife were you to have one. The two of you would starve together." The thought saddened her, though she knew it was true. She could never marry him and drag him down into the poverty she had only just escaped herself.

He came and stood behind her, his hands on her shoulders. "No wife of mine would ever starve while I was alive to care for her."

She looked up into his green eyes, shining in the firelight. A marriage between them was impossible. If she had not known it before, she knew it now. "You do not even like me. I am a thief, do not forget. You have fought me nigh on every time we have met."

"That was before I knew you were a woman."

"Does my being a woman make it all right again? Just like that?"

He creased his forehead as if in pain. "Damn it, all I can think of now is your red lips, and the way they would feel against mine were I to brave that 'friend' hidden in your boot and try to kiss you."

Slowly she removed the knife from her boot and tossed it on the floor. It skittered over the bare boards and came to rest in the corner. A marriage between them might be impossible, but there was nothing to stop her from becoming his mistress—even if only for one night. She wanted him so badly she would take whatever she could get and try not to pine for what was beyond her reach. "I will take the gamble that you will not hurt me."

He fixed her with his gaze. "Stand up next to me." The force of his will was almost tangible in the air.

It was an order she could not refuse, that she did not

want to refuse. Slowly she got to her feet and turned to stand in front of him.

He held on to her arms as if he was fighting for his sanity. "You are a liar and a thief and a soldier. I should not desire you still, but I do. God help me, but I do."

She tipped her head back to look at him. "It was not all lies. I wore a gown the first time only for Sophie's wedding, but the other times I wore it just for you. It took more courage than I knew I had. I have been a boy for so long—for most of my life. I have not worn a gown since I was little more than a child."

He looked puzzled. "I do not understand. Wearing a gown takes courage?"

If he once knew about Rebecca, he would know her innermost soul. He would have all her secrets. She was not yet ready to tell him. "I cannot tell you now. One day I might explain to you why, if you care to know."

"Even when you talk in riddles, I want you all the more." He nuzzled his face in her hair, breathing in the scent of her. "The first day I saw you sitting in the church, I thought you looked like an exotic madonna. You looked so pure and sweet, with those rosebuds in your hair. I thought I had never seen anything so beautiful."

His foolishness made her smile even as her skin warmed with his words. "Not even Francine?"

"You were different. Francine is like a rose in full bloom—her charms are obvious, and will soon become overblown. But you, you were as sweet and unripe as a rosebud, promising delights that no one else had shared." He raised his head and looked sorrowfully at her. "Is that, too, a lie?"

"I have never—"

He cut her off with a hand over her mouth. "Hush, do not speak. I could not bear it if you told me more lies."

She tossed her head to remove his hand from her mouth. "I will not—"

He silenced her with a shake of his head. "If I cannot stop you from talking any other way, I will stop you like this."

Slowly he bent his head towards her and she lost the will to speak. A lock of golden hair fell over his eyes and she reached up her hand to smooth it back again.

His hair was as fine and silky as it looked. She ran her hands through it, delighted by how it felt beneath her fingers.

She was almost taken by surprise when his mouth reached hers. He kissed her closed lips, then her cheeks, her chin, and, at last, her lips again, with soft touches that sent a shiver of pleasure down her spine. She turned her mouth wordlessly towards his, shuddering with need, wanting his kisses with a desire she had never felt so strongly before.

Her hand settled instinctively at the nape of his neck, and she pressed her mouth more firmly against his. She wanted only to feel his body against hers, from the breadth of his shoulders all the way to the floor. She wound her other hand around him, stroking the planes of his back with the tips of her fingers. She hardly believed she was here, in his chamber, touching him and being touched in return. He was so strong and yet so tender, everything she could have desired in a lover.

Miriame pressed her breasts, covered only with the thin linen of her shirt, against his chest. Her nipples, happy to be freed from their confining wraps, peaked and hardened at the touch. They had been ignored for too long, hidden away in the dark, their very existence denied. Their new-found freedom brought a sensitivity that made her nearly faint with pleasure as they rubbed against the roughness of his jacket.

Her mouth opened to give a tiny exhalation of delight, and he took advantage of it to enter her mouth with his tongue, tasting her very soul.

Kissing with open mouths? It did not take her long to learn that such kisses were sinfully delicious. Tentatively she moved her tongue against his, exploring the sensations that burst in on her as she explored his mouth with her own.

She felt him hardening against her belly and she rubbed herself shamelessly against him. Virgin though she was, she was not a complete innocent. She had grown up on the streets, and was on friendly terms with several whores. She knew that a man showed his passion for a woman by the hardness of his prick when he touched her.

She laughed deep in her throat as he kissed her. Judging by the rod of iron he was holding against her, Jean-Paul must want her very much indeed. Her legs turned boneless, barely keeping her upright, as she gloried in his need for her. She might be a liar and a thief and a soldier, but she could make this man desire her all the same.

He groaned as she pressed herself up against him, tantalizing herself with his hardness. "You are a witch to enslave me like this."

She was not a witch. Churchmen burnt witches at the stake. She did not need to be tied to a stake in the marketplace with a pile of faggots around her feet to feel almost dead with fiery heat. She did not need flames licking her toes and ankles and up her thighs to feel hotter than she could bear. She was sure if she got any hotter she would burst into flames all by herself, without the need for a cruel priest to hold a lighted torch to her.

Miriame did not protest when his hands moved to touch her breasts under the linen of her shirt. She arched her back, thrusting them into his hands. She would die if he did not touch her, if he did not take her breasts into his hands, and smooth his callused palms over her sensitive nipples.

It was as if he read her mind and knew every desire that she felt but could not put into words. His hands moved exactly where she wanted them to go. They touched her just where she ached to be touched.

His hands moved down to the waistband of her breeches, and paused. For one heartbreaking moment, she thought he would stop there, but he did not. "I cannot think of you as a wench when you are garbed as a man," he growled into her ear. "You will have to take those breeches off, or I shall do it for you."

Never had she been happier to oblige him. She moved backward a few steps until she felt the end of the bed bang against the backs of her knees. She slipped out of his grasp, sliding her body against the length of his, sat down on the bed and held out one leg. "My boots first. I cannot take my breeches off while my boots are still on."

He knelt down in front of her and pulled off first one boot, and then the other, tossing them into the corner of the room without hesitation. With a sigh, he ran his hands along her slender ankles and up over her knees.

Her feet and legs felt so naked without her boots. She shivered. This was real. She was in his chamber and he was undressing her, inch by inch. She bit her lip, feeling suddenly vulnerable.

He nudged her knees apart and moved in closer between her thighs. "Now for your breeches," he said, as he bent his head to begin work on the laces.

His fingers fumbled with the knots, unable to work the stiff leather. With a curse of frustration he grabbed his dagger. She flinched away from the blade as, with one quick tug, he slit through the leather ties.

Slowly he drew them over her buttocks and legs, discarding them into the corner on top of the boots.

His teeth grazed her thigh, and she whimpered part in pleasure, part in apprehension, and clenched her thighs together. Surely he was not going to hurt her now? Surely he would not hurt her as Rebecca had been hurt? He could not be that sort of man. Surely he could not be.

The thought of Rebecca was like being doused with cold water. What was she doing, opening herself to a man she barely knew? She sat up again and pushed him away, clutching her shirt to her breast and waiting for the explosion of anger that was sure to follow.

The explosion she feared never came. "Are you frightened?" His voice was gentle.

She nodded, unable to find her voice, looking at his knife.

He followed her gaze, understanding on his face. He held it up by the tip of its blade and offered it to her handle first. "Take it from me."

She took it, feeling the comforting weight in her hand. Slowly her fears started to ebb away. He would never have given her his knife if he intended to hurt her.

"You have my knife." He held his arms open, baring his chest. "I am in your power. You can stop me whenever you want to, and I shall not dare protest."

She had no need to be afraid. Jean-Paul was not like André. He would not hurt her. She tossed the knife away in the corner. "Don't stop," she whispered. "Not yet."

"Your wish is my command." He gave her a wicked grin before bending down to untie the faded ribbons holding up her stockings—with his teeth. The ribbons undone, he drew the stockings down over her ankles, and threw them off into the corner as well.

He sat back on his heels, looking at her with new appreciation. "I like you better like this. You look all woman to me now."

She crossed her arms over her breasts, feeling suddenly chilled despite the heat of the fire in the grate and the smoldering furnace blazing inside her own body. She felt so exposed, sitting in front of him naked but for her linen shirt and drawers. "I have always been all woman."

"Your breeches concealed that small detail from me for some weeks," he said with a grin. "You cannot blame me for holding a grudge against them."

"You should be thankful to them. They have kept me safe for years."

"Do you feel in danger now that they are gone?"

She looked at the predatory gleam in his eyes. He wanted her, and was not afraid to show it. Yes, she was in danger, but not as Rebecca had been. Never that. "Never more so."

"You know I would not hurt you."

"Maybe not now," she teased. "Now that you know I am a woman and have stopped trying to kill me in your spare time."

"I would not hurt any woman, if I could help it. Not even you, you minx, though heaven knows you have done your best to torment me." He reached out and touched her breasts with his hands. "Just as you are tormenting me now."

She shivered at his touch. "I am not teasing you now."

He pulled the shirt over her head. "I am glad of it. I could not bear it if you were to mock me now."

Her breasts were on the small side for a woman—certainly she could not compare them to the lush flesh that spilled out of the bodices of the gowns of the whores she knew. They had mountainous breasts. She had barely a couple of molehills. She was shy under his scrutiny, feeling suddenly inadequate as a woman, but he seemed to find no fault in her.

He moved his hands over her breasts and then bent his head to taste them. She gasped at the shock of his mouth on her nipples, gently pulling and tugging them, suckling on them, licking around the hard, pink center until she could hardly bear the rush of sensation in her body.

He took away his head, and she felt the breeze of his movement on her wet nipples.

With his back to her, he pulled off his own boots, tossing them in the pile on top of hers, flung his jacket off his shoulders, pulled his shirt over his head, then unlaced his breeches and kicked them off as well.

He paused for a moment, clad only in his linen drawers, and then they, too, were discarded to lie on top of the pile.

She watched with wide eyes as he freed his body from its coverings. His back was smooth and brown in the flickering firelight, the muscles well-defined. His thighs looked as strong and beautiful as if they had been carved out of marble by a master craftsman. She wanted to reach forward and touch them to make sure that he was indeed made of living flesh.

Slowly he turned around to face her and she gasped with shock.

His chest sported a long raised scar, puckered and red and raw in its newness, that marked the wound that had nearly taken away his life. She had known that he must be scarred, of course, but knowing it was different from seeing it.

She raised a forefinger to touch it. "Does it still hurt?"

He made a wry face. "Not nearly as much as this does right now," he said, indicating his erection.

She traced the outline of his scar and then slowly

moved her hand down his belly to his jutting cock. There would be time enough to weep over his scar later. She had other things on her mind for now. "Will it hurt more if I touch it?"

He grimaced. "Undoubtedly." But when she went to take her hand away, his own hand moved over hers, holding it where it was. Slowly he lifted her hand and brought it down again, teaching her how to touch him to give him pleasure.

She relished the lesson, glorying in the feeling of power over him, delighting in the groans of pleasure that she drew from him as she stroked along the thick, hard length of his proud cock.

He lay back on the bed and drew her down beside him. "You are still wearing too many clothes," he murmured into her ear. "Take them off for me. Please."

She wriggled her hips and slipped out of her linen drawers. "Is this better?"

He murmured his agreement and pulled her body close to his. Her breasts pressed into his chest and their bellies were joined together as they kissed with a growing ardor.

His cock pressed into her belly with a delicious hardness and she wriggled against him to feel it all over her, as much of it as she could reach. He gave a moan of pleasure at her movements, and moved one hard thigh in between her legs, rocking it gently against her.

Then his fingers crept down to touch her in the place where she ached for him. She arched her back to give him room to touch her there. He did not need to be invited twice.

His fingers slid easily over her, moistened with her liquid heat, and then into her. She gasped at the invasion of her most private space, but his hot breath in her ear made her want only more. "You are wet and ready for me, Miriame, my love . . ."

She could only gasp as he slid a second finger in to join the first. She thought she would die with the wonderful fullness of it.

"You want me to take you now, don't you? You want me to put my cock inside you, to stroke you as far and as high as I can reach, to fuck you until you scream yourself hoarse with pleasure for me."

She did not answer. She could not. She hardly had enough air to breathe with, let alone to talk.

He took his hand away, leaving her bereft. "Tell me you want me, Miriame. Tell me."

"I want you. God, I want you." She had never wanted anything more than she wanted him to take possession of her body.

His fingers crept back again, stroking her until she was mindless with desire. "You are not lying to me now, are you?" His voice was thick with masculine satisfaction.

She could hardly get the words out, but she knew he would stop if she did not speak. More than anything she wanted him not to stop. "No, I'm not lying to you."

He nudged her over until she was lying on her back, and spread her legs wide apart. "No second thoughts?" he asked, as he straddled her, his cock poised at the very entrance to her body.

She shook her head and lifted her hips off the bed to meet him. He already possessed her heart, and she longed for him to take possession of her body as well.

He thrust into her a little way, then a little more, slowly but surely sinking deep into her body until he was inside her up to the very hilt. He rested there for a moment, his weight on his elbows, and looked into her eyes. "By God, Miriame, you test my self-control."

The fullness she had felt before was nothing to what she felt now. What was one finger, or even two, compared with the long, hard cock she felt inside her now?

She moved tentatively against him, exploring the sensation of having him inside her. It felt strange somehow, as if he were a part of her and yet not a part of her all at the same time. She had thought that having a man inside her would be brutal—that she would feel invaded and violated by his presence. Instead, she felt completed, as if this was how she was meant to be.

Slowly he withdrew and then moved into her once more, setting her nerves on fire with the slow, tantalizing friction of his desire. He set a gentle rhythm, rocking first into her and then out again with deliberate slowness.

She thrust her hips up to meet him, eager to join with him, to experience this wonder together.

His thrusts became slowly more urgent and more demanding. Slowly but surely she spiraled higher and higher, until she was no longer in control of the feelings that flooded her body. Harder and harder he plunged into her body. His breath grew short and his body started to shake until he gave one last thrust and held himself there, flooding her body with the essence of his. She felt herself falling, falling, into a well of indescribable pleasure, until she cried out his name at last. . . .

They huddled together in the aftermath of their loving. Jean-Paul drew a blanket over them both and held Miriame in his arms.

Too limp to move, she lay still and watched the flames leap in the grate. She felt as though her body had been wrung out and left to dry, but her mind was alert now.

A shame, she thought to herself, that it had not been some minutes before—before she had allowed, nay, welcomed, Jean-Paul spilling his seed into her. What would she do if she was with child?

A moment's softness stole over her as she imagined a boy with golden curls like his father, or a little girl with dark eyes just like her darling sister Rebecca. How she would adore to have a daughter to love and to care for.

She stifled the emotion deep within her. She could not afford such weakness. She was alone in the world, and her only livelihood was her wits—and her sword. With a child in her belly, she would have no way of using either to her advantage. Besides, who was to say she could look after a child of her own any better than she had looked after her sister? She could not bear to lose a son or daughter to the cruelty of poverty.

Jean-Paul was handsome, certainly, but he could not support her, especially not if she were carrying his babe in her belly. She would not drag him back down into the misery she had only just escaped herself.

She looked again around his meager chamber but saw no evidence that he had any hidden wealth. She had been naive enough to think that because she had stolen a handful of gold from him once, that he had money enough to spare. He was foolish in the extreme to think that he could take a wife.

She sighed and rolled over, her back toward him. He was not as foolish as she was. She was three times a fool not to look deeper into the matter before she became so involved with him. In her innocence, she had thought that all musketeers, save her alone, would have apartments like those of Courtney, where comfort and luxury were treated as a matter of course. She had not thought that many of her comrades might be quite as poor as she was, with nothing to live on but their soldier's pay.

She had had her pleasure with Jean-Paul and she must now take her leave, with her fingers crossed that she would not take away a lasting memento of their momentary passion. With a sigh she kicked off the blankets and slouched over to the corner where their discarded clothes were tangled all in a heap, in a parody of their own coupling.

Jean-Paul rose on to one elbow and blinked sleepily at her. She could not read the expression on his face. Was he, too, regretting their moment of shared lust? If so, she did not want to know. She did not want to leave him with any regrets on her account.

He cleared his throat and then hesitated as if he, too, didn't know quite what to say. "You are leaving?" he said at last.

She slipped on her linen drawers and breeches, knotting the cut laces together until she had long enough pieces to hold them up around her waist. Haste made her clumsy. She did not want to create a scene—just to leave without a fuss. She hoped he would not make it more difficult for her than it was. "Yes. I think it is best for me to go now." She had bedded him with her eyes open, and had no one but herself to blame for any consequences that might ensue.

He stared at her as she pulled her shirt over her head and buttoned up her jacket over her breasts. "Goodbye," he said simply, his eyes not leaving her for a moment.

She looked over at him in surprise. Did he not care that she was going without a word after all they had shared?

How contrary she was. Now that he had accepted her departure so easily, she could wish that he show some sorrow at least: maybe to get on his knees and beg her to wed him, rise up and bar the door against her and forbid her to go, even just ask her nicely to stay a few moments longer. "You do not care that I am leaving?" she said, as she tied up her stockings and pulled on her boots.

He closed his eyes as if in pain. "I cannot ask you to stay."

She buckled on her sword. "I did not want to be asked," she lied.

"You are a desirable woman, but you are also a liar and

a thief. You have hidden your real self from me for weeks, until tonight, when you chose to confide in me somewhat. But how do I know what other secrets you are keeping from me? How can I truly know you? And how can I trust you?"

He sat up on the bed, letting the blanket fall off his naked shoulders, and forced himself to look at her. "I am sorry to see you go, but in truth I do not want you to stay. You are too beautiful, too seductive for a man such as me. I cannot bear to fall in love with you." His face was contorted as if he were in pain.

"I do not want you to fall in love with me."

He turned his face to the wall, unable to bear looking at her any longer. "Please, Miriame. Just go." The words sounded as though they had been dragged from the depths of his soul.

She could not bear the suffering she heard in his voice. Closing the door quietly behind her, she walked out of his life without looking back.

In the weeks that followed, Miriame threw herself into life again with a passion. Who knew how much longer she could remain a musketeer? Who knew how soon she might have to lose all that she had gained? She would make the most of every adventure that came her way while she could. Her new friends were only too glad to help her out.

Sophie, now returned from her mission to England, wanted to rescue a prisoner from the Bastille. Miriame agreed to help her, just for the hell of it. At the very least the excitement would help to break up the monotony of her days and ease some of the ache she felt in her heart at Jean-Paul's rejection.

Courtney wanted to foment a rebellion against the

King to put his spineless younger brother upon the throne of France. Why should she not join it? The pay was good, and her sword was for hire to whoever would pay her best. If she could not have Jean-Paul, she might as well have excitement and danger and the chance to earn her fortune instead.

The prisoner died before she could be rescued, and the ill-conceived rebellion failed before it had even begun. Sophie had to flee to Burgundy and soon after Courtney was forced to join her. They both had to give up their lives as musketeers and live as women again.

Miriame grieved their loss. They had been her comrades and her friends. She had given a piece of her heart to them, though she had sworn she would not. When they were gone, a part of her went with them.

Even as she mourned the loss of their company, she shuddered at their fate, hoping never to have to join them. Not that she minded the thought of living in Burgundy—indeed, she heard travelers' tales that made her wish to see the place—she just could not conceive of giving up soldiering and having to wear a gown. As a musketeer she had an adventurous life and the faint possibility of hope for the future. As a woman, she had nothing—not even the love of the man she had once sighed over in secret.

Her folly was past now. Jean-Paul was not worth sighing over. She ignored him when they passed each other in the practice yard. Sometimes he looked as though he would speak with her, but she looked through him as if he wasn't there. He was nothing to her. Nothing.

He had spurned her and she would not give him another chance, just to have him reject her once more.

She gambled at cards and dice, she even cheated at times—but either her life was charmed or her cheating so adept that none suspected her. She felt no guilt. She only played with those who could afford to lose, and who could pay the forfeit out of their pocket change without blinking. The coins they lost to her were a fair enough payment for an evening's entertainment.

Besides, she evened up the score by deliberately losing on the odd occasion to a thin, hollow-eyed new recruit, barely out of his boyhood, who looked as though he never got enough to eat.

Each night she counted her winnings and added them to the pile behind the loose brick in her chamber. Heaven help her but she would not starve, even if she were to bear a babe for her folly.

She counted the days with growing anxiety. Would she have to pay for her sins, or would God overlook her sin this time? Would he take pity on her and show her mercy? She was not a hardened criminal, after all. She wondered, then, how the marquise managed to keep her shape—she had borne several children to Louis, after all. She would have to ask next time she paid the woman a visit.

If the Madame de Montespan ever asked for her again. Francine had not sent for her lately—the marquise must be piqued over Miriame's failure to turn up the last time she was called, on that fateful night that she gambled with Fate itself and opened her heart to Jean-Paul.

Twenty-one days came and went without a spot of blood. Miriame's fingernails were bitten to the quick.

On the twenty-second day, the bleeding came. She fell on her knees in thankfulness when she saw the telltale spots of red appearing between her thighs. Feeling as though she had just received a reprieve from an execution, she bounded into the barracks, ready for the first time in nearly a month to start to live again, to care about her life.

No more would she pass the days in a frantic whirl, deliberately courting danger, as if keeping close to death was the only way she could feel more than half alive.

From now on she would keep herself to herself. She would not admit her sex to anyone else—never. She had escaped this time by the grace of God, but He might not take it kindly were she to make a habit of it.

No more loving for her. No more frantic tumbles in a darkened chamber. She was a man again, and a man she would remain.

Jean-Paul Metin stared after Miriame as she turned on her heel and strode away from him, ignoring his plea to talk to her, as she had ignored all his pleas for the past week. God damn it, but he was a fool to have let her alone for so long. He had let her stew for a fortnight or more, too proud to ask for her forgiveness for his cruelty. She would not find it easy to forgive him now.

He had been so angry with her when he had first found out that she and the young musketeer who had stolen his name were one and the same person. He had taken her to bed out of lust, true enough, but also out of anger. He had wanted to bury his rage in her body, to punish her for making a fool out of him for so long, and she had willingly accepted him. Too willingly for his peace of mind.

The thought of how he had used her so cold-bloodedly made him cringe. He had not done right by her. He was a soldier and a musketeer, not a brute who treated women like dirt under his feet.

He still could hardly believe how she had fooled him—and all their comrades—for so long. He watched her as she strode away, her legs straight, her hips hardly moving from side to side, moving just like a man. If he had not seen her naked body with his own eyes, tasted the delights of her very womanly body with his eyes and hands and cock, he would doubt his own senses.

No, he could never doubt those. She had been unforgettable—a mixture of sweetness and spice, of innocence and eroticism, such that he would never forget her again for as long as he lived. He felt himself growing hard again at the memory, and he turned away to shift his privy parts to a less obtrusive position.

As soon as he could move again without discomfort, he strode after her. This time he was not going to let her get away with slighting him. This time he was going to force her to sit down and talk with him. By heaven, he might owe her an apology for his rudeness, but she owed him some answers to his questions. He would not wait any longer for them.

She was walking quickly, but not fast enough to avoid him. He strode up behind her. "I want to talk to you, boy." He could not call her by her assumed name, but neither could he call her Miriame when they were in the middle of the barracks. That was more than his life was worth.

At the touch of his hand on her shoulder, she snapped her head back with a scowl. "What do you want from me?"

Not exactly the reception he would have chosen, but at least she was talking to him again. And her eyes were still the most beautiful deep brown he could imagine. Even knowing what he knew about her, he could willingly lose himself in her eyes. "You owe me some answers."

The scowl on her face deepened and she spat on the ground at his feet. "I owe you nothing."

She certainly had the manners of a musketeer—and those were nothing to boast of. He hated to imagine what his mother would think of her. His poor parent would be truly scandalized and think the wench was possessed by devils, no doubt. She'd have the priest around with bell, book, and candle to exorcise her in a trice. "That is where we disagree."

Her face lit up with an impish grin and she put her hand on her sword with a threatening look. "Do you want to fight about it? I'm itching for a good fight."

He'd rather have her looking full of mischief than scowling any day. "I'd rather kiss you instead."

Her grin vanished at his words and he could see her hand creeping perilously close to her boot, where she hid her knife. She certainly had a temper, his Miriame. She would keep him on his toes once they were wed. She did not look impressed at the thought of him kissing her. "Don't forget that I'm a soldier."

"I'm not likely to forget it, with the way you are dressed." Even as he spoke the words, he knew they weren't true. He liked the look of her in her red dress, her breasts spilling out of the top of her bodice, but now that he thought about it, he liked her equally well in her breeches. They clung to her hips and legs, showing off a part of her figure that would normally be shrouded in a skirt. "Though I have to say that you're definitely the best-looking soldier in the barracks."

"That's where we have to disagree again," she said, the grin beginning to creep back. "I would give that honor to Javert De Toile."

"De Toile?" He racked his brains, but he couldn't match a face to the name. What was Miriame doing looking at him anyway? Whoever De Toile was, he might just find himself with a new scar shortly that would spoil his beauty.

"You must have noticed him. He's the one with the dark curling hair, the elegant moustache, and those glorious muscles."

He most certainly did not like Miriame noticing any

other man's muscles. "I thought you had turned musketeer to fight, not to ogle men's bodies on the sly."

She shrugged. "I don't bother with most of them, but some of them are more worth ogling than others."

He touched his fingertips to his chest where the livid red scar ran across his body. Had she been revolted by it? The idea had not crossed his mind before, but now he could not shake it. She could not have received any pleasure from looking at his mutilated flesh. The thought gave him pain, especially since her beautiful body had given him so much pleasure. "Does he know you are a woman?"

The look she gave him was pure disdain. "Do you think I am an utter fool?"

He shrugged, hardly knowing how to answer her. She was still alive, which said much for her wit and cunning. Foolhardy in the extreme? Absolutely. He had never met a woman, or a man, for that matter, who took such huge risks so blithely.

"Well, I am not," she hissed furiously as he remained silent a moment too long. "Nobody here knows I am a woman."

"Except me."

"I didn't bother to count you. As far as I am concerned, you are a nobody." Her voice was vicious.

He did not like being dismissed so readily. "I have kept your secret."

She looked briefly down at her boot in a warning. "And if you hadn't, you would be sorry."

Did she think he had kept her secret out of fear? "I would?"

"There's a lot a woman can do with a knife when a man is sleeping." Her smile as she looked up at him was cold and hard.

The tone of her voice, even more than her words, sent

shivers of unease down his spine and quieted his restless arousal. That in itself was a blessing. He was finding it difficult to concentrate on being angry with her when his body was demanding quite a different reaction.

As far as her threat went, he didn't know whether or not she meant it, but he was not about to take the risk and find out. Her secret was safe with him. "I would never give away your sex," he said loftily. "I would hate to miss the opportunity of ogling you in those delightful breeches you wear."

She looked momentarily taken aback at his jest. "You are not serious."

"Are you?"

"Always. I never jest about dismemberment." But she was at least smiling again—a real smile of warmth and laughter, not one of cold, hard threat.

He was surprised how much he liked to make her smile. He would have to come to terms with his anger at her deception and learn anew how to deal with her not only as a woman but also as a soldier. God knows, but she was glorious whatever she was wearing. He reached out and twirled one loose curl around his finger. How he loved her hair, so smooth and soft. He wanted to bury his face in it and breathe in her sweet scent. "It's just lucky for me that you like my member enough not to dismember it."

She snorted and tossed her head, pulling her curl out of his fingers. "So you like to think."

"So I know. But I still have some questions that I want answered."

"Ask away."

"Not here. Not now."

She shrugged. "Suits me."

"Come to my chamber this evening, so we can talk in peace." Remembering how carried away he had become the last time she had visited him, he hated to suggest it, but there was nowhere else for them to go. Nowhere else could they spend time together with any privacy, unless she were to invite him to her small apartment. Somehow, he didn't think that such an invitation was likely to be forthcoming.

She looked at him out of the corner of her eye. "All you want to do is talk?"

He nodded. "Just talk. I promise you." He would act more honorably this time and not leap on her and rip her clothes off the moment he had her to himself again. He would control his urges if it killed him.

Still, the thought of her so close to him again was almost more than he could bear. How could he remember the sight of her lying naked across his bed, the feel of his cock stroking inside her, wet and warm, the sound of her harsh breathing in his ears as she moaned in pleasure at his touch, the sweet taste of her honey golden skin on his hungry lips. How could he remember all this and not want to repeat the experience?

She hesitated, obviously unsure as to whether she should agree or not.

Suddenly it was more important than anything that he talk with her once again, that they be together, just the two of them, where no one else could see or hear them. "I swear to you that I am telling you the truth. I will not take advantage of you. I will do my best to forget that you are a woman." He could not resist adding a little jab. "Unlike some of my comrades, I do not make a habit of deceit."

Her cheeks became tinged with a rosy pink. "We each choose our own path in life. What makes you set yourself up so high as to judge what I do?"

He squirmed a little uncomfortably at the deserved rebuke. He should not simply assume that her motives were wrong. She was a thief, true, but she had become one out of sheer necessity. He owed her the courtesy to listen to her explanations before he condemned her. "So you will come tonight?"

"Maybe." She turned on her heel and started to walk away. "Or maybe not," she said over her shoulder. "You never can tell with us deceitful people. I suppose you will simply have to take it on trust."

He had no choice. He could not compel her if she didn't want to come. Perhaps a friendship at the very least could be salvaged from the wreck of their relationship, but what chance did even a simple friendship between them have unless he could trust her to keep her word?

He bit back the angry retort on his tongue. Maybe if he trusted her a little, she would learn to trust him in her turn. "Until tonight."

Chapter 9

Francine leaned back on her pillows and allowed Berthe to smooth some almond oil into her white hands to keep them soft and supple. Now that she was the King's mistress again, in fact as well as in reputation, she could afford such luxuries whenever she pleased. She often pleased.

She had it all back again—the bowing and the scraping, the fawning and the flattering, the snide whispers about her in corners when she was not quite out of hearing. Not even the cardinal could spoil her moment in the sun, despite his power and his web of informants. If he had the incriminating letters, he had been wise enough not to use them against her as yet. Her triumph was complete. How she loved it.

Unfortunately the King was just as cold and haughty as ever. She sighed as she watched Berthe attend to each cuticle with painstaking exactness. Why had it not been her lot to become the paramour of a king who was handsome and attentive, witty and entertaining, instead of pompous and obsessed with etiquette?

She was weary of masques and formal balls. Even in the center of the glittering court of Louis XIV, she needed constant distractions: a group of tumblers or even a naughty Italian puppet show was just what she felt like seeing . . .

She needed livelier pastimes than the intellectual Louis, patron of Molière and Voltaire and scads of other brilliant minds. It was all very impressive, of course. As long as his courtiers shielded their eyes at the sight of him, pretending that they were dazzled by the brightness of his glory, by the glory of the Sun King, he seemed content.

"*L'état, c'est moi.*" *I am the state*, indeed. She was tired of ceremony and such ridiculous playacting, and of having to defer to the King as if he were next to God Himself. Perhaps she should get herself a jester, or even a dwarf, to keep her merry. Or do what she had always done before, take a new lover . . .

That reminded her—Jean-Paul Metin, the second, had not been to see her for some weeks. Mayhap he had heard the news that she was reinstated in the King's favor again and had wisely kept his distance for the moment. Yes, that must be the reason.

He was a practical fellow, to be sure—too practical for her liking? She would not believe that he was tired of her—not for a moment. She knew how to play the game better than that. Men did not tire of her. She kept them dangling after her until she was tired of them.

Now that she had brought the King to heel again and her star was blazing even brighter than before, she had the leisure to please herself a little more.

She sat up and snatched her hand back again. Having her nails done had become tiresome. She was sick of being fussed over and pampered and petted like a lapdog. "Peacock quill and a sheet of rose paper, Berthe."

"Yes, Madame."

She tickled her cheek with the brightly colored feather as she thought what best to write, what would best lure him in to her web again, and yet promise him nothing. A veiled invitation, but no more than that.

"Have you forgotten me so soon? Your friend, F." Yes, that should do the trick.

She folded it in two and sealed it with a blob of hot wax, pressing her ring into it to leave her own distinctive mark. "Have it delivered to Jean-Paul Metin in the King's Guards," she said, as she handed it to Berthe. "And for God's sake don't let the messenger boy get them muddled this time," she added irritably. "Give it to the dark one, not the blond one." She didn't want her former lover back again: she wanted the mysterious young boy with his dark curls and golden brown skin and eyes as dark and deep as one of the King's dungeons.

If nothing else, his ridiculous stories of brave deeds in battle made her laugh.

At the sound of rough knocking, Jean-Paul opened the door of his chamber and peered out into the gloom.

Miriame stood in the shadows, her brown eyes shining almost yellow like those of a cat. "You wanted to talk to me?"

In the dimness of the half light he noticed something that he had never seen before. "You're wearing my boots."

She looked down at her feet and wriggled her toes. "They're a little long for me, I have to admit, but other than that I can hardly fault them. You have excellent taste in footwear."

The little minx. She had robbed him blind while he had been lying wounded and dying in the inn. "You even stole my boots."

"I had none of my own. I hardly thought you'd be needing them while you were lying in a coffin."

How low could a woman go, robbing a corpse before it was even cold? She was such a little opportunist it was almost funny. "You really have no morals, do you?"

"Not when I'm hungry. Now that I'm well-fed and warm most of the time, I suppose I could afford one or two. I just haven't yet decided which ones I should choose."

He was torn between irritation at her levity on such a serious matter and amusement at her wit. In the end, amusement won out and he had to laugh. Miriame was so unlike every other woman he knew. She danced to nobody's tune but her own. He hardly liked to admit, even to himself, that he rather liked her that way. He opened the door wide. "Please come in."

She bent her head to pass under the lintel and came into his chamber, throwing herself into one of the chairs in front of the fire.

He'd tidied his chamber in the hopes that she would come that night—even going to the effort of borrowing one of his landlady's chairs so they had one each. Judging by the way her eyes swiveled around the room, noting each of the changes, his effort had not been wasted.

"Well?"

"Those men who want to kill me. I believe they really are after my letters." He had thought long and hard about the reason why he had been jumped in the street—twice—and this was the only explanation that made sense. The man whom Miriame had wounded must have spoken truly.

There was no other cause he could see. He had no jewels or money to make it worth a robber's while to waylay him. His parents were not wealthy enough to make it worth holding him for ransom. He didn't even have any enemies to speak of—other than the brigands who had tried to murder him. He couldn't think of any reason why anyone else would want to kill him.

Francine had called for him specifically to ask for her letters back. She would not have bothered if they had not been very important to her.

Someone must want those letters very badly—someone besides Francine. They wanted the letters enough to kill him for them.

Miriame shrugged. "That's hardly news. The man said so himself when we had him cornered. He had no reason to lie."

"Which means I shall fear more attacks until something is done about the letters." He took the chair opposite her. "Now that you've muddied the waters by claiming to have them yourself, you are in danger as well."

She leaned back in her chair and stretched her legs out in front of her. Her body looked quite at ease, if one did not catch the watchful look in her eye. "You'd simply hand them over to the men who tried to kill you for them? You surprise me. I thought you had more fight in you than that."

He smacked his hand against the arm of his chair, irritated at her assumption that he would cave in to his enemies out of fear. "Of course I don't want to give them to the cardinal. For one thing, he would use them to ruin Madame de Montespan."

She had the gall to laugh at him. "Ah, so now we have the real reason. You are still pining for the fair Francine."

Not true. Especially not when Miriame was in front of him, her legs hugged by her tight breeches, looking infinitely desirable and even more unobtainable. "Damn it all, I am not pining for that woman. She has nothing to do with anything." He had promised not to touch Miriame, but he could not stop himself from thinking about touching her. His lust for her was making him irritable.

She sat at her ease in her chair by the fire and held out her hands to the flames. "Actually, she has quite a lot to do with everything. If you had never crawled into her bed in the first place, you would never have come to Paris and been wounded, I would never have robbed you or joined the musketeers, and we would not be sitting here in front of the fire together."

"All right, so Francine was the cause of all our problems," he admitted grumpily. "That still doesn't mean that I am pining for her."

She grinned at his frown. "I rather liked her myself, when she wasn't trying to kiss me, of course. That part was a bit of a nuisance."

"She tried to kiss you?" He loosened the neck of his linen shirt a little, suddenly feeling even more hot and bothered than ever.

"We were alike in so many ways," Miriame said easily. "Both of us are adventurers, determined to make our own way in a man's world. We just chose different ways of going about it."

Alike? He shook his head. Never were two women more unlike, except of course, that they both seemed to take an inordinate amount of pleasure in tormenting him. "Francine is a heartless bitch."

"She broke your heart. I robbed your corpse. There is little to chose between us."

No, Miriame was not like Francine. Francine kept her place at the top heedless of those she had to step on to it. Miriame, for all her toughness, had a heart—a heart that he was determined to claim for his own. "Maybe so," he conceded, not caring to argue the point any further, "but I have made my choice. I want no other woman but you."

"I thought you didn't trust me."

He gave a wry smile. "I don't. But I want you anyway."

"Sorry, not interested," she said carelessly, as she rose to her feet. "Now, was there anything else you wanted to talk with me about, or may I go now?"

She wasn't as impervious to his words as she tried to make out. He knew it by the way her legs shook slightly as she moved toward the door.

He took her by the shoulder and steered her back towards her chair. She made no protest, but sat down again. This time he drew his chair close to hers so she could not leave before they had finished. "There is something else we need to discuss. The letters."

Her face wore a look of determined unhelpfulness. "What about them?"

He could tell that in such a mood as this, she would shoot down anything he suggested on the instant, just for the sake of being contrary. He decided not to give her the satisfaction. "What shall we do with them?" he asked instead.

"Returning them to Francine is the obvious solution," she said reluctantly, after it became clear that he would not offer a suggestion of his own until he had heard hers. "Indeed, now that you mention it, I received a summons to wait on her in her apartments later this week. I could take them with me and deliver them with all due ceremony."

The idea sounded plausible enough, but he shook his head. He would not have Miriame put herself in danger. "That is far too dangerous."

She shrugged. "I've visited her several times in the past. What makes it too dangerous for me to see her now?"

"The men who attacked me when we were fighting at the western gate know you have the letters in your possession, but they evidently don't know much more about you. I have been watching them. They have been waiting there for the last few weeks, hoping to ambush you with the letters on you. Were you to pay a visit to Francine now, you would be dead before you knocked on her door."

"Waiting to ambush me? In this foul winter weather?" She laughed, a low, melodious chuckle that made him want to take her into his arms and feel her laughter vibrating against his chest. "I'd just die laughing if they all got frostbite in awkward places."

No doubt she would, too. So would he, for that matter. "We need to get rid of the men before we return the letters to Francine. Permanently."

She shook her head, her lips pursed together. "I cannot kill them, if that is what you are suggesting. I've seen too much death already. Besides, the cardinal would only send more men out after us and we would be no better off than we are now. Worse, in fact, for we would have the blood of three men on our hands."

He did not understand her sudden reluctance. "You have killed before. You told me so."

She shuddered. "A man who deserved death many times over." There was a distant look in her eye, telling of a sorrow that she had not revealed.

"And they do not? They have tried to kill me twice over. Both times you saved me or I would be dead. I have no doubt they would kill you, too, without a second thought, should you ever cross their path."

"If they die at my hand in a fight, then so be it." Her voice did not waver in its determination. "I will not grieve for them, but neither will I deliberately set out to kill them."

She was in no less danger than he was. He did not understand her unwillingness to shed blood. Certainly Miriame was no coward. Did she not see that if he were to fail in this mission, they would eventually come after her? "I will see to them alone then, if you will not aid me."

"You misunderstand me. I will help you dispose of them, and more effectively than if you had killed them."

Much as he misliked the thought of deliberately butchering his enemies, he could not see any other way of being free from the danger of an attack in the night.

He had been lucky twice to escape with his life. He could not count on Fate to help for a third time. He had to choose now—to kill or be killed. Better that he kill them than die himself. He would not go meekly like a lamb to the slaughter. "How is that?"

Miriame gave a smile that boded ill for those who would cross her. "Ridicule is a far more potent weapon than even your sword could be. We shall make them the laughingstock of all Paris. They will not dare to lift a sword against us ever again, and neither will any of their fellows, for fear of meeting the same fate."

He thought of the way Francine had humiliated him in her chamber at her levee and held him up to the ridicule of the whole court. Miriame was right. He would rather die a thousand times than face such shame again. "Tell me more."

Miriame opened the door a crack to peer inside. A thin beam of light escaped into the street where she stood in the shadows. "Here goes," she muttered to Jean-Paul, who stood at her shoulder. "I hope they haven't forgotten me, and are willing to do an old friend a favor."

With those words, she squared her shoulders and stepped into the light.

Two seconds later she was enveloped in an enormous hug. "Dan, you scoundrel. We haven't seen hide nor hair of you for weeks. I thought you'd done a runner. Where have you been hiding?"

Miriame extracted herself from the large woman's embrace before she gagged on the heavy musky perfume she was drenched in. "You know me, Nicole," she prevaricated. "I've been here and there, out and about. Not staying too long in any one place."

"It's agreed with you, surely," Nicole said with appreciation, holding her at arm's length to get a better look. "You've filled out, got a bit more flesh on your bones. You used to be such a skinny mite a strong wind could've blown you away. Half starved you were."

Miriame laughed and flexed her recently grown muscles. Training with Renouf every day had filled out her puny arms until they looked quite respectably strong, even for a woman. "Only on a good day. The rest of the time I was three-quarters starved."

"You were, you were indeed." Her eyes flicked past Miriame to Jean-Paul, who was standing just behind her. "Who's this handsome fellow you've brought along with you tonight? Has he come for a taste of our girls?"

She was glad to see out of the corner of her eye that Jean-Paul's face was red as he stammered a hasty denial.

She shook her head. "We're here on business tonight— not pleasure, I'm afraid."

Nicole raised her eyebrows and gave a fat chuckle. "Business? You've come up in the world, young Dan. Time was the only business you ever had with me was begging a crust of bread."

Miriame shuddered as she remembered how desperate she had been for a scrap of food, a spot in front of a fire, or even a kindly word. Nicole's casual kindness, the smile that accompanied the crust of bread or morsel of cheese, had meant more to her than the older woman would ever know. Thank the Lord that those days were behind her now—never, she vowed, ever to return.

Nicole was looking at her strangely. Miriame gave herself a little shake to bring herself back from her evil memories. No good ever came from dwelling on the past.

Jean-Paul stepped forward and pressed a couple of gold *pistoles* into the woman's hand. "We're looking for somebody. Three somebodies, in fact. We hoped you might be able to tell us where to find them. They're worth that again if you can tell us where they are."

Nicole bit on the *pistoles* with one of her few remaining teeth, and, satisfied they were real, tucked them into her bodice with a gleam in her eye. "Who are they?"

"I don't know their names, but I can tell you what they look like right enough."

Nicole shrugged. "Names ain't much use to me anyway. I never can remember them, though I've got a knack for not forgetting a face once I've seen it. Comes in handy in my line of business."

Jean-Paul described the three men who had attacked them in the street some weeks before.

Nicole listened carefully, but at the end of his recitation she shook her head. "There's so many that would answer to that description. Just about every rogue in Paris, I'd warrant. Was there nothing in particular that set them apart from other men?"

Jean-Paul shook his head. "That is all I can give you. The night was too dark to see more."

Miriame clenched her fists into tight balls. She had hoped that this moment would not come, though all along she knew it would. "Yes, there was one more thing about them. Their leader. You may have known him. He was tall and thin, angular almost. His skin was as white as a ghost and he had grreasy black hair that fell to his shoulders. His fingers were long and he carried a knife." She shuddered at the memory of those fingers. "He was a cruel man. His name was André."

Nicole's ear pricked up at this description. "He talks like he was a gentleman? As if he'd sprung from the King's court, but his voice makes your blood run cold?"

Miriame nodded. She felt icy as death even thinking about him.

"I know the man, though I haven't seen him around here for some time, thank heaven. We had to turn him out on his ear last time he came. He had Jeni round the throat with those long, white fingers of his and was trying to choke her to death. She couldn't scream. She couldn't even breathe.

"Lucky I had some customers who'd paid to watch the two of them together and they ran to tell me, otherwise the poor girl would never have made it. The lads got to her only just in time. They had to pull him off with main force and kick him out the door. Since then I've lived in terror of him coming back again."

Miriame dug her nails into the palms of her hands. Why had Jeni been saved, and not Rebecca? "You won't see him again."

Nicole gave her a piercing look. "Why not? Where's he gone?"

She thought about the thud his body had made as it hit the floor. "To hell," she spat, "where he belongs."

Nicole looked as though a real monsieur, pockets bulging with gold, had just walked in through her door. "He's dead?"

"As a doornail."

"Are you sure we're talking about the same man?" She looked suspicious, as though Miriame's news was too good to be relied upon. "He was alive and kicking not six weeks ago."

"As sure as can be." She shrugged uneasily at the look of uncertainty that still haunted Nicole's face. The woman deserved the truth. "I was the one who killed him. I slit his throat and watched him die at my feet." She no longer felt sick to her stomach at the thought. She had managed to distance herself from the act. It seemed almost as though someone else had killed him, and that she had merely been a spectator to the grisly deed.

Nicole's face cleared. "By God, Dan, but you've done the world a favor, and me in particular." She put her hand into her bosom and pulled out the gold pieces she'd tucked away there earlier. She pressed them into Miriame's hands. "Take your gold back and welcome," she said, in a voice of heartfelt thanks. "Heaven help me if I ever take a penny of yours. Jeni will be that glad to hear of his death. She's not been right in her mind since he abused her so. Now, then, these others you was looking for, they're friends of André's?"

Miriame nodded. "They followed his lead. One of them will have been hurt badly and limping lately, from the last time we tangled a few weeks ago."

Nicole's face burst into a smile. "By God, I think I do know the three you mean." She bustled to the door. "Here, come with me and take a look. You'll see right enough if them's the ones."

Out of the corner of her eye, Miriame saw Jean-Paul gulp. "You mean they're here now?"

"If them's the ones I'm thinking of, then they're right here upstairs with the girls. Come here a lot they do, when they've the money to pay for it. One of them in particular likes summat a bit special, and there's not that many girls in Paris who are as willing as our Eloise. 'Course, she makes a fortune out of it. She'll be able to retire young, that one will."

A flickering rushlight in her hand, she led them up a pair of back stairs to a narrow corridor. "You might want to take off your boots about here," she said in a low whisper as they reached the top of the stairs. "The floor's as bare as my old granny's bones and the noise carries something terrible." She gave a low chuckle. "It would never do to disturb the paying customers as they go about their business. I takes a great deal of care of my customers. The girls they can get anywhere—it's the care that I takes of my customers that keeps 'em coming back."

Miriame stopped and took off her boots in the darkness. Behind her, she could feel Jean-Paul stop and do the same. Boots in hand, they tiptoed quietly on.

Nicole stopped at the first black curtain and twitched it aside for a moment before muttering to herself and passing on. The second curtain she passed without any comment, and the third also. The fourth she twitched back again, and then held the rushlight up and beckoned Miriame and Jean-Paul towards her, her finger to her lips. "Is this one your man?" she whispered.

Miriame stood close to the wall and peeped through the hole that had been placed strategically opposite the mattress in the bare chamber. At the sight of the couple entwined on the bed, she opened her eyes wider than she thought possible and gave a gasp of shock.

Nicole could not quite suppress a wheezy laugh as Miriame stepped back again and let the curtain fall. "A few strange ones around, aren't there?"

Miriame nodded, speechless. She hardly counted herself a prude, but still . . .

"Is he the one you want?"

"I don't know," she confessed. "I didn't get around to looking at his face." By heaven, her imagination would never have come up with that on its own.

All the same, her awareness of Jean-Paul was heightened as he gave a grunt of annoyance and stepped up to the curtain in his turn. His arm brushed against her breasts and she felt the tips of them tingle at his touch.

He didn't seem to notice the effect he had on her, or the way her breathing had quickened. He picked up one corner of the curtain gingerly and peeked through. His shoulders straightened and his neck suddenly went rigid. "Yes, that's one of them," he said with a look of disgust on his face as he dropped the curtain again.

Nicole padded along a few steps on her slippered feet and pulled back another curtain. Miriame and Jean-Paul followed, walking side by side in the narrow corridor, taking great pains not to touch each other.

Miriame peeked through where Nicole held back the curtain, a little more prepared in her mind for what she might see this time. "Ouch," she whispered with feeling once the curtain had gone down again. "I recognize that one. You'd think his legs would have given him pain enough without paying extra for a woman to whip him. If I'd known he actually *liked* being hurt, I would've gone more gently with him."

A couple of curtains later and the third of the party was also located, in an equally compromising position.

Miriame and Jean-Paul followed Nicole back down again to the kitchen. Nicole sat herself down in a large armchair in front of the fire. "So, you've found them," she said with satisfaction, wheezing from climbing up and down the stairs. "What are you going to do with them?"

Jean-Paul paced up and down, his brows knitted together in a frown. "How often do they come here?"

"Once a fortnight or so, I suppose, though not always all three of them at once like tonight. They're good enough customers on the whole, though the girls don't like 'em much, 'specially after that business with André."

His boots rang hollowly on the flagstones as he continued to stride up and down. "We can't afford to wait another fortnight or longer for them," he said at last. "We'll have to take them now. Tonight."

Miriame felt a familiar curl of excitement start to unfurl in the pit of her belly. By heaven, if she could not tumble Jean-Paul on the flagstones of the kitchen and make violent love to him as she wished, then a good fight was just what she could wish for instead. That would put all thoughts of Jean-Paul out of her mind, at least for the moment. When the excitement of the fight was over, that would be another matter . . .

She turned toward Nicole, excitement brimming in her body. "Do you mind if we take the three of them with us? We have some unfinished business to settle."

"You could do away with a dozen of my best customers and I'd not mind, seeing as André is dead and gone. What are you going to do with them?"

Jean-Paul was muttering to himself. He lifted his head to ask, "Do you have some strong rope?"

"As much as you need."

"Good," was all he said before he went back to his muttering.

A prickle of unease suddenly attacked Miriame. She didn't want innocents caught in their feud. "Will the girls not be alarmed if we burst in on them without warning?"

Nicole shook her head. "We'll get them one by one, quiet-like, so as not to startle the others. I'll go with you to take care of the girls. As long as I'm there, they'll know everything is fine."

"I'll go first," Miriame offered. "I'm the quietest. The men will never hear me coming until I have my dagger on their throats. Then you can come in behind me and tie them up." Indeed, in the fever of excitement she was in, she would find it easier to fight than to be silent.

Jean-Paul looked like he was ready to argue the point, but Nicole's enthusiastic agreement settled the matter.

Miriame didn't bother to take off her boots again before she climbed the stairs once more. She could move as silently as a cat, boots or no. Now that they had everything ready, she was eager for the action to start.

The chambers had no locks or bolts to contend with—

they didn't even have doors. Only a thin curtain was draped across each opening to give a modicum of privacy.

Miriame drew back the first curtain without a sound and stole quietly into the room.

The first of the men had finished his business with the whore and was lying, stark naked, on his back on the grubby mattress in the corner, his eyes closed and a blissful smile plastered on his thick-set face.

The smile turned to a look of abject fear when Miriame squatted by his ear and dug the point of the knife into his throat. His eyes sprang open and he made a choked noise. "Don't make a sound," Miriame advised him in a hissing whisper. "That might annoy me, and I'm unpredictable when I get annoyed."

The man's eyes bulged and he swallowed any noise he was going to make before it could come out of his mouth.

Miriame wrinkled her nose at the acrid smell of his sweat and beckoned the others in.

The girl by his side had huddled in the corner at the first sign of trouble, keeping out of the way of both of them. She seemed neither particularly curious nor particularly afraid at the interruption—just glad that whatever quarrel going on had nothing to do with her.

Miriame kept the knife at his throat while Jean-Paul hauled him roughly to his feet, hacked off a length of rope, and tied his hands behind his back. He gave the other end to Nicole. "We'll be back in a moment. Slit his throat if he makes a noise."

Nicole gave a wide grin that showed her cracked and missing teeth. "Be glad to. I haven't killed a man for all of five or six years. I'll get rusty if I don't keep my hand in."

The captive moaned.

Nicole tsked with disgust and gave the rope around his hands a sharp tug. "Quit that, you filthy bastard, or I'll put my knife to you."

The girl meanwhile had flung a wrap around her shoulders and was sidling out of the chamber. "Don't go yet, Kate," Nicole said. "Come here and hold the rope for me a minute. There'll be more before they're done."

The girl shrugged, but did as requested.

The second man was captured with almost as much ease. Jean-Paul hauled him into the first room and gave the rope to Nicole to hold. As an afterthought, Miriame tossed in the horsewhip she'd found there as well. She'd wager that a few flicks of the whip on their bare skin would be enough to keep them quiet if they started protesting.

Time for the third man—the first one she had spied on through the hidden holes in the walls. She swallowed as she pulled back the curtain, hoping they had given him enough time to finish what he had been doing.

They had not. She turned back to Jean-Paul. "We can't go in and get him now. They're still at it."

Jean-Paul grunted. "We haven't got all night. Sooner or later the other two will get restless. Nicole and the girl can't hold them there for much longer."

Miriame poked her head through the curtain. No, she couldn't do it. Jean-Paul would just have to go first. With all the noise their quarry was making, there was no need for silence anyway. It wouldn't matter if Jean-Paul stormed in wearing hobnailed boots. She held the curtain back and gestured him through. "After you."

He grinned at her as he passed. "Embarrassed? You?" he whispered. "I never thought I'd see the day."

Miriame made a rude gesture at his back. She didn't look again until the grunts and groans had been replaced first with a cry of horror and then a tense silence and some banging and shuffling as both parties righted themselves. Finally a low call of "All clear" came from Jean-Paul.

Even then she gave it another few moments before she dared to lift the curtain and stride in.

The man was sobbing gently as he crouched on the ground, his face gray with shock. The girl stood by looking mostly bored as she nimbly unbuckled the leather harness she wore around her waist and tossed it on to the ground in front of her.

Her face averted from his naked backside, Miriame bent over and tied the man's hands behind his back.

Jean-Paul picked the harness up off the floor and turned it over in his hands. "I've never seen one of these before," he remarked, with a grin in Miriame's direction. "Interesting. Very interesting."

"Costs double," said the girl, reaching to take it out of his hands again. "Wanna try it?"

Jean-Paul shook his head. "Thanks, but no." He flicked a couple of coins at the girl. "I'll be taking it with me, though."

Miriame made a strangled noise. "You what?"

Jean-Paul's grin grew wider as he slung the harness around the man's neck so that the phallus on it stuck up into his face. "It'll be a grand decoration for his night in the stocks."

The man started to whimper. "No, not the stocks. Anything but the stocks."

Jean-Paul tugged the rope. Their prey had to get to his feet and follow him out of the chamber, or be dragged out on his knees. "I don't recall giving you a choice in the matter."

As they reached the curtain to the chamber, the man started to whimper more loudly and pulled against the rope. "What have I ever done to you?"

What had he done? Miriame thought of the sight of Jean-Paul lying on the cobbles, bleeding to death on the street for the sake of a few pieces of paper he carried. She had no pity for scum who killed innocents and no patience, either. She gave him a swift kick in the backside to hurry him along.

He gave an anguished yelp as her boot made contact with his naked buttocks and shuffled out, tamed for the moment.

Nicole handed over the other two they had captured. "We're quits then, Dan?" she asked with a shrewd look in her eye. "You won't be wanting to kidnap any more of my customers, will you? These three will do for André."

Miriame spat in her hand and held it out to Nicole. "We're quits."

Nicole gave a broad grin, spat in her hand, and they sealed the bargain with a handshake. "It's not that I mind about these three, but if word gets out of what happened, it'll be bad for business."

"I won't say a word. And I doubt that these three"— she gave the ropes in her hand a quick jerk so that her captives stumbled—"will be in the mood for boasting, either."

The wind outside was cold for early spring and the cobbles wet from a light rain.

Miriame turned her collar up against the cold and hunched her shoulders in her jacket, feeling a certain amount of vicious satisfaction in the bad weather. Naked as they were, a night in the stocks would be no gentle punishment for these three.

They deserved death, for sure. After the punishment they were about to undergo, no doubt they would wish for death, but killing them was too easy. They deserved to suffer a little first.

The marketplace was only a few minutes' walk from the brothel. Their unwilling captives grew more and more truculent at every step that brought them closer to the shame of the stocks. Twice Miriame had to stop and tickle her man with a knife to his privates. The second time she grew impatient and drew a trickle of blood. Her captive's face went green and he soiled the cobbles in his fear. She had no trouble with him after that.

The stocks were set right in the middle of the market square. They loomed up out of the night, black, menacing shapes in the darkness.

Their subjects needed some not so gentle coaxing to put their heads and arms through the holes in the stocks that would keep them there once the irons were locked. Jean-Paul held them there by sheer strength and the point of his dagger, while Miriame slowly lowered the heavy block of wood that would imprison them until the morning came, then she locked the irons with a bolt. Eventually some petty official would want the stocks for some other malefactor, notice their plight, and set these three free.

The harness with the eternally erect phallus had fallen to the ground, shaken off by its owner as soon as he bent his head to put it into the stocks. Jean-Paul picked it up gingerly by a strap, and put it around his neck once more. "All of Paris will see what your favorite game is."

Miriame had to cover her mouth to stifle a derisive laugh. The early morning crowds in the marketplace would be merciless. He would never dare show his face again—not in the whole of Paris.

Jean-Paul looped the whip he had taken from the girl around the neck of the second man. "The good people of Paris may as well understand your favorite pastime also, my friend. That way your fellow will not be the only one held up to mockery."

Despite the cold air, the first man was sweating when Jean-Paul came to stand in front of him. Droplets of moisture fell in rivulets from his face and into the wood of the stocks, stained dark from the sweat and blood of countless others. "You're in luck today, my good man," Jean-Paul said in a conversational tone. "I don't have anything to hang around your neck today so the morning crowds can jeer at you. Of course if you are foolish enough for there to be a next time, you may not be so lucky . . ."

He tucked his dagger back into his belt and stepped back to admire his handiwork. "We should be safe enough now, wouldn't you say?"

Miriame shrugged. "I doubt they'll bother us again. And if they do," she deliberately raised her voice so the three men could hear her, "I'll cut their manhood off before I put them in the stocks next time." With that parting shot, she turned on her heel and began to walk away.

A chorus of protests greeted her departure. "You can't mean to leave me here all night."

"The crowds will crucify us!"

"I'll freeze to death before morning . . ."

"I'll kill you for this, you stinking bastard!"

"I'll give you anything you want to let me out. Anything at all."

"Name your price. I'll double it."

"Just you wait until I'm out of here, you poxy son of a whore. You'll regret this, I swear you will!"

"Don't leave me here . . ."

Their voices bullied, threatened, cajoled, and whined in equal measure.

Miriame looked up at the sky, whose edges were even now tinged with the pinkish gray of dawn. "Yes, we do mean to leave you here. Nothing on earth would induce me to let you out. Unfortunately for me, though fortunately for you, I suppose, I doubt that any of you will be crucified."

Jean-Paul got into the game with her as they walked

away from the square. "So, what do you think will happen to them, then? Rotten cabbages thrown at their heads?"

"Probably. Of course, they'll be luckier than they deserve if it's only rotten cabbages aimed at them, and not stones."

He creased his forehead in thought. "A slap on their naked buttocks with a dead fish?"

She laughed. "Highly likely. Fishwives aren't known for their subtlety."

"Crucifixion?" he asked hopefully.

She shook her head. "Too much effort for the crowd, I would wager. And a waste of good wood."

"Freezing to death?"

"No—it's not cold enough. Frostbite maybe, but nothing worse than that."

The desperate shouts of the men still carried through the still night air as the two of them walked away.

Miriame felt little triumph in their victory. The men were no more than the hirelings of a greater man, who used his brain and their brawn to bludgeon his opponents to death. Her quarrel was not so much with them as with their master. The cardinal would find other dupes for his purpose—though maybe not as easily as he might have done before the news of tonight's events spread through the underclass of Paris.

She felt a savage satisfaction that the square would not remain empty for long. As the first light of dawn erased the night, the early risers of the city—the fishwives, fruit sellers, flower girls and rag-pickers—would make their way through the brightening streets to the market square.

Let those three reap a taste of the misery they had sown in the jeers and catcalls of the crowd that would soon gather there. They would think twice before they next waylaid strangers in the street and tried to murder them for a handful of gold pieces.

Miriame suddenly felt weary unto death. She yawned and stumbled over an uneven cobblestone.

Jean-Paul caught her arm before she could fall. "Are you all right?"

She nodded. "Just tired, that's all." Now that she thought about it, she was so tired she could hardly walk another step. She concentrated on plodding along, one foot after another, not thinking about how far she had to go or how she was going to make it home. She wanted to fall to the ground and curl up where she lay.

Just as she felt she could not go on and was about to stop for a rest, she felt herself being lifted up by a pair of strong arms. "Put me down," she protested weakly.

Jean-Paul took no notice of her protests. "No."

"Where are you taking me?" She was almost too tired to care.

"Home to my bed."

She shook her head, even though she knew she did not have the strength to fight him. Her weeks of restless energy and her nights without sleep had finally caught up with her. "I don't want to go to bed with you."

"I don't recall giving you a choice in the matter." His voice was dry. She realized with a start that he was repeating word for word his earlier threats to the men they had just locked in the stocks.

"I won't fornicate with you," she warned. At least she hoped she wouldn't. She doubted that she had the strength to resist him if he really pushed the point.

"The thought hadn't even crossed my mind. Besides which, fornicating with you tonight would be about as exciting as fornicating with a corpse."

"I'm offended," she said, but his words had calmed her fears. She relaxed into his arms, no longer even trying to fight him.

By the time he reached his apartments, lugged her up

the stairs, and placed her gently on the bed, she was fast asleep.

Jean-Paul pulled off her boots and breeches, carefully averting his eyes from her stockinged legs. There was no point in getting all steamed up about nothing—Miriame was dead to the world for hours yet. She would probably sleep until doomsday if she could.

She muttered sleepily as he pulled off her jacket and rolled her between the blankets to keep her warm.

The fire had died down and the room was chilly in the light of early dawn. He eyed the sleeping form on his bed enviously and yawned. Chairs were not made for sleeping in, and his bed was plenty wide enough for two if they huddled close together.

He shrugged off his own outer clothes and crept in next to her, eagerly sharing the warmth of her body. God, but he had grown colder than he knew, sitting there in the icy room, as the warmth seeped out of him.

She had brought warmth to his soul as well as to his body. He hated to admit as much, even to himself. He had been lost and alone without her. With her, he felt as though he could conquer the world.

She was his friend, his companion, even his comrade. He desired her body as he had never desired another woman before. Not even Francine, with all her paint and perfume and whore's tricks, could hope to match the fire that he felt for Miriame.

Heaven help him, but he had fallen in love with the wench all over again. He lay there in the growing light, the thought running through his brain over and over again. He had fallen in love with Miriame.

She was a beggar and a thief—with one hand she had robbed him of all that he owned, while with the other she had saved his life—twice. Without question she was a beggar and a scoundrel, but she was more honest and loyal than Francine, for all her airs and graces, had proved to be. She had killed a man in a fight—the man who had tried to kill him.

She was not the woman in the velvet dress he had first thought she was—she was far, far more than that. She was more beautiful than an angel and as deadly as a viper. She was sweet and gentle and loving, and swift and brutal in her defense of the innocent. She would trade passionate blows with him one moment, and kiss him just as passionately the moment after. Through it all, she was the woman of his heart.

He did not want to love her. He did not want to love where he could not trust, but he could not help himself. Fate had played a cruel trick on him.

Her body was warm and soft. His arms crept around her almost of their own volition to keep her close to him. He did not want to love her, but he could at least find a measure of warmth and happiness in her embrace.

Miriame awoke to a luxurious feeling of warmth. Her bed felt softer than usual, and the blankets smelled different from hers. Not bad or wrong, just different. Nicely different.

She reached out an arm and touched a body, a warm body. She knew without even opening her eyes who it belonged to. The planes of his back, even through the rough linen of his shirt, were implanted in her memory. She knew every ridge and hollow of his shoulder blades. Her hands stroked up and down his back, reminding her of all that she had once possessed, that she had had to give away.

Realization of her danger struck almost at once. Her sleep-befuddled brain was awake and alert on the instant, and she threw off the blankets that covered her, grabbed her clothes from the floor, and dressed herself in a matter of seconds.

Thank heaven she had woken up in time. She was still clothed in all her linen so they could not have been fornicating—heaven save her from that. She could not afford to bear a child. She could not bring up a child to live on the streets, cold and hungry as she had been— such a life was no life at all. She would sooner throw herself in the river and be done with it all right away.

Jean-Paul would have to go. As long as she was in his company, she would be a prisoner of her own desire. The Devil would tempt her and tempt her and tempt her until sooner or later she would give in to his lures. She knew herself well enough to know the limits of her own strength. She laced her breeches and pulled on her boots as fast as her fingers could fumble. Better that she remove herself from temptation right away before the devil got the better of her.

"There's no need to look quite so panic-stricken, my dear."

Miriame peeked at Jean-Paul out of the corner of her eye as he leaned on one elbow to gaze at her frenzied dressing. She resented the description. "I am not panic-stricken. Just in a hurry."

"In a hurry for what?"

She could not confess that she wanted to get out of his company. She could not confess to her weakness for him, or he would use it to weaken her resolve. "To break my fast," she improvised. "I'm starving."

"Wait with me. We'll go together."

She couldn't think up any excuse not to wait so she waited, tapping her foot impatiently on the wooden floor as he drew his breeches over his firm thighs. She tried not to look at his half-naked body, but her eyes were drawn almost irresistibly to the sight of him.

He looked up from lacing his breeches and smirked at her when he caught her peeking at him.

She dropped her eyes to the ground and made sure they stayed there from then on.

They'd slept away a good part of the day. It was well past noon already and the evening shadows were starting to lengthen. The cook shop at the end of the street was doing a roaring trade, filled with shopkeepers and apprentices with shirt sleeves rolled up and aprons tied around their waists, tradesmen and journeymen lugging the tools of their trade, and peddlers with their heavy packs.

Jean-Paul handed over a handful of coins in exchange for a couple of meat pasties and tankards of small beer and they squeezed into a corner to eat them and drink.

A burly blacksmith with arms the size of a normal person's legs and hands as wide as trenchers elbowed her in the crush.

She glared at him as threateningly as she could. He took one look at her uniform and the long sword by her side, mumbled an apology and moved away.

Miriame bit into her meat pasty with satisfaction. She liked being a man and a soldier. No one looked down on her or treated her as dirt beneath their feet. As a soldier, she was the equal of anyone in France.

The meat pasty was good. She wolfed it down in no time at all and licked her fingers. Only when every crumb of pastry and every drop of gravy had disappeared did she sit back and wash it down with a swig of ale.

Jean-Paul was staring at her in amazement. She noticed with some embarrassment that he had hardly touched his pasty. He raised an eyebrow. "Do you always eat like that?"

She crossed her arms across her chest to ward off his criticism. "I told you I was hungry." She didn't know why she cared what he thought of her. Growing up on the street she hadn't acquired gentlemanly manners, far less ladylike ones. "Besides, where I came from, if you didn't swallow your food down quick, it would be stolen from your mouth as you were chewing it."

He took a massive bite of his own pasty. "Fair enough," he mumbled through the crumbs. "I'll make sure to watch my dinner while you're around."

She screwed her nose up and made a rude gesture at him. "I wouldn't touch your leavings. I earn my own bread now."

"You could have earned your own bread on the streets, too, doing what Nicole and her girls do. Instead, you were a virgin when we first met. You were a virgin until I took you to my bed."

She lifted her chin. "I am not ashamed of what I have done."

Jean-Paul shook his head slowly from side to side as he looked at her. "Why did you not take that path instead of turning soldier as you did?"

Miriame's defiance turned to disbelief. "You are suggesting I should have made my living on my back," she whispered, "whoring for whoever had two coppers in his pockets to rub together?" She banged her fist on the table, heedless of the eyes that turned her way at the ruckus. "Damn you, I should slit you from end to end for that insult."

He raised his hands in front of him. "I did not mean the question that way, believe me."

She stared at him, her fury still bubbling over in her mind. How could he think that whoring was more suitable for a woman than soldiering? Could he not imagine the desperation, the utter despair, a woman would feel before she opened her legs to a stranger and catered to his every filthy whim?

"Most women would have taken the easy way out—earned money in their sleep. You, alone out of so many, chose not to take that path."

No, she had never chosen the path of a whore, she never could. As afraid as she was of the hangman's noose, she would rather risk death every time she picked a pocket or lifted a length of cloth to sell. Anything, anything but whoring. Her soul would never have survived that.

She stood up and began to shoulder her way to the door through the crowds. The secret was not hers alone, but Rebecca would readily forgive her, she knew, for what she was about to divulge. "You ask me why I did not choose the life of a whore to fill my belly with bread? Come with me and I'll show you."

Chapter 10

She wasted no time, but strode through the darkening streets as fast as she could. Her old haunts were less than pleasant places to be when night fell, especially for those foolish enough to carry anything of value on them. She didn't want to have pulled herself out of the gutter only to be knifed in the end for the price of the fine linen shirt on her back.

She met Jean-Paul's questions and his attempts at conversation with silence. Idle chatter seemed sacrilegious at such a moment as this.

He soon understood that she was in no mood for talking, and walked beside her as quickly and quietly as she could wish for.

Miriame stopped outside a ramshackle church set in a plot overgrown with weeds. She had not been here for she didn't know how long—the grief and guilt of Rebecca's death was too much for her—but her feet still knew the way without being told where to go.

In the weeks she had been absent, the church had fallen into even more disrepair than ever. It was a far cry from the beautiful stone cathedrals, monuments to God created by kings and princes for the glory of their souls. The walls of this poor church were made of mud bricks and the roof thatched haphazardly with bundles of reeds lashed together with a thin rope.

She pushed open the door, hoping that the wall did not cave in at her touch. It looked as though the slightest breath of wind would topple it. "Let's see first if the priest is here." The priest had buried Rebecca in hallowed ground, and done his best to comfort Miriame in her sorrow at her sister's death.

The priest was indeed in. The rasping noise of his snores and the choking fumes of cheap Spanish wine hit them the moment they walked inside. He was lying on the muddy ground in front of the makeshift altar, his robes spread out around him in the mud and the ragged altar cloth pulled over him for a blanket, fast asleep.

Jean-Paul gave a start of surprise and disgust at the sight. A priest lying asleep in the house of his Lord in a drunken stupor, keeping himself warm with the altar cloth? His foot itched to kick the old man into wakefulness, and into a sense of his dereliction of duty, but Miriame did not seem to feel any such desire.

She merely shrugged and turned away again. "Father Jacques is in his usual state, I see. Drunk on communion wine. A pity. I would gladly have talked with him if I could."

He had been brought up to revere the cloth. Priests like this made a mockery of God and religion. He was a disgrace to the cloth he wore. "He's always like this?" said Jean-Paul.

"I don't think I've seen him sober twice in my life. No wonder, is it, with the misery he has to deal with in this parish. Come, let's go into the churchyard."

The fresh air outside was a blessing compared with the stench inside the building. He followed Miriame past the church and into the churchyard beyond.

A few gravestones stood here and there in the long

grass. Others, cracked and weather-beaten, lay on their sides, half hidden by the ivy that crawled over them, fastening rootlets on to everything in its path.

Miriame stopped in front of a small headstone in the corner. The inscription was simple. It was only a name. "Rebecca."

She stood in front of the gravestone in silence, her head bowed, her lips moving as if in prayer. At last she lifted her head and looked straight into Jean-Paul's eyes. "She was my sister."

He did not know what to say in the face of her grief. He felt helpless even to offer a word of comfort. "I am sorry for her death."

"She was my very best friend, the only friend I ever had," she went on, as if she had not heard his pitiful attempt to comfort her. "I loved her dearly, and she loved me, too. When our mother died, there were just the two of us. She was all I had left. I promised my mother on her deathbed that I would take care of Rebecca. I promised, but I could not keep my promise. I could not protect her, even though I tried my very best. I failed. She is dead because I failed her." A tear slid out from under her lowered eyelids and trickled down her face until she wiped it away absentmindedly with the back of her hand.

Jean-Paul watched the meandering path of that lonely tear in fascination. He was more shocked by the sight of it than anything else. Miriame had faced death without flinching, but the sight of her sister's grave had undone her composure. He reached one arm around her shoulders to comfort her, but her shoulders were as stiff and did not bend into his embrace. "How did she die?"

Her face was pale and set. "I killed a man not so long ago."

"So you told me. The man who knifed me in the street,

I believe. You also told me that he had deserved death many times over."

"He did. I would kill him a thousand times, though each time were to doom me to everlasting damnation in the hottest fires of hell. He murdered my sister. I killed the man who murdered Rebecca."

There was no need for her to feel guilt on that score. She had done the world a service by ridding it of a man who had murdered a defenseless girl, among many others. "He deserved no better. I would have killed him myself, if I could. I owe you my thanks."

She shrugged his arm off her shoulder. "I did not kill him for your sake," she snapped at him, her eyes flashing. "I killed him because of what he did to Rebecca."

He had never before seen her so dangerous. In a mood like this, she could easily kill someone again. "Tell me about your sister."

She calmed immediately. "Rebecca loved being a girl. She was sweet and dainty and pretty, with long, black ringlets that fell down to her waist. She never got dirty playing in the streets like I did." She smiled, her eyes soft at the memory. "I was always rushing around, as bad as any boy—climbing trees to steal apples, throwing stones at the miserly landlord who came to collect our rent every Friday, stealing nuts from the market stalls. How Rebecca would scold me when I came home with a pocket full of stolen nuts. But then she'd forgive me, and help me eat them all anyway, even though I'd stolen them. She would never stay angry at me for long."

He stroked her hair, giving her the comfort of his touch. "You must have loved her very dearly."

"I did. I did." She wiped away another tear as she looked at the gravestone in front of her. "For all the good it did her in the end."

He led her across to a low stone wall a few feet away

and sat with his back against it, taking her with him and holding her in his arms. She was cold and unresponsive to his touch. "You were not to blame for her death. You told me yourself that she was murdered by an evil man. That was none of your doing."

"When mother died, I took to wearing breeches. They were easier to run in, easier to climb walls in, easier to blend into the crowds in. I would be the man of the house, I decided, and take good care of Rebecca."

He leaned his head into hers, stroking her hair as one would do to calm a child. "How old were you when your mother died?"

She shrugged. "I don't really remember. Twelve, maybe, or thirteen, and Rebecca was a year younger than I. Luckily I was strong and wiry and underdeveloped for my age, so I had no trouble passing for a boy."

His heart ached for the child she had been then, left all alone in the world after her mother's death, save for a sister even younger than she. She had never had a proper childhood—Fate had robbed her of it too early. "You were left to look after your sister all by yourself? You had no family, no friends you could turn to?"

"There was no one. The landlord turned us out on the street before our mother's body was cold. He didn't want a couple of pauper brats left on his hands."

His heart shuddered in his breast with futile rage. How he would like to take that miserly landlord and squeeze his neck until his eyes popped out of his head. To turn two young girls out onto the streets? Such an act was little short of murder. "How did you survive?"

"We begged what we could. When we couldn't feed ourselves by begging, we started to steal." Miriame turned her hands over in her lap, looking at them as if they belonged to someone else, not to her. "My hands were nimble and quick enough from long practice, but Rebecca was no good at all. She was nearly caught a couple of times—we only just managed to get away.

"After that, I had to forbid her to steal, or she would get herself hanged, and me alongside her." She shuddered, her face gray with remembered agony. "I spent so many nights huddled against her side to keep warm, frightened of the hangman, terrified that he would put the noose over Rebecca's head and push her off the cart to dangle in the wind."

She had been only a child herself. Jean-Paul hugged her close to him, wanting to chase away her fears. "How did you manage then, when you forbade Rebecca to steal?"

She shrugged. "When we couldn't feed ourselves by stealing, we started to starve. That's when Rebecca decided that she was a burden to me, that she had to earn her keep the only way she could without putting herself in danger. She decided to become a . . . a whore." Her voice broke and she began to weep noiseless tears.

He stared at the battered gray tombstone half hidden in the long grasses. "But she was only a child."

"The madams were always on the lookout for new girls for their brothels." Her voice through her tears was bitter. "Young ones, especially if they were virgins and guaranteed to be free from disease, fetched a good price from the customers. Some of them believe they can cure the pox by fornicating with a virgin." She snorted an angry laugh that sounded more like a curse than anything else. "If they'd kept their pricks inside their breeches to start with, they wouldn't have the pox at all."

He shifted uneasily on the hard ground, remembering with a sense of guilt how he and his brother had treated the subject as a joke, laughing about which local virgin they would like to ravish if they were ever afflicted with the pox themselves.

She did not seem to notice his discomfort. "One of the madams befriended Rebecca when I was out thieving scraps for our dinner," she continued. "My luck had been bad for some days, and we were ravenous. I walked the streets, light-headed from hunger, hardly even knowing whether what I was seeing in front of me was real or whether my brain was playing tricks on me.

"But I was in luck that day. I managed to make off with a quarter wheel of cheese from a market stall, and then out the back of the boulangerie, I found three stale rolls. They were as hard as rock, but I knew that if we soaked them in a bit of water, we'd be able to eat them right enough. They'd fill a hole in our bellies, anyway."

She had been so hungry she had been glad to find some refuse to eat? His grip on her tightened. No wonder she had robbed him while he lay wounded. His imminent death must have seemed like a godsend to her starving self.

"I rushed back to where I had left Rebecca that morning still sleeping under the bridge that we now called our home. She wasn't there. One of the others told me she'd gone off with Fat Adèle, the madam from the brothel on the corner. I'd told her not to go. I'd told her that I'd get enough food for the two of us, that she just needed to trust me, but she'd gone anyway.

"I ran off after her, terrified to think of what I would find, but I was too late." She put her head in her hands and her shoulders heaved with dry sobs. "The bastard had already gotten to her."

He held her in his arms as tightly as he could, forcing her to take some comfort from him. "You don't have to tell me any more."

She shook her head and carried on regardless. "Rebecca had been determined, Fat Adèle told me when I screamed at her until I was hoarse, but scared, too.

When Adèle had cleaned her up a bit to get the grime of the streets off her and sent the first scumbag with money in his pockets in to deflower her, poor Rebecca had lost her nerve. The customer had not taken no for an answer. He had knifed her to stop her struggles, and then raped her while she lay dying. I came too late to save her. She died in my arms."

Her shoulders shook with sobs. He kept a lid on his own rage and anger to stroke her soothingly. "And the man who had killed her? Was he not taken up by the watch and delivered to justice for killing an innocent young girl?"

She gave a bitter laugh through her tears. "Who cares aught for the life of a young whore? He walked away from her body with nothing but my hatred as payment for her death."

He stared at the headstone marking where the body of young Rebecca lay, killed on the vicious whim of a stranger. "He paid the price in the end."

Her shaking was growing less now. "Yes. I slit his throat as easily as he slit hers. I thank God every waking moment that his blood is on my hands. I have taken a life for a life. But nothing will ever bring Rebecca back to me."

How could Miriame blame herself? She had been a child, nothing more. "She chose her own path in life, as you chose yours, and God saw fit to take her. You cannot blame yourself for that."

"Few women willingly become whores. They do it out of desperation, out of despair, out of hunger and cold. If I had been a better thief, Rebecca would live yet. I failed her."

He grimaced as he looked down at the boots she wore. His boots. She had managed to steal the very boots from his feet, yet she considered herself a poor thief. "If you had been a better thief, not even the King's jewels, though they were locked up in the palace and surrounded by armed guards, would have been safe."

"There's many a day I would have traded in all the King's jewels for a loaf of bread and a dry blanket. We were always cold, so cold . . ."

Indeed, her skin was ice-cold to the touch as she leaned into him. "Rebecca is in her grave now, and through no fault of your own. You looked after her as well as you could while she was alive, though you were both mere children. You risked your life every day to feed you both. She risked her life one time too many, and Fate took her away from you."

"Fate had nothing to do with her death. André did." Her voice was tired, as if she no longer had the energy to carry her hatred and bitterness around with her.

"You have avenged her death on the man who killed her. Put all that behind you now, Miriame, my love, and do not grieve for her any longer. She lives with God now in heaven. She would want you to be happy."

"You are right. She has gone to a better place where she will never be cold or hungry or scared again. It is time for me to say my final adieus to her." She shook off Jean-Paul's embrace, knelt down in front of the grave-stone and kissed it reverently. "May God be with you, Rebecca, on your soul's final journey," she whispered, as if the stone had ears to hear her with. "Keep watch over me, still wandering here on earth until my time comes to join you. We shall meet again in heaven, I swear. I shall try not to miss you too much until then."

When she stood up again and brushed the dirt from her knees, her face was pale and composed for all that it was wet with tears. She seemed to stand taller and straighter, too, as if a heavy burden had been finally removed from her shoulders.

The graveyard was silent and cold in the stillness of

early evening. He took her by the hand as she stood there saying her final, silent adieu. For once she did not object, despite being dressed as a musketeer.

Hand in hand they walked out of the churchyard into the gathering gloom. Miriame kept hold of his hand as if it were her lifeline. He laughed to himself to think of the sight they must present to strangers on the street— two soldiers walking hand in hand along the street, for all the world like a pair of lovers.

He did not let go her hand. Let the world think of them what it may, he loved Miriame and he would fight for her with every last drop of blood in his body.

Only when a passerby looked at them, blinked, then spat at them as they passed, did she come to herself and snatch her hand away from his as if his touch pained her.

"So, to Francine's?" she said, not quite back to her old light-hearted self. "We should deliver the letters while the cardinal's minions are still recovering from last night's jaunt."

He could not help but smile at the thought. "Do you think they ever will?"

She grinned widely, her tears buried deep within her once more where no one would ever guess at them. "I will never forget the sight of their naked buttocks sticking out behind them as they stood in the stocks. If I live to one hundred, I will never see a more ridiculous sight."

At least a couple of villains had gotten what they deserved. "I doubt we will have any trouble from the cardinal for some time. It's a pity we cannot serve him as we served the men he paid to kill us both."

They walked along in silence for a few steps. "Mayhap we cannot put him naked in the stocks," she said, scuffing the toes of her boots against the cobbles as she walked. "But I think I can see a way in which we can make him look just as ridiculous in the eyes of the King as those poor fools looked to the folk in the marketplace."

If anyone could think up a way of getting even with her enemies, he would lay a wager it would be Miriame. "How?"

She hesitated before she spoke again. "We would risk making an enemy of Madame de Montespan."

He shrugged. "Does that matter?"

"Not to me."

"Then let's hear this plan of yours. I would sleep easier in my bed if I thought the cardinal could be made to pay for his sins in the same manner as his men."

Jean-Paul swept the hat from his head and bowed low, trying to keep the trepidation he felt from showing on his face. His stomach felt as though he had a whole swarm of horseflies in it, buzzing around in their eagerness to get out. By the end of the night, the cardinal would be his deadly enemy. He only hoped that by the end of the night, the cardinal would no longer have the power to wreak any vengeance on him. He hid his thoughts the best he could as he straightened up again. "Your Excellency."

The cardinal gazed steadily at him, not the slightest wrinkle of emotion showing on his weathered face. "What do you want with me?" His voice was as cold as the winter wind that whipped over the icy mountains and blasted the plains below.

Jean-Paul hoped that this was the cardinal's usual demeanor, not the one reserved specially for those he knew were about to betray him. "I hear you have no great love for the Marquise de Montespan."

The cardinal examined his fingernails with an abstracted air. "Whoever told you so is mistaken," he said, his voice not changing in the slightest. "The marquise and I understand each other perfectly."

So perfectly that the cardinal was willing to murder innocent men to ruin her. He bowed again. If the cardinal would not admit his dislike of Francine openly, he would have to call his bluff. "Then I can only apologize for my intrusion and bid you goodnight."

The cardinal looked up from his fingernails. "There's no need to be so hasty," he said, as if he were conferring a gracious favor on Jean-Paul out of the goodness of his heart, and not in the least anxious to hear what he had to say. "Come tell me what is bothering you and I will do all in my power to help you."

Jean-Paul breathed a sigh of relief that the cardinal had not simply sent him on his way without hearing him out. Their plan depended on his talking to the cardinal and convincing him of his sincerity. "I know a few tales about the marquise," he said craftily, "which I thought might be worth something to the right person."

"Tales about the marquise?" The cardinal shrugged. "Any poor fool can make up a tale. Such tales are not worth the breath used to tell them."

"Even if the tale is true?"

"True? False? What does it matter? A tale is still only a tale."

"Even if the tale can be proven?"

The cardinal's eyes gleamed with a spark of interest which he quickly hid behind half-closed lids. "Proof would be another matter. Depending, of course, on what was to be proven."

Jean-Paul paused for just the right amount of time, until the air in the chamber grew heavy with expectation. "The marquise has a new lover," he said at last, into the waiting silence.

The cardinal sat back again, disappointed with the

news. "So it is often rumored. I pay no heed to such rumors myself. She is too canny a woman to risk the affections of the King on a mere whim." He ran the palm of his hand over his wispy beard in a thoughtful manner. "Even were your tale to be true, she is as slippery as an eel. Catching her in the act would be no easy matter."

"I know who her new lover is. I know where they meet, and when."

The cardinal grew suddenly still with suspicion. "Why are you telling me this?" he asked. His voice was light, as if the answer was of no moment, but his face was watchful.

"I was her lover once."

The cardinal dismissed his claim with a wave of his hand. "Pshaw. Any fool can claim as much. Have you any proof of what you say?"

"We became lovers when she was banished to the South of France. I fell in love with her, and I thought she loved me in return. The King recalled her to court and I followed her soon after, thinking she would be as glad to see me as I was to see her."

The cardinal's face wrinkled awkwardly into a rusty smile, brimming with malice. "And when you arrived you found out how mistaken you were?"

"I came to see her at her levee. She disclaimed all knowledge of me, dismissed me as though I were a bad-mannered puppy. She shamed me in front of the whole court."

"Ah, so you are the man who tried to make love to her in public, the man she swore she'd never seen in her life before." He gave a wheezy chuckle. "Anyone could see you were a newcomer to Paris, expecting a highborn courtesan like the marquise to take notice of you in public. You were lucky she did not have you whipped."

Jean-Paul shrugged. "Men in love often do foolish things."

"Jean-Paul Metin, are you not?"

Jean-Paul nodded.

"I have heard of you." The cardinal paced up and down the room, his red robes swishing to and fro. "Did the marquise not write you some letters? Letters that she might not want the King to know about?"

He shrugged again. "She did write me some affectionate letters, true, but they were stolen from me weeks ago when I first came to Paris. It saved me from the trouble of burning them, I suppose. I would not want to keep any remembrances from such a whore as she."

The cardinal's pacing came to an abrupt halt. "Who took them?"

"Common thieves and cutthroats from the gutter, I suppose. I was lucky to get away with my life."

"Interesting." The cardinal did not look interested so much as he looked murderous. "Very interesting."

Jean-Paul had to fight to keep his grin suppressed. Without even planning to, he had dropped the men who had tried to kill him in even more trouble. A night naked in the stocks would be as a fleabite to the punishment that the cardinal would hand out to them, if the look on his face was anything to go by. "The marquise shamed me," he said, returning to the point of his visit. "I am a soldier and a musketeer. No woman should treat me so shabbily."

"So now you want revenge." The cardinal nodded as if he could well understand Jean-Paul's motives now. "You want revenge on both her and her new lover."

"She cast me off as if I were of no account. I would have given my life for her and she treated me with nothing but contempt. She is a worthless, faithless woman, and deserves to be punished for her fickleness."

"She is a whore at heart," the cardinal agreed, "as all women are. Tell me, when will she next meet with her new love?"

"He will be there tonight."

"Tonight? So soon? How do you know?"

Jean-Paul drew his dagger and tossed it spinning into the air. "I intercepted the messenger," he said with a grin, as he caught the glittering blade by its handle and tucked it back into his belt again. "He talked fast enough with my blade held at his throat."

The cardinal had drawn back a few paces at the sight of the blade. "Who is he then, this new lover of the marquise?"

Jean-Paul shrugged. "He's a musketeer in the King's Guard like myself. Scarcely more than a boy—I doubt if he is even old enough to shave his chin yet—and slightly built. Long, black hair that he keeps tied at the nape of his neck, and a crafty, malicious face. As quick on his feet as a deer—not a comrade I would trust to fight by my side in battle." He gave a snort of disgust. "I dare say he and the marquise deserve one another."

"It seems she has a penchant for uniforms." The cardinal went to his desk and drew out a heavy-looking purse. He handed it to Jean-Paul. "Your news has pleased me well. Take this for your pains."

Jean-Paul hesitated, his hands held firmly behind his back. "I did not tell you for the sake of a reward. I told you for the sake of my revenge."

"I know you had no thought of a reward for your information. It was freely given, and received with gratitude." The cardinal pressed the bag into his hands so he could not refuse to take it. "In my eyes that makes you even more deserving of a reward than one who thinks only of his fee."

Jean-Paul left the cardinal's luxuriously appointed apartments and sauntered back to his chamber, the bag of *pistoles* giving his pocket an unaccustomed weight. He could not wait to see Miriame again. How she would appreciate such a grand jest. The Cardinal had paid him royally for the news he had brought him. Little did the prelate know just how royally he was about to be cozened in return.

Miriame kept a wary eye out for spies as she knocked on the door at the western gate. A figure moved in the shadows to one side of her and her whole body tensed, her hand moving to the dagger at her side. She could feel a stranger's eyes on her, watching and waiting. The very air smelled of tenseness and danger.

The maidservant Berthe opened the door and Miriame scuttled past her, glad to be inside. Any attack on her now would come face on in the light, and not at her back in the dark. If Jean-Paul Metin had delivered his message to the cardinal, no doubt she would be left to enter the marquise's chamber undisturbed. *If* he had delivered his message, and *if* the cardinal had taken the bait . . . There were too many ifs for her to feel quite comfortable.

The figure behind her had already melted away into the shadows again. One of the cardinal's spies, she was sure of it. No thief would dare to ply his trade so close to the royal walls, and no one else would be lurking in the streets at such an hour. How she hoped that Jean-Paul had carried out his mission well and primed their target ready to strike.

The corridors were equally quiet as she and Berthe padded their way along, but their very silence made the hairs on the back of her neck stand up. Not even the merest rustle of clothes or a creaking of hinges disturbed her ears. That in itself was eerie. Berthe plodded along as stolidly as ever, not seeming to notice the sense of danger hovering in the air. Miriame followed her, every sense on the alert.

The cardinal must have well-trained spies on his pay-roll who knew how to observe their prey without making a sound, but Miriame could still feel the weight of their eyes on her. Not until she had reached the marquise's chamber and Berthe had shut the door behind her did she lose the feeling of being watched.

A fire burned merrily in the grate. Miriame strode over to it and stood with her back to the flames. If the cardinal had taken the bait that Jean-Paul had offered him on a platter, it would not be long before a much larger conflagration than this simple fire broke out. She crossed herself nervously, praying that both she and Jean-Paul would avoid getting singed.

Madame de Montespan did not keep her waiting for long. She barely had time to collect herself before the marquise was upon her with a flourish of perfume and curtsies.

"My dear Jean-Paul," she cried, sweeping gracefully up to Miriame and taking her hands in her own. "How have you been keeping these long weeks?"

Miriame extracted her hands, swept her hat off her head, and made a low bow. "Very well, I thank you, Madame." She was too much on edge to be overly eloquent.

The marquise pouted and batted her eyelashes. "I thought we were friends, you and I, but you have neglected me most shamefully these past weeks."

"I have had much to keep me busy. As have you, Madame, or so I have heard."

Her fan fluttered swiftly about her face. "You are talking of the King, I suppose?"

"Of course. Who else would I give up the pleasure of your company for without so much as a murmur of complaint?"

She gave a delighted laugh. "Yes, dear Louis has been

paying me far too much attention of late. He is so fond that it positively bores me. I am so glad that I have a few friends that I can call on to entertain me when I simply have to escape his company before I scream."

Miriame took the proffered hand and raised it to her lips. "I am at your service, as always, Marquise."

Madame de Montespan pressed Miriame's hand with her own and pulled her over to the sofa. "Come sit beside me and entertain me," she simpered, showing as many white teeth as she could possibly display at one time. "The King has been boring me silly all day with talk of his tedious hunting parties. I am positively dying for the company of a real man."

Miriame grinned as she sat down beside her. The marquise would just have to keep on dying for a real man for a while longer. "I would be pleased to do so."

Francine leaned back into the corner of the sofa and closed her eyes. "The life of a courtier is so hectic," she said, throwing her arms behind her head and thrusting out her breasts with a theatrical yawn. "I am sure being at court is turning me into an old woman. I can feel the wrinkles forming on my face and my hair turning gray with worry as I just sit here at my ease. I am getting so old."

Miriame looked idly at the woman's pearly-white complexion. She could wish for herself such clear, white skin tinged with pink. Francine was as unwrinkled as a young girl. "I hardly think you have anything to worry about."

Her voice came out as sarcastic rather than flattering, as she had intended. Francine pouted.

"I mean, you are still so young. You can hardly be more than fifteen, I swear."

"Indeed, I am older than you suspect," she said, her pout vanishing and a smile returning to her red-painted lips at this arrant flattery. "And I am sure I have a wrinkle forming on my forehead, and another one right here, by the corner of my eye," Francine said, half opening her eyes again and gazing at her from under her eyelashes.

Do I hear a noise from the far side of the door? Miriame couldn't be entirely sure, but she thought she heard the sound of muffled footsteps, the noise of heavy men unused to softening their tread. "I cannot see a thing," she answered, all her attention on her ears.

Francine gave her hand a gentle tug. "You cannot see anything from that great distance. Come a little closer. I'm sure I have a wrinkle there." She was leaning right back into the corner of the sofa, her skirts showing more than a little of her ankles, her breasts just about bursting out of the low-cut bodice that barely covered them.

For Miriame to get any closer to look at these phantom wrinkles, she would have to be half lying on top of her. No doubt that was Francine's intention all along.

She definitely heard noises now, the sound of a door quietly being unlocked and pushed open. She did not so much as turn her head to look at the intruders as she leaned over Francine. "We have visitors, it seems," she hissed in the marquise's ear.

Francine's eyes grew wide and her face paled under her layers of rouge. "Who?" she croaked in a tiny voice.

"Hold your tongue and follow my lead if you want to get out of this unscathed," Miriame whispered in a tone that brooked no dissent. "Do you understand?"

Looking as if she was going to be ill, Francine gave the tiniest of nods.

"No, Madame," Miriame continued in a loud voice. "Not the smallest wrinkle that I can see—"

She was not able to finish her sentence. "The cardinal spoke true, we see," came the cry from the door. "You are a vile fornicator, committing indecencies with our own guards while our back is turned."

Miriame sat back on the sofa and turned to face the speaker. Jean-Paul had primed their target well. The cardinal in his red robes of office was there, an unholy glee on his wrinkled face. With him was King Louis himself, his royal robe draped over his bony shoulders and his royal face purple with rage.

Miriame rose to her feet and squeaked in a high voice. "Your Majesty," before sinking to her knees in a rather awkward curtsy.

The King ignored her, focusing all his rage on the marquise. "What is the meaning of this?" he thundered. "What is this young pipsqueak of a soldier doing in your chambers with you, alone and at night?"

Francine's face had gone a sickly shade of green that no rouge could hide. "We m-meant no harm by it."

"No harm? You call cuckolding your King meaning no harm?" The King's eyes looked close to popping out of his royal head in his royal rage. "We would rather call it treason."

Miriame giggled, the sound loud in the quiet that followed the King's furious outburst.

Finally he noticed her and turned his rage on her. "Do you think it a small matter to cuckold your King? The hot blood of your youth will not protect you from the wrath of the mightiest King in Europe, the Sun King himself!" he thundered, in a voice that threatened an evil death to anyone who crossed him. "You will be tossed into a dungeon until your once hot blood is frozen in your veins."

Miriame gave another giggle, though her stomach was churning inside. She hoped the King's anger would not last, but vanish as quickly as it had been summoned. "You think I am a man?" she squeaked, in the most girlish voice she could muster. "You really think I am a man?"

The King looked confused for a moment. "You are not a man, you are a boy," he replied at last. "But boy or not, you will not live to boast of your misdeeds with our chosen mistress."

"Oh, a boy is good enough," Miriame giggled, bouncing up and down on the sofa as if she found the jest too amusing to let her sit still. "Come now, Francine, you must pay me now. Fifty gold *pistoles* we bet that I could not pass myself off as a man and have anyone believe me. I think you should pay me a hundred *pistoles* at least, for my disguise has fooled the King himself."

The King looked momentarily confused. "What do you mean? You are not a boy? What devilry is this?"

He winced as she giggled again and clapped her hands in a transport of delight. "Oh, Francine, I am sure I should demand one hundred *pistoles* at least."

The cardinal's face was growing as red as his robes. "Enough of this tomfoolery," he barked. "Anyone can see the boy is pretending to escape the punishment that he and his whore richly deserve. Just look at his breeches. Whenever did you see a girl who looked like that?"

Miriame gave another giggle. "Oooh, yes, that was a good trick, wasn't it?" She reached one hand down into her breeches and unpinned the pair of rolled-up stockings she kept there and waved them about. "I knew no one would suspect me of being a girl if I looked like a man down there."

She pulled off the leather thong that kept her hair tied back and shook her curls over her face to emphasize the femininity of her face, taking the opportunity to look at each of them in turn.

Francine sat on the sofa, her mouth agape, looking as if she had just been delivered from the Devil himself and couldn't quite believe her good luck. Her painted face, now back to its usual pink-and-white, was the very picture of astonishment and disbelief.

The King's rage was dying down, slowly replaced by obvious bewilderment. Confusion and affronted dignity warred in his sallow face, but it looked at least as though the dungeon would be forgotten for the moment.

The cardinal was a red as a turkey cock, his Adam's apple bobbing up and down as he swallowed convulsively. "Pah, what does that prove?" he spat, as Miriame dropped the stockings at her feet. "Any boy could do as much."

"One hundred and fifty for sure, for fooling the King and the cardinal together," Miriame crowed. "I never dreamed my disguise would work half so well as that."

She shook off her jacket and unbuttoned her shirt enough to show off her naked breasts that she had left unbound specially for the occasion. Underwhelming as they might be, they were unmistakably those of a woman. She shook them at the cardinal, who had turned an unbecoming shade of puce. "Will that convince you, Monsieur Cardinal, that I am a woman in earnest, or would you have me disrobe from head to toe?"

"A woman," Francine breathed in a tiny whisper, her cheeks flushed. "You were a woman all along."

The King peered shortsightedly at Miriame's breasts. "A woman indeed, and a fine one at that. Who ever would have thought it? Indeed, Francine, you should pay your little friend what you have promised her. She fooled even the King of France with her disguise. There are few living today who can boast of so much."

"It cannot be a woman," the cardinal thundered. "This . . . this thing, be it man or woman, I know not, is the marquise's lover."

"My lover?" Francine stood up, her back straight, her composure now completely returned. "What nonsense is this? How dare you accuse me of unnatural acts with another woman?"

The King was equally unimpressed with the cardinal's claim. "Francine is our mistress and we are fond of her," he proclaimed sternly. "It is not your place to question the authority of your King. You displease us with your wild talk. May we suggest that you absent yourself from our presence until you have come to a better understanding of the good sense and discretion we require in our servants." He shook his head. "Pah, shame on you to be tricked by a girl in man's dress and to drag your King out on such a fool's errand as this."

The cardinal's face grew gray as he realized the enormity of his mistake. He had played for high stakes, and he had lost. "But, sire—" There was a quiver in his cold voice that took Miriame quite by surprise. It was time for him to pay the forfeit for his failure.

Francine had recovered enough from her surprise to revel in the downfall of her biggest rival. She shot the cardinal a malicious smile as he tried to stammer out a belated apology.

The King was not in a forgiving mood. "On second thoughts, may we suggest that you absent yourself not only from us, but also from Paris, until we choose to forgive you." He waved the man away with a flick of his wrist. "Begone with you! Go off to some country monastery—somewhere where you cannot bother us with your foolishness. You have displeased us greatly this night."

Miriame heaved a sigh of relief that all the King's anger at his affronted dignity had fallen on the cardinal's head and not on her own. Royalty made her nervous. It was too easy for them to ruin, even kill, a man with a click of their fingers.

The cardinal gathered his robes around him, bowed

to the King, and backed out of the chamber. The glance that he directed at Francine as he left was so poisonous that Miriame expected to see her keel over where she stood.

Francine was unmoved by the venom her defeated rival shot her way. "The serpent has lost its fangs," she whispered into Miriame's ear. "By heaven, that is worth one hundred and fifty gold *pistoles* to me to witness such a sight."

"Come, pay the pretty wench what you owe her," the King said, making his way over to the door, "and send her on her way again. We have had enough tomfoolery for one night and we would speak with you further this evening."

Francine beckoned Miriame over to a cabinet in the corner of the room. "I will forgive you for tricking me, you man-woman," she said, as soon as the door shut behind the King. She used a small silver key on a chain around her neck and unlocked one of the drawers. "Even though you delighted in making a fool out of me."

"No one knows that but you and me," Miriame reminded her, "while the cardinal will have the whole court to bear witness against him."

"I shall be sure to spread the news myself." Francine laughed out loud with the joy of her triumph. "The look on his face was priceless. Just as he thought he was about to dispose of me forever, just as I thought he was about to succeed, you snatched victory from his hands. Masterfully done, Mademoiselle Dardagny, masterfully done."

"Why, thank you, Madame Marquise. I am much practiced at the art of pretending to be a man."

Francine's curiosity made her eyes sparkle. "You did not don that disguise just to fool me?" she asked. "Do you really live like that all the time?"

Miriame nodded.

"But why?" the marquise asked avidly. "Surely there are other things you could do, other ways of earning a crust?"

"Walking the streets?" Miriame asked with distaste.

Francine shook her head. "You could always find yourself a rich man, as I have done." She gave an evil smile. "None dare call me whore—at least not to my face."

"Why do you whore for the King?" Miriame asked idly in her turn. "Surely you do not need to earn your bread on your back?"

Francine was not offended by the question, though Miriame had expected her to be. "For the glamour, I suppose," she said, her head on one side. "And for the excitement. And the danger. Definitely the danger."

"For the excitement and the danger?" Miriame shrugged. "You would make a good soldier, I imagine, if you were ever to tire of the King. Or he of you."

Francine shook her yellow curls. "I do not think so. I would not know what to do with a sword. My battles are fought with words and glances." She turned her attention back to the cabinet. "Come, let me give you your due, and then you must be gone, Mademoiselle Chevalier. The King is expecting me in his chambers." She made a face. "And if I have learned one lesson in life, it is that a monarch does not brook disappointment easily."

Miriame reached into her pocket and drew out a packet of letters. "Before I go, I believe you were wanting these?"

Francine's eyes grew wide as she saw what lay in Miriame's hands. "My letters," she exclaimed in a low tone. "However did you get them?"

Miriame grinned. "Never mind that." There was no time to go into the story right now, even if she wanted to. "I believe you were looking for them?"

Francine took hold of them gingerly and riffled through the pages. "They are all there?"

"Every last one of them. I like the cardinal no more than you do."

Francine clutched the papers to her bosom as she made her way over to the fire. "I forgive you a thousand times over for making a fool out of me." One by one, she fed the letters to the fire, watching each one as it briefly flared up in flames and was reduced to ashes. When all the paper was gone, she stirred the fire with the poker that lay on the hearth, to make sure that not a single scrap of half-burned paper remained.

When all the letters were disposed of to her satisfaction, she dusted her hands off briskly. "God help me, but I will be more careful next time. Never again will I leave such evidence lying around for the cardinal's spies to find."

"You would be better not to run the risk in the first place."

Francine grinned—the first smile of hers that Miriame had seen without any artifice in it. "But without the danger in life, where would the pleasure of living be?"

She had a point—Miriame conceded with a shrug.

"I knew you would understand me," Francine went on. "What else but the love of adventure would make you turn musketeer?" She gave a low laugh, returned to her cabinet and began counting out a pile of gold *pistoles* into a large leather pouch. "No wonder I found you so attractive. You and I are kindred spirits. We would not be happy with a tame life of dullness such as most women lead."

"True enough." Miriame swallowed hard. Now that the time to ask her question had come, her throat was so dry she could hardly croak it out. "But tell me, how do you manage to keep your shape so well?"

Francine gave a puzzled frown. "Corsets, of course. I have borne children. The King's, of course."

Miriame could feel her ears grow hot, but she had to explain what she meant. Just the merest thought of Jean-Paul's hands on her body, teasing her and pleasing her, taking her to heights she had never before dreamed of, and she screwed up her courage to explain. "I know—ah—that you are not a virgin, but you are not always pregnant, either. How do you manage it? Do you have a secret charm to keep the babes out of your belly?" What wouldn't she give to possess the charm for herself, to be able to lie with Jean-Paul without fear of ruin.

Francine looked sideways at her. "I see you have the heart of a woman underneath your manly uniform, Mademoiselle Chevalier. No wonder I could make no impression on it, try as I would. I gather you have a practical interest in the answer?"

"I have been lucky once," Miriame admitted with a blush that set her face on fire. "I would not care to trust my luck too often."

Francine laughed. "It never pays to dice with Fate. She has a warped sense of humor and in one foolish moment you will find yourself with exactly what you wished above all to avoid." She left the pile of *pistoles* she was counting for a moment and rummaged around in her cabinet, finally emerging with a small cloth bag which she handed to Miriame. "Soak these in vinegar. Place them inside you beforehand and, God willing, you will not conceive."

Miriame peeked inside the bag, which turned out to be filled with sponges. Plain sea sponges as one could buy from any market stall. She picked one out and held it up to the light. There didn't seem to be anything special about it. Was it really as easy as that? No special prayers to be said every night and morn? No herbs to be picked in midwinter and eaten during a full moon? "Sponges soaked in vinegar? That really works?"

"It has so far for me." Francine made the sign of the cross on her chest. "God willing that it works for a while longer. I shall never keep the King if I am big with child all the time. Louise de la Valliere, the poor silly girl, bore him half a dozen children, and he quickly tired of her when her figure became fat and bloated and her face red and blotched as any common fishwife's. I cannot be always *enceinte*."

She finished counting out the *pistoles*. She rummaged around in her cabinet, found a piece of parchment, and tucked it into the bag along with the gold pieces. "A token of my gratitude for the letters," she said with a smile at Miriame's querying look. "My luck is riding high for now. You may as well have a share in it. I have no doubt I will be able to wheedle twice that out of the King tonight, now that the cardinal has been sent away to a distant monastery."

Miriame took the pouch and tucked it into her jacket, along with the bag of sponges. "I meant no harm to come of my deception . . ." She let her voice slide off into nothingness, wondering how to explain what she really felt without rudeness.

Francine understood her only too well. "But the lure of the gifts I gave you was too much for you to resist?" she suggested with a twinkle in her eye.

Miriame nodded, slightly ashamed for the first time of her greed. "I was so poor."

"You don't need to explain." Francine looked slightly shamefaced herself. "They were given with that intention. I meant them as lures to hook you with." She sighed. "It is such a pity you are not a man after all. You told the most absurd stories of your exploits in battle that I have ever heard. They made me laugh for days afterward."

Miriame gave an affronted harrumph as she made her way to the door. "Here I was doing my best to impress the Marquise de Montespan, and she was laughing at me behind my back? I swear, that is the last time I try to make eyes at a woman."

The Marquise laughed. "Fare thee well, Mademoiselle Chevalier. You have done me a service tonight that I will not soon forget. Take care of yourself and remember, I may have an excellent memory for those who do me evil, but an even better one for those who do me a good turn. I will not forget you."

Miriame doffed her hat for the last time. "Adieu, Madame Marquise. May you find the dangerous joy you are seeking and live happy."

Chapter 11

Jean-Paul was waiting for her outside. He rushed up to her as soon as she appeared through the doorway. "Miriame," he said, taking her shoulders in his hands. "All is well with you?"

She felt her heart constrict at the sight of the worry on his face. She had been so foolish to give him an entrance into her heart. She had thought she could displace him again when she pleased, but he was so firmly entrenched there now that to root him up again would take all the courage and strength of will that she possessed—and more. "Yes," she said, as lightly as she could manage. "Our plan worked as well as we could have possibly hoped."

He looked searchingly into her eyes as if to make sure she told him true. "The cardinal?"

She managed a real grin at the thought of the cardinal's final exit. He would not be back to trouble them for a long while. If Francine's star remained in the ascendant, she wouldn't like his chances of ever returning to Paris. "The cardinal is disgraced and banished."

Jean-Paul heaved a sigh of relief. "The King believed your story?"

"He saw the evidence with his own eyes, and blamed the cardinal for misleading him. You have made an enemy of the cardinal, I fear. After tonight's work, he would murder you himself, were he to get half a chance."

Jean-Paul's forehead creased, but not with worry about the cardinal. "Did Francine forgive you for tricking her? Indeed, I never would have agreed to it if it had not been for the best."

Francine, always Francine. Did the foolish boy not think of anyone else save his precious Francine? Would he never forget her? Was the lure of her pink-and-white beauty more than enough to make up for her disloyal heart that thought only of itself? Would he never stop pining for what he could not have?

Her heart was heavy when she spoke again. "The King is content and the marquise is triumphant. She would have forgiven me a thousand times over to have the cardinal out of the way. We have nothing to fear now. No more dark assassins lurking in the shadows of the street, waiting to knife us while our backs are turned."

He seemed puzzled at the dullness she couldn't quite disguise in her voice. "We have won," he said, jubilation in his voice. "Our enemies are defeated." He looked at her more carefully. "Yet something is still troubling you?"

There was no need for them to work together any longer to defeat a common enemy. No need even to talk to each other when they passed in the street. No need for anything when they met save a slight nod of the head, maybe, to acknowledge their acquaintance. Already she felt the pain of his absence gnawing a hole in her heart.

Miriame forced a smile, not wanting him to guess the wayward turn her thoughts had taken. He had asked her to leave him once already—she could not bear to have him ask again. "I tricked Francine into giving me one hundred and fifty gold *pistoles*," she said, with as much enthusiasm as she could muster. "Since I had just saved her from the wrath of the King, she could hardly refuse me, and I felt it was fair enough payment for disposing of her friend the cardinal with such flair." She jingled the bag of money in her pocket, thinking of the bag of sponges hidden in her other pocket. How foolishly optimistic she had been to think that she might ever need them. "Come, let's go somewhere quiet and split it up."

To her surprise, he shook his head. "Francine gave it to you, not to me. Keep it all."

"Don't be a fool. You had an equal share in the plan. I owe you an equal share in the booty before we part and go our separate ways."

His brows drew together in a frown at her words. "Is that all you owe me?"

"A new pair of boots, too, I suppose," she conceded. "I'll throw in another *pistole* for those, if that makes you happy."

"Damn and blast the boots," he said, suddenly angry. "I don't want you to pay me for them. At least not with Francine's gold. You can't buy me off as easily as that."

She glared at him, unhappiness making her voice sharp. "I'm not giving your boots back again, so don't even think about asking for them. I like your boots. They're mine now."

"I told you. I don't want the damned boots." He grabbed her by the arm and started to pull her along the street. "Come with me. I swear we are going to sort this out once and for all."

Miriame dug in her heels. "Where are you taking me?"

"To my chamber," he said between clenched teeth. "Where we can talk in peace."

She allowed herself to be dragged along. His chamber would be as good as any other place to divide their takings for the night. Heaven knows they couldn't do it in plain sight, in the street or in a tavern. One hundred and fifty *pistoles* was more than most people ever saw in a lifetime of labor.

He stomped up the stairs to his apartment, not troubling to soften his footsteps despite the lateness of the hour. Miriame followed behind him, trying to make up for the fact that Jean-Paul was making enough noise for both of them.

Jean-Paul slammed the door behind her as soon as she entered and whirled towards her, his face dark with suppressed emotion. "Are you ready to listen to me now?"

All she wanted to do was to get out of the torment of his company and go back to her tiny attic where she could be miserable in peace. Why had she even bothered getting the sponges from the marquise? She shouldn't take the risk anyway, even if Jean-Paul were to want her. Not that he did . . .

"Forget about the talking," she said, plunking down the bag of coins on the table. "Let's just divide up the gold and be done with it."

He didn't move towards the bag. "Take off your boots."

She stood her ground, wondering what strange fancy had gotten into him now. Whatever it was, she wasn't playing. "No."

As if by magic, a knife appeared in his hand. "Take off your boots."

She reached one hand towards her boots where she hid her own knife. If he wanted a fight, she would give him one, and heaven help her if she didn't leave him with another scar or two as a memento of her foolishness in loving him.

"Don't even think about it," he warned her, his brows drawing together as he saw her reach for her own knife. "Just do as I tell you for once in your life and nothing will get hurt. Not even your precious boots."

She looked at him suspiciously. "I have your word on that?" He was a musketeer and a soldier. She was beginning to learn that their word of honor counted for something with them.

"My word as a gentleman."

What harm then in doing as he had asked? She took off her boots, taking only the precaution to slip the knife into her jacket without his noticing. She would not be totally without resources if their disagreement became physical. Her trust only went so far.

"Toss me your boots."

Who did he think he was? "Come and get them yourself if you want them so badly," she said, feeling sulky.

He shot her a grin that made his angelic features light up with an unholy light. "So you can stab me while I'm bending over? You must think I'm daft."

"How can I stab you? You know I keep my knife in my boots."

"If your knife is still in your boots, I will eat it, blade and all."

She gave him an evil look and tossed him the boots one after the other.

He caught them, looked inside them, shook them upside down, and felt around inside them with his hands. "Hm. Just as I thought—empty."

She glared at him again, her knife a comforting weight in her pocket.

"Can I trust you not to stab me while my back is turned?" he asked conversationally.

Her glare grew more pronounced than ever. She didn't trust *herself* not to stab him while his back was turned. It would be no more than he deserved.

He shrugged. "I guess I will have to take the chance." He crossed to the casement window, opened it, and tossed out the boots.

Miriame squealed with outrage and rushed over to the

window. Her boots were lying on the street, a couple of black shapes outlined in the cobbles.

Behind her she heard the key click in the door. She whirled around to see Jean-Paul pocketing the key. She advanced on him dangerously. "I want my boots."

"I'm sure you do."

She held out her hand. "Give me the key. Now."

"No."

They stood there for a moment, staring at each other, neither of them prepared to back down.

She thought of her boots, lying abandoned in the road. She wanted them back. "Give me the key, or I'll take it from you."

"You can try. Of course, I shall fight you for it. It will take you some time to beat me. Your boots may well be gone by then."

She took her knife out of her pocket and held it up in front of her. "I'm not afraid to fight you."

"Naturally, there is an easier way to get your boots back, if you choose to take it."

She looked at him, not deigning to answer.

"I want to talk to you. I want you to listen to me. Once I have done, you can have the key with my blessing."

"You did not have to steal my boots for that."

"I would not have you walk out in the middle of what I have to say to you. This way you will be quiet and listen to me without interrupting, for fear that your boots will be stolen if you waste too much time."

Miriame cast an anguished glance out of the window, hating the way he had trapped her so easily. Fighting him for the key was tempting, but if she really wanted her boots, she would have to hear him out.

She put her knife away, crossed her arms in front of her chest and stood at the window, tapping her stockinged foot. "Well, hurry up and say what you have to say. I haven't got all night."

"Good. I have your attention at last." He cleared his throat. "Miriame Dardagny, will you marry me?"

Did he think to make her laugh with such a foolish jest? She was in no mood for his foolishness. "No," she said baldly.

"Wrong answer," he said cheerfully. "Try again."

She grimaced. "Ha-ha. Very funny."

There was silence in the chamber, broken only by the sound of their breathing. "I gather you have finished saying what you meant to say to me," she said after a few minutes in which neither of them spoke, and she held out her hand. "Give me the key so I can retrieve my boots."

"Will you marry me?" Jean-Paul repeated.

"No. Now give me the key." She began to advance on him threateningly. If she had to fight for her boots, then so be it.

He shook his head. "I fear you don't quite understand," he said calmly. "You need to answer my question before you get your boots back."

"I have answered it. Twice."

He shrugged. "I don't like that answer. Try another one."

She gaped at him, her mouth falling open. She shut it again with a snap. "You won't give me the key until I promise to marry you?"

He smiled. "Ah. I knew you would catch on eventually. You're quick-witted, you know. I like that in a woman."

With a quick flick of her wrist, she drew her knife out of her jacket and held it in front of her once more, advancing on him with fierce determination. She would promise nothing, and she would not lose her boots. "Give me the key."

"Come and take it from me," he taunted her.

She made a sudden rush at him, but he sidestepped quickly and she met nothing but air. Only a quick piece of footwork stopped her from falling over on her nose.

Breathing heavily, she came to a halt, forcing herself to calm down before she faced him again. Anger only made her hasty and careless. She would need to keep a cool head if she wanted to beat him quickly.

"Promise to marry me and I'll give you the key."

Even before he had finished speaking, she sprang at him again, but he was watching her and circled behind the fireside chair, using it as a shield between them.

"You are a soldier and have nothing but a soldier's pay. You cannot afford to take a wife," Miriame said, as she plotted her next move. "We would be as poor as church mice. I will not drag you down into the gutter."

"Not so poor as all that," Jean-Paul said in a voice full of laughter. "Not after the cardinal paid me so well for his own undoing." His face grew serious again, his eyes never leaving hers for a second. "I have been living on my soldier's pay, true, but out of choice rather than necessity. I thought that the family acres could go to my brother Augustin untrammeled, but he will not begrudge me the wherewithal to keep a wife. And children, too, should we ever be fortunate enough to be blessed with them."

Her eyes closed for just a moment at the thought of children. Her children and Jean-Paul's. How she would love to have a child.

A foolish mistake, to dream of what could never be, in the middle of a fight. In that instant Jean-Paul was upon her. A blow to her wrist and the knife fell from her fingers to clatter uselessly to the floor. His greater weight bore her to the floor and pinned her there.

She lay there with him on top of her, unable to move.

"You've won," she said lightly, trying not to feel the hardness of his body against hers. She did not want to think about how good she felt with his body pressed to hers, or of the special hardness of his that was nestled snugly in the juncture of her thighs. "I suppose that means I will have to give you back your boots after all."

His breath was hot against her cheek. "I was fighting for a far greater prize," he murmured into her ear. "A prize that I intend to claim right here and now."

Miriame arched her back under him as he pressed his lips to her cheek, with every kiss drawing closer to her mouth, resisting him with all of her strength. She knew only too well that he had chosen the one weapon against which she could not fight. She knew, too, that in a moment all her will to resist would be gone, and she would be vanquished indeed. "Let me go," she whimpered. "Let me go."

"Not yet," he whispered back. "Not until I have claimed a forfeit for my victory."

His lips touched her mouth, and Miriame knew she was lost. As his mouth kissed her tenderly, with growing passion, she responded in kind, not even caring any more that she had surrendered to his demands.

She wanted him, oh, how she had ached for him in those long, lonely weeks since first they had touched. She had no strength left to fight her desire for him. All she could do was give in to the feelings that raged through her, the urgent need for the touch of his hands on her body, the delight of holding him in her arms once more. She thrust her hand under his shirt, caressing the planes of his back, loving the smoothness of his skin, the curve of his firm buttocks, the harsh angles of his shoulder blades. She wanted to touch everything, all of him, everywhere.

He had caught her own urgency, seeming to feel the

same need to touch her, skin to skin. He shrugged off his jacket and pulled his shirt over his shoulders, his torso gleaming silver in the moonlight that glimmered through the open casement window.

She cast aside her own shirt and jacket with feverish hands and pulled him down on top of her once more, his chest on her breasts.

His face in the moonlight was contorted with painful desire. "Heaven help me, Miriame," he muttered, "but I want you badly. If you are going to refuse me, then for the love of God, say it now."

Her tongue could not utter the words. Her heart would not allow her to deny him what they both so desperately wanted. "I will not say nay. Not tonight."

He raised his head to gaze at her. "Never?"

She could only promise him tonight. Nothing more. Not even her desire for his body could make her forget her love for him, for his soul. She was silent. Stubbornly silent.

"I will have you yet," he muttered, wresting control over himself with an iron will and raising himself over her.

She cried out as his body left hers, but he did not go far. He bent his head to her breeches, unlacing the ties that kept them on and pulling them down her thighs and over her ankles. Her drawers and stockings followed an instant after.

She was naked, utterly naked. She held out her arms to him to come and possess her, but he would not be cajoled. Not yet.

Jean-Paul bent his head to her belly and began, slowly but surely, kissing his way down past her navel to the mound of hair between her thighs. She squirmed at first, not knowing what to think of such intimacy, but then the pleasure of his tongue on her secret places, kissing and licking the sensitive nub of flesh, made her forget all her caution.

She lifted her head back and moaned aloud, letting herself float away on the wave of delight that engulfed her, swallowing her whole, drowning her in its depths until she could not breathe.

Higher and higher he took her with his tongue and fingers, each time taking her to the brink of climax before letting her down, gently, until she was shaking with the need for completion.

"Please, do not stop now," she begged him, when she could stand no more of his torment. "Take me all the way. Please."

He raised his head and smiled at her, a wolfish smile that spoke of his joy in having her just where he wanted her. "Promise to marry me, and I will."

She shook her head, not yet ready for a complete surrender.

"No?" He got awkwardly to his knees, astride her body as she lay prone on the floor. His hard cock was nudging demandingly at her opening. How she longed to have him inside her, to feel him filling her once more with his seed. "Then I suppose I will have to leave you."

He paused there for a moment. She did not say a word. Slowly he began to get to his feet.

She couldn't bear it any longer. "I will marry you," she promised, grabbing him and dragging him down to her. "God help me, but I will marry you. Just do not leave me this way."

His smile now was a smile of triumph. "I will never leave you again, my love." Without another word he lowered himself over her and, with one long, slow thrust that seemed to Miriame as if he were piercing her very soul, took her for his own.

She had never felt so complete before, so whole. Not

even the thought of the child she might grow in her belly from his seed could dissuade her. Let the child be born if God willed it to be so. She would look after it and protect it with her life, while she had breath in her body. She would love it, take care of it, keep it safe.

Then even the thought of a child left her, as Jean-Paul began to take her higher and higher, stroking her as he thrust in and out of her welcoming body.

In mere moments he had her teetering on the brink yet again. This time, she knew with a savage satisfaction that filled her heart with joy, there would be no turning back for either of them.

One more thrust, and she climaxed again, her hands clutching him as if he were her lifeline. She never wanted to let him go.

He held himself inside her as she spiraled downwards into the darkness of satisfied desire. Then with one last thrust, he joined her there, his hot breath caressing her face, his cries of passion singing in her ear, and his warm, wet seed flooding her womb.

They lay together on the floor, spent, their breathing the only sound in the darkness. Miriame did not feel sleepy—her heart was too full for sleep. She wanted only to enjoy these moments before they were over, these moments with the man she loved.

"I'm glad you are a soldier," Jean-Paul said at last, just as she thought he had fallen asleep.

"Why is that?"

"You promised me that you would wed me. A soldier, especially a musketeer in the King's Guard, cannot go back on his word. Or her word, as the case may be."

"You took advantage of me in a weak moment," she protested.

"A promise is a promise. It was freely given and I intend to hold you to it."

She sighed into the darkness. "You do not have to wed me."

"I want to," he said simply.

"You are in love with Francine."

He put his finger on her lips. "Hush, my love. Do not speak her name. This is about you and me—no one else."

"But—"

"I thought that I was in love with her—until I met you."

"I am a liar and a thief."

"You had no other choice but starvation," he reminded her.

"I stole from you."

"I have forgiven you long since. Besides, you have given me something far more valuable than what you took from me. You have given me love."

There was silence in the chamber as she thought about what he had said.

"You do love me?" he asked, his voice suddenly unsure.

She took his hand in hers and laid it on her breast so he could feel her heart beating. "With all my heart."

What a relief it was to have the words spoken aloud, the words that she had hugged to her chest for so many weeks, not daring to whisper a hint of them even to the wind.

"And you will wed me?"

"I will."

She could feel his smile though she could not see it. "You will never regret your promise, I swear it. I will work hard for you and earn gold enough even for your mercenary little heart."

She dug him in the ribs for his teasing. "If I conceive, I will have to leave off being a soldier. You may well have to feed more than two mouths before you are much older."

"Would that pain you, to give up your sword and dagger?"

She fell silent, thinking of the respect she had earned as a soldier. Yes, she would miss the free and easy life she had lived, the excitement of danger, and the pride she took in a task well done.

The thought of André's body lying on the wooden floor was another matter. She would not miss the blood, the pain, and the death. She had killed once for the sake of Rebecca's life, and to give her soul ease from the hatred and despair that had once consumed it, but she would not gladly do so again.

With a happy heart, she would swap her sword for the sake of holding a child of her own in her arms. "No, I will not miss my sword. But as for my dagger," she added, her voice alight with mischief, "why would you think I would ever give that up?"

Jean-Paul shifted slightly and Miriame was suddenly aware of the hardness of the ground under her back.

He pulled her gently to her feet. "Come to bed, sweetheart, before you freeze down there on the floor."

They fumbled their way over to the bed in the darkness and crept under the covers.

A muffled jingle sounded as she knocked the bag of gold that Madame de Montespan had given her off the bed onto the floor.

She took no heed. Her arms held all that she had ever wanted in the world. They held the man who loved her, and whom she loved in return. Poor though they were, and struggle though they might, they had each other. She could want for no more.

A single shaft of moonlight crept in through the window as they lay sleeping, shining on the golden coins scattered over the floor, lighting up the writing on the parchment that Francine had given her.

A small gray mouse crept in from a hole in the wainscot, its paws scuffling a little on the bare wooden floor.

It looked at the paper with its beady eyes, but it could not read the writing on it, the writing that deeded a fine manor house in Burgundy and all its rents to Miriame, the writing that would make her a wealthy woman, come the morn.

The mouse twitched its nose and nibbled on the edge of the parchment, but the taste was not to its liking.

On silent paws it crept out again, leaving the lovers entwined in each other's arms, asleep in the moonlight.

Contemporary Romance By
Kasey Michaels

Discover the Thrill of
Romance With

Kat Martin

__Hot Rain
0-8217-6935-9 $6.99US/$8.99CAN

Allie Parker is in the wrong place—at the worst possible time . . . Her
only ally is mysterious Jake Dawson, who warns her that she must play
the role of his reluctant bedmate . . . if she wants to stay alive. Now, as
Alice places her trust—and herself—in the hands of a total stranger, she
wonders if this desperate gamble will be her last . . .

__The Secret
0-8217-6798-4 $6.99US/$8.99CAN

Kat Rollins moved to Montana looking to change her life, not find
another man like Chance McLain, with a sexy smile of empty heart.
Chance can't ignore the desire he feels for her—or the suspicion that
somebody wants her to leave Lost Peak . . .

__The Dream
0-8217-6568-X $6.99US/$8.50CAN

Genny Austin is convinced that her nightmares are visions of another
life she lived long ago. Jack Brennan is having nightmares, too, but his
are real. In the shadows of dreams lurks a terrible truth, and only by
unlocking the past will Genny be free to love at last. . .

__Silent Rose
0-8217-6281-8 $6.99US/$8.50CAN

When best-selling author Devon James checks into a bed-and-breakfast
in Connecticut, she only hopes to put the spark back into her
relationship with her fiancé. But what she experiences at the Stafford
Inn changes her life forever . . .

Available Wherever Books Are Sold!

Visit our website at **www.kensingtonbooks.com**.